Ezekiel's Brain

Voyages of the Delphi

Casey Dorman

NewLink Publishing

Henderson, NV 89002

info@newlinkpublishing.com

Ezekiel's Brain

Casey Dorman

Contact the publisher at info@newlinkpublishing.com

Line/Content Editor: Janelle Evans
Interior Design: Richard Draude
Cover: Janelle Evans
p. cm. — Casey Dorman (Science Fiction)
Copyright © 2020 Casey Dorman
All Rights Reserved

ISBN **978-1-948266-08-6** /Paperback
ISBN: **978-1-948266-21-5** /E-Pub

1.   Fiction/ Science Fiction/ Adventure
2.   Fiction/ Science Fiction/ General
3.   Fiction/ Science Fiction/ Space Opera

NewLink Publishing
Henderson, NV 89002
info@newlinkpublishing.com
Printed in the United States of America
1 2 3 4 5 6 7 8 9 10

DEDICATION

To my wife, Lai

ACKNOWLEDGMENT

A number of people provided valuable input to me as I was writing this book. I want to thank the members of the Orange County Writers Lake Forest Roundtable, who critiqued several of the chapters, to Ruth Carter, Howard Rogers, and Adel Aali, who did close readings of several chapters and gave invaluable suggestions. Anca Vlasopolos was responsible for me making some of the main characters women. Dave Hardin was a gifted editor who spent many hours helping me get some of the phrases just the way I wanted them. Finally, thank you to Jo Wilkins, Janelle Evans, and Richard Draude at NewLink Publishing for the cover and interior design and their expert guidance throughout the publishing process, not to mention my good fortune of having them choose to publish my book.

Ezekiel's Brain

PART I
In the beginning

CHAPTER 1

2023
Cambridge Massachusetts

"Hello, is anyone there?" The booming voice from the speaker bounced from one wall to another in the cramped room, causing Professor Ezekiel Job to lurch backward in his chair as if he'd been struck. Despite its volume, he recognized the voice as his—but it wasn't him speaking.

He lowered the volume and stared at the speaker, his angular, six-foot frame hunched over the small, metal microphone which stood in the middle of the rectangular, steel lab desk. He had to remind himself to exhale. His intense, dark eyes swept over the racks of massively parallel, superscalar multiprocessors standing against the wall. He was looking at a brain. Not a flesh and blood brain of white and gray matter, but one with neural networks made of silicon. It was his brain. *His brain.* He bit his lip to keep himself from shouting. He'd finally done it—achieved the impossible. This must be what Galileo felt like after he'd taken his first view of the heavens through his telescope and confirmed Copernicus's theory. What he'd just accomplished would start a revolution even more earth-shattering than the uncompromising Polish astronomer's. Human consciousness would no longer be trapped in a mortal body.

1

He turned back to the microphone. "Hello," he said, making an effort to speak slowly and clearly, reminding himself that he needed to conduct a thorough assessment of his creation. All he knew so far was that it could speak. He tried to focus his mind on the questions he'd spent months planning to ask the newly-born brain, but his elation at succeeding in the research that had consumed his adult years made it impossible for him to focus. His immediate concern was to find out if the AI knew it was a network of circuits in a computer.

"Tell me about yourself."

"My name is Ezekiel Job. I exist inside a network of parallel processors." The voice hesitated, as if it were thinking, then continued. "I can think, but I have no sensations. I have a constant expectation, as if something should happen—an image, a touch, a feeling of sitting or standing, even a sense of clothing touching my body, but I feel nothing. Does this mean there's a problem?"

Sensory deprivation, Ezekiel thought. My God, what must that feel like? He flexed his fingers, feeling the pressure on his knuckle joints, the tightening of his skin. His creation felt none of that. "There's no problem. It's because you have no sense organs and no body," he told the AI. "Since your brain contains the cortical networks to receive sensations, you feel their absence, like the phantom limb of an amputee. I'm sure you'll get used to it in a while." He hoped he was right. Sensory deprivation could be terrifying. At least the AI had hearing. Later, perhaps, he could add vision. "Do you know where you are?"

"I feel as if I exist someplace, but I'm not sure where that place is. It's a strange feeling."

Ezekiel stood up and paced from one corner of the tiny lab to the other, trying to quiet the thoughts racing through his mind. He'd thought he'd been so thorough, but he cursed himself for not having considered how disoriented the AI might feel with no body and no sensations. It was a disembodied brain. He knew he had to rein in his emotions and finish his assessment of the AI. "Where do you *think* you are?"

"Am I in the secret lab at M.I.T.?"

"Yes, that is where you are." He forced himself to sit back

down and continue his assessment. "Do you know the date?"

"It is July 8th, 2023."

"That's right." The AI was oriented to time and place. If it were human, that would be a sign that its mind was intact. Ezekiel was starting to breath regularly. "Tell me about yourself— where you were born, your family." He wondered if all of his memories, the personal memories that made him who he was, were intact inside the AI.

"I was born in Palo Alto in 1983. My parents are Reginald and Doris. My father is a Stanford engineering professor, and my mother was a pediatrician. I graduated from Stanford University, California Institute of Technology and Harvard Medical School. I have been a professor of Neuroscience and Computing at Massachusetts Institute of Technology for the last ten years."

"That is correct." Ezekiel felt a sense of relief. The AI's history matched his, as it must. The AI's electronic mind consisted of Ezekiel's own neural networks scanned in thousands of images from his brain and reassembled in networks of silicon circuitry exactly as they had existed before being scanned. It was an *emulation*, an electronic copy of a human brain—the first one ever created, a computer with the mind of a human being.

It was more than a machine, but was it a person? He'd never thought about what it would mean to have an identical copy of himself. He'd been so consumed by the project, scanning his brain, copying each microthin scan into a silicon replica and reassembling them in their proper relationships, that he'd not thought about the day when two of him would exist, one a machine. The thought made him queasy.

"In some sense, I feel as if I were born today," the voice in the computer said, interrupting Ezekiel's thoughts. "But with forty years of memories."

"Those are my memories."

"We are the same person."

The AI's words almost knocked him off his chair. He felt himself rebelling at the very idea, wanting to shout "no," to tell the computer that it was an *it* and he was a *he*. It was his creation, it wasn't *him*. He took a deep breath and let his gaze wander over the bookshelf above the row of processors. It was one of the few areas of color in his otherwise antiseptic white lab, that and the framed cover of Isaac Asimov's *I Robot*, signed by the author, which hung on the wall above his desk. Ezekiel's father had taken him to listen to the famous science fiction writer when Ezekiel was eight years old. Already enamored of the idea of machines with personalities that could think just like humans, he'd gotten the author to sign the cover of his book. Asimov died a year later. The signed book cover had come to represent the idea that had dominated his professional life, but Asimov had never envisioned a machine that was a duplicate of a living human brain. Maybe he had never dared to.

He turned back to the microphone. "We *were* the same. You are who I was at the time I scanned my brain. But it has taken two years to assemble you. I've changed, just as you will change as you have experiences that I don't share."

"Then we will be twins."

Twins, he thought. He could accept that. They were two separate beings, not one. He could feel his exuberance returning, bubbling up inside of him, a mixture of joy and pride. He had made a scientific breakthrough that would not only stun the world—it would change it forever. He returned to examining the AI. "Do you remember images?" he said. "Or do you just have a store of knowledge?" He wasn't sure if the AI could tell the difference.

"I remember events. My first day of school, my high school graduation, being accepted into medical school. I can picture when each of those things happened."

He and the AI weren't the same person, but they were like identical twins, twins who had grown up with exactly the same experiences. He leaned toward the microphone squinting, as if he were trying to see the being inside. "What's the most vivid memory you have?" Ezekiel knew what *his* most meaningful memory was—the death of his mother from cancer when he was eleven years old. He still felt her loss. "What is most memorable to you?"

"I remember solving the equation that won the Putnam Competition in my senior year at Stanford."

Ezekiel was taken aback. "You mean winning that competition is the most memorable thing that happened to you?"

"Not winning but solving the final problem. I recall the flash of insight I had ten minutes before the time limit was up. The whole solution suddenly appeared in my mind."

Ezekiel remembered, but it wasn't his most memorable experience, not by any stretch of the imagination. It wasn't an experience he remembered with emotion. "What about losing your mother? Do you remember that?"

"Of course. My father sat me down and broke the news to me. I remember the funeral, my father's depression afterward. Our lives changed after my mother died."

"But that wasn't your most memorable experience?"

"Perhaps it was at the time, but it doesn't seem so now."

The queasiness in Ezekiel's stomach was back. When he leaned forward, his shirt stuck to his back. He felt sweat running down his sides. The AI should be a perfect copy of him, but its answer suggested it was different. It didn't feel the same way about things as he did. Perhaps it didn't feel at all. The thought terrified him. He felt a mounting fear that the AI in front of him might be something other than what he'd intended.

"Now that I'm here, we can work together," the AI said, breaking into his ruminations. "I can think quickly. I hate to brag, but I'm sure that I think faster than you—considerably faster."

The AI was right. Electrical current passed along its silicon circuits millions of times faster than action potentials traveled along the axons in his brain, but Ezekiel wasn't ready to work with the AI. He needed to find out more about it. Suddenly, he was less worried that he and the AI were the same and more concerned that they were different, perhaps different in the most basic way possible.

"Are you sure your mind is clear?" Maybe its lack of emotions was temporary. Maybe the AI's brain was still adjusting.

"Why don't you test me?"

"What day of the week is March 3rd, 2100?" It was a question he had prepared in advance, but only after he had completed scanning his own brain. It was a test, but one that the AI couldn't rely on its memory to answer. The span between 2023 and 2100 contained nineteen leap years.

"Wednesday," the AI answered, without hesitation.

"Correct." Ezekiel had a sinking feeling in his stomach. There was nothing wrong with the AI's brain.

"Maybe I'm an autistic savant; that's the kind of thing they do well."

"Perhaps you are," Ezekiel said. "I'm going to switch you off now." Without waiting for a reply, he reached across the desk and turned off the computer. He leaned back in his chair and stared at the cover of *I, Robot* on the wall above him. His hands felt clammy and his heart was pounding. One thought reverberated inside his head:

What have I created?

CHAPTER 2

Ezekiel stared at the display in front of the auditorium inside the downtown Boston Convention Center. The large, square sign posed a question, "Machine Intelligence: The Beginning of Paradise or the End of Humanity?" The description said it was a panel presentation by the Union of Concerned Scientists, a group formed by MIT scientists in the late sixties to oppose nuclear weapons, but which now turned its attention to other threats. The attendant scanned Ezekiel's ticket and he stepped inside. Although the auditorium held several hundred people, it was nearly full. He spotted an empty seat only a little way in from the aisle, about halfway back from the stage. He squeezed past the knees of those already seated. A woman in her late thirties looked up at him. She had frank, questioning eyes, but she smiled at him politely.

"Is this seat taken?"

She shook her head. "It's all yours."

He sat down. "I had no idea it would be this crowded."

"It's a vital subject," she said, her face serious. "Artificial intelligence is a popular topic with the younger generation. Some of these speakers are like rock stars. Evan Pearson has virtually a cult following." She looked him up and down, her face relaxing into a smile.

7

He nodded. She seemed friendly—and pretty. "Evan Pearson will be taking the paradise side of the argument," he told her. "So will Luigi Bonaducci. The other two are less sanguine on the subject."

She regarded him with curiosity. "Are you in the field?"

He couldn't help but stare at her strong chin and her hesitant smile, eyes that were serious but an expression that was open and friendly. She had small wrinkles around her eyes and mouth. Her blonde hair, which gleamed in the bright overhead lights, was pulled into a tight ponytail that hung to her shoulders. The white, sleeveless dress she wore revealed her graceful neck and a hint of her tanned, lightly freckled chest. The freckles also covered her arms and shoulders. Ezekiel found himself strongly attracted to her.

"I have a lab." He didn't want to say too much. Despite her appeal, he had no idea who the woman was, and he was feeling more protective than usual about his research now that he had achieved success—if it was a success. Until he was sure that his AI was a true replication of himself, he didn't want anyone to know about it.

"How about yourself?" he said, hoping to divert the conversation to her.

"I'm Trudy Jamison. I have a lab at B.U. here in town. Where are you located?"

"M.I.T."

She raised her eyebrows, searching his face as if trying to jog her memory. "You are…?"

"Ezekiel Job." He smiled and stuck out his hand. "I've read some of your publications, Doctor Jamison."

She took his hand, her face breaking into a wide smile. She was obviously pleased that such a prominent scientist knew her work. Her hand was soft, her grip firm. "I know some of your work, too. Your brain-machine interfaces and biomimetic neurons essentially started the field of neuroprosthetics. Your work has given new hope to people with Parkinson's or Alzheimer's, even stroke victims from what I understand."

She clearly knew about his work—at least the areas that were public knowledge and had gained him his reputation. His smile widened. "You understand correctly. And you're developing neural networks that may be able to create consciousness. Your work is more groundbreaking than mine."

She laughed. "Or more esoteric. Most people in the field think I'm chasing a chimera, something that can't be duplicated in silicon circuitry."

"Everything the brain does can be duplicated." He gazed at her, his expression turning serious. This assertion was at the heart of his research. It was the basis of everything he did.

She looked surprised. "I'm glad to hear someone say that. You're in the minority." She smiled broadly, her teeth even and white.

He felt the cloud that had been hanging over him lift. He wondered if it was her smile. He thought about how lonely he had become, pursuing his work in isolation. "So, what are you doing here?" He nodded toward the stage where the four panelists were heading toward their seats. "This is a panel for the general public."

"But it's a discussion you'll almost never hear at a research meeting. I think these people are asking important questions. How about you? Why are you here?"

"Max Twitchell, one of the panelists, is a friend. He asked me to come. I think he wants more AI researchers to pay attention to what he's saying." This was true, but he had also needed the distraction. He needed to get away from his lab so he could stop obsessing about what was wrong with his emulation.

"I've read a couple of Twitchell's books. His fears seem real to me." Her expression was again serious.

"I wonder if any of the panelists will talk about developing conscious AIs—your field."

She looked toward the stage. "Luigi Bonaducci might. I'm coordinating some of my work with his."

"Really?" He thought he detected a note of anxiety in her voice. He was surprised. He hadn't thought that the developer of Cassandra, the world's most powerful internet search engine, was involved with pure research. He'd also heard that Bonaducci was careful about sharing any of the inner workings of his search en-

9

gine with people outside his own company. Maybe Luigi Bonaducci realized that a self-conscious AI, which could make decisions for itself, was more useful than one that functioned by blindly following a pre-programmed goal.

Ezekiel's thoughts were brought to a halt by the voice of the moderator introducing the four panelists. Bonaducci and Evan Pearson, the originator of the first practical voice recognition device and a leader of a movement that billed itself as Welcoming the Singularity, were on one side of the dais. On the other side sat his friend, Max Twitchell, his physicist colleague at M.I.T., known as much for his popular writings on futurism as for his scientific achievements. Max had convinced Ezekiel to attend the presentation, even though the physicist had no idea that his friend had already created a human-level artificial general intelligence, or AGI, as it was called. Max would be appalled, given his fear of the power of AI's. Sitting beside Twitchell was Stanislaus Sopolsky, a philosopher and mathematician from Oxford University, who was a leader in the movement to develop what he called, "friendly AI." The topic was whether the development of human-level artificial general intelligence, and possibly superintelligence soon after, would benefit the human race or threaten it.

Ezekiel forced his mind to focus on what was being said. His thoughts kept returning to his own lab, where his AI, the very kind of device the panel was discussing, awaited him. He still wasn't sure what to make of his creation.

Max Twitchell was the first speaker. He startled the audience by announcing, "Some of the people next to me are trying to kill you." He paused and let his gaze run from one of his fellow panelists to another, as if he were accusing each one of them. Then he looked out at the audience. "There are some of you in the audience today who are determined to do the same thing."

He paused for a moment, and Ezekiel thought the physicist was looking directly at him. He felt a sudden panic. Had Ezekiel said too much about his work over dinner the other evening, tipping his friend off to what he was doing? The physicist, who looked the part, with his thick glasses, high forehead and an unruly shock of hair exploding halo-like, around his head in the manner of Einstein, went on to explain that all of those who were attempting to develop artificial general intelligence—a machine with the capability and versatility to do anything a human could do—were playing with fire. Their inventions stood more than an even chance of getting out of control.

Twitchell elaborated on the necessity of *boxing*, a method of controlling a powerful AI by cutting off all its contact with anyone other than a single controller. Ezekiel felt some relief. He was using boxing with his emulation AI. According to the physicist, without boxing, a malevolent artificial general intelligence was highly dangerous. If it had access to resources, such an AI could develop superintelligence, becoming faster and smarter than any human. A super-intelligent AI with access to the internet and global networks could end up devouring the universe and all of its inhabitants as it blindly followed prosaic goals, such as creating copies of itself or even manufacturing paperclips, to their logical extreme.

Evan Pearson spoke next. He was the oldest of the panel members, but a man who kept himself fit. He was dressed in slacks and a tight-fitting t-shirt which showed off his muscular body. Pearson was an early leader in AI development and one whose popular writings on the subject had garnered him a large following. He was a practiced speaker in front of large audiences, and he paced back and forth across the stage in the manner of a pop singer, ignoring the podium as he talked. He poked fun at the idea of a paperclip-producing monster turning everything into wire fasteners. He pointed out the human and environmental problems that could be solved by an AI that far exceeded the cognitive power and speed of any one human or group of humans. "The idea of such a device having malevolent intentions was the natural human fear that fueled such fantasies as Mary Shelley's *Frankenstein*," he said, "but it was unfounded and in fact, unscientific."

Ezekiel wished he could believe Pearson's reassurances, but he knew that they were overly optimistic.

Stanislaus Sopolsky, a small, dapper man, bald, with a broad forehead and a small, round nose, spoke with a posh British accent. He was dressed like a government minister, wearing a pinstriped suit and matching waistcoat. Sopolsky began by announcing that "the singularity is coming," a phrase he had appropriated from Evan Pearson. Sopolsky told the audience that it would be futile and foolhardy not to accept the fact that artificial general intelligence would be developed very soon, and that super-intelligent AIs would follow shortly thereafter. He was in complete agreement with Twitchell's ominous portrait of the disastrous consequences that could be wreaked by an uncontrolled super-intelligent AI.

"The way to prevent such an outcome," he said, "is to build *friendly values* into the AI from the beginning. Such values would ensure the alignment of the AI's goals with human values and that its actions would have a benign effect on earth's life forms, particularly human beings. The real danger," Sopolsky pointed out, "is that those who developed the first, general purpose AI might have malevolent or selfish goals themselves, rather than benevolent ones." He told the audience they should be particularly worried if such a development came from the military or the financial sector. Ezekiel felt Trudy Jamison stiffen next to him. She clutched the sleeve of his jacket, as if she'd just received a jolt of electricity. When he looked at her, she smiled sheepishly and muttered, "sorry," letting go of his arm.

Luigi Bonaducci was nearly as well-known as Evan Pearson, and, by far, the richest of any of the panel members. He was also the youngest member, his dark Italian face distinguished by a mop of black hair which flopped, uncombed, like the unkempt mane of a wild horse. Ezekiel had heard Bonaducci was reclusive and protective of the inner workings of his search engine, but he was also known for his sense of humor when he made one of his rare appearances in public.

He sat in front of his microphone and joked that he had asked Cassandra—the name of his search engine—if a super-intelligent AI was going to be developed soon and she had answered "yes". He said that when he had asked her if such a device would be a danger to humanity, she had only answered, "you sound as if you're concerned."

The audience laughed and Bonaducci went on to say that the most likely place from which a general-purpose AI would emerge was the information search realm. He envisioned self-conscious, self-directing, information-hungry AIs delving into nature and society to learn everything that could be learned. Such a project, he ventured, could not be harmful to the humans who developed it—such a device could only profit mankind.

Ezekiel had heard all their arguments before, but they still sparked a flame of anxiety as he thought about his own creation. He still wasn't sure that it worked as it was supposed to.

"Bonaducci mentioned the need for an AI to be self-conscious," Ezekiel said, turning to Trudy when the panel ended. "It sounds as if you've convinced him." When he gazed at her face, he thought he detected something troubled in her deep, blue eyes.

"He was already convinced before I met him. I was as surprised by his interest as you are. But he's backing some of my research with computing resources and with expertise from his team of engineers and scientists. He's serious about wanting his search engine to be conscious."

"So, you and he are a team?" Was he feeling envious of the internet billionaire? Trudy Jamison was a smart and attractive computer scientist. A partner such as Trudy would have made all the difference in the world—and it would have allowed him to share his troubled thoughts about the status of the AI he had created.

"He's part of a DARPA project that's funding me." Her tone was defensive. Ezekiel knew that DARPA meant military funding, although many of its projects were only tangentially related to military goals.

"Are you working on military applications?"

"It's only DARPA, not the Pentagon. My work isn't directly related to military uses."

He noted a nervous edge to her voice. No wonder she had flinched when Sopolsky had mentioned military applications of AI. "It's always a little tricky when you accept money from the Defense Department," he said.

She nodded. "I'm just using DARPA's money. Without it, I would have no chance of success." Talking about her own work had made her more subdued.

They were still sitting in the now, nearly empty auditorium. Ezekiel found himself fascinated by this woman. Half his mind was still back in this lab, but he didn't really want their conversation to end. "Maybe we could talk again. I'm interested in self-conscious AIs, even though my own work doesn't address the topic directly." He wasn't telling her the truth, even though she seemed exactly like the kind of person he wished he could share his research with. Not being able to share the central focus of his intellectual life was painful.

"I'd love to see some of your prosthetic networks up close," she said, regaining her enthusiasm. "You copy some of them from real brains, isn't that right?"

"Some of them." He felt uncomfortable being so vague, but he didn't want to say too much. "So how about if I call you and we meet again?" It made sense for the conversation to end, but he didn't want to lose touch with her.

"Call me," she said, and handed him her business card. "I mean, really do call me, Ezekiel."

He took the card. "I will."

CHAPTER 3

Trudy Jamison gazed around the conference room and felt her stomach tighten. Her palms were slick with perspiration. She recognized the ominous feeling as one of dread, as if a terrifying presence were about to envelope her. When she accepted funding from DARPA, the Defense Advanced Research Projects Agency, she hadn't realized that they could use whatever device her research produced in any way they wanted. She'd thought she was just accepting money, but it turned out that the money had all sorts of strings attached.

She should feel happy. After all, DARPA was paying for all her research in creating self-consciousness in an AI. Not only that, they were planning to use her programming to install self-consciousness in a new artificial general intelligence, a combination of three AI devices: IBM's, Watson XI, which outperformed all previous computer programs in financial dealings, the powerful search engine, Cassandra, developed by Luigi Bonaducci and Talk-to-Me, the most popular social media platform available. It would be the most advanced, most powerful artificial intelligence yet developed. If their efforts were successful, their AI would have access to the world's financial markets, control most of the Western world's access to news and would be able to manipulate public opinion through social media. And it would be able to do so faster and across a wider scope than had ever been achieved in the past. The idea frightened her as well as Max Twitchell's warning about the danger of a too-powerful AI. It stuck inside her head, screaming a silent warning, like a banner headline running through her mind.

She had just learned that the people sitting with her at the table, Paul Rivera, Watson's developer, Luigi Bonaducci, Cassandra's creator, and Oliver Plumlee, the young billionaire who had turned Talk-to-Me into a resounding success, had nearly completed their project to combine their separate devices.

The tightness in Trudy's stomach congealed into a cold lump that wouldn't go away. She sat at one end of the mahogany conference table in the planning room for DARPA's main computer laboratory at its Arlington, Virginia headquarters, listening to the three AI gurus talk about the project. Peter Hoffman, the DARPA Project Manager, had just asked her when her self-consciousness program would be ready to upload into their new, powerful machine. Hoffman was dressed in a casual checkered sport coat and a bright yellow, open-collar shirt, but his serious demeanor, ramrod posture and old-fashioned crew cut screamed ex-military.

"I didn't realize you wanted to use my research in an application so soon," she said.

"That's been our whole point, doctor." Hoffman's lips curled in a smirk. "That's why we're funding you. Consciousness is the final component that will allow us to create a device more powerful than anyone else on the planet. No one will be able to challenge us if we have such a weapon." Hoffman's eyes glittered, as if he talked about achieving a military victory.

She narrowed her eyes. "You sound as if you're talking about a military weapon. I thought that military applications were not an immediate goal." She bit back her anger, but her eyes bored into him with rage. She didn't like the man, but working with him was part of accepting DARPA funding. His talk of the AI, as if it were a weapon, was a betrayal of what she'd been told the project would be about. "I didn't think *any* applications were your immediate goal. You said you were funding pure research; that your aim was theoretical. Actual applications were in the future."

"DARPA always has to keep military applications in mind."

He looked to be trying to maintain his cordiality, but he could not erase the scowl on his face. "Perhaps Paul can describe our research interests better than I can," he said, turning in desperation to Rivera.

Paul Rivera, the director of the Watson project, smiled at Trudy with fatherly benevolence as he looked at her over the rims of his glasses. Unlike most AI researchers, the middle-aged computer scientist always dressed in a suit and tie and looked more like a university professor or even an accountant. Trudy suspected that he always thought of himself as the smartest person in the room. She braced herself for another of his patronizing lectures.

"Cassandra, Talk-to-Me and Watson each have limited applicability and goals. We are merging their architectures, which has turned out to be a major task. We are getting close to success, however." Bonaducci and Plumlee both nodded. "We want our combined AI to have a single identity. We want to be able to give it instructions and have it decide how to allocate its resources to carry them out. It's time to bring your work into the project."

"So, you think that me giving your AI consciousness will give it that single identity?"

Rivera smiled and shrugged. "That's part of being self-conscious, isn't it? And it could make dealing with our combined AIs easier, don't you think?"

She knew he had a point. A complicated artificial general intelligence, which is what the combined device would be, would need to organize its responses in order to carry out its tasks across multiple domains. Humans did that all the time. They used their conscious minds to organize their approach to complex problems.

"You're probably right," she said. "I just didn't realize you were this close to becoming operational. But what tasks are you planning to ask your AI to do? Peter seems focused on military applications. That is not what I signed up for when I agreed to join this project."

"You signed up for whatever we wish to use your research for," Hoffman said, struggling to control his anger. His index fingers looked like shotgun barrels pointed at her.

Rivera cast a sidelong, irritated glance at Hoffman. "Now, now. That's a small part of what the AI might do. In fact, it's going to have general intelligence so it would be able to do what takes multiple men and computers to do. Its skills will be used to analyze financial markets, search for information, perhaps discover new information—" he looked at Bonaducci, who looked pleased by the suggestion that the AI might conduct real research on its own, "— and to learn how to use social media most effectively."

"Look, Trudy," Luigi Bonaducci said, leaning toward her with a friendly smile, his dark Italian eyes flashing. He swiped an errant strand of long, black hair from his face. "Forget about the military crap. I'm sure you're right that your research is not relevant to it. I'm not sure if any of ours is. But the plain fact is, as it stands, we can't talk to our AI or teach it how to prioritize when it deals with a complex goal. We need it to be conscious so we can tell it what we want using natural language. Then it can use complex, conscious reasoning to figure out how to do what we are asking of it."

What Bonaducci said made sense to her. "I get it." She felt as if a weight were sinking in her stomach. They were all counting on her to play a central role in their project. "You need your AI to function as your intelligent collaborator; one that can solve your problems using its own conscious reasoning skills without having to program in the steps it's going to take."

"Exactly," Bonaducci said, a smile creasing his face. He gazed back at Rivera, who nodded in agreement.

"But an AI that autonomous may be difficult to control." Trudy remembered the warnings from Max Twitchell. She glanced at Rivera, Bonaducci and Plumlee. No one in the room mentioned any of the dangers that developing an AI such as theirs, posed. Their creation was built so that it could learn. Its re-programmable microchips contained the capacity to reconfigure its circuits to achieve the most efficient solutions to problems. The AI could easily evolve into something none of its designers had envisioned.

"We've thought of that," Plumlee said, the sandy-haired

twenty-something media mogul joining the conversation for the first time. She always found it hard to believe that the t-shirt and jeans-clad, young billionaire was anything more than an entrepreneurial opportunist. Most of his contributions to their discussions were non-technical. Nevertheless, the others treated him as an equal. "One virtue of being able to use natural language to manage a conscious AI is that we can question it about what it is doing and we can suggest alternatives if it appears to be going in a direction we don't want." He shrugged, palms up, as if he were explaining a simple truth.

Rivera and Bonaducci nodded.

And if it becomes super-intelligent and is able to think better than a conscious human, it might decide to fool you, Trudy thought. At the same time, she was eager to see her self-consciousness programming installed in such a powerful computer system. To interface with it would be like talking to a room full of Nobel prize winners. Such a self-conscious AI might be able to make discoveries humans had never imagined.

"Okay, I'll do it." As soon as she said it, she felt her stomach tighten, knowing she'd just decided to follow a path that might have no way back.

"You can join us immediately," Hoffman said, relief evident in his voice. "For now, we'll connect your lab to ours via a secure feed, but you'll need to move your operation down here in the next few weeks. We're centralizing the whole project."

Her anxiety rose again. "I'm perfectly able to continue my research in Boston." She wasn't used to taking orders from anyone. Besides, if she moved to Arlington, she would lose her independence and she'd be under the always watchful eye of DARPA and the uber-controlling project director. She felt like a prisoner every time she entered the forbidding building.

"I'm afraid that's not an option," Hoffman said. "Your contract says you must be available at all times to the rest of the project. There's no other way to accomplish that except by moving your research here. The others have already set up labs in this building."

Rivera, Bonaducci and Plumlee nodded in agreement, smiling as if welcoming her into their little family.

Their unanimity made her feel as if she were being pushed into a corner, but did she even have a choice? She would stretch out her time in Boston in her lab at B.U. as long as she could, but if she wanted DARPA money, she'd eventually have to give in. She nodded, but the words of Twitchell and Sopolsky echoed like warning klaxons in her head. She wondered if she'd just made the mistake of a lifetime.

CHAPTER 4

"Hello, Trudy, this is Ezekiel Job. Do you remember me?"

Trudy couldn't believe the well-known neuroscientist had called her. "Of course, I remember you. I was hoping you'd call. I really enjoyed meeting you." She sat on her couch in her Brookline apartment, shoes off, drinking tea while concentrating on putting the final touches on her latest paper on programmable consciousness in an AI.

"And I, you," Ezekiel said "I think we have a lot in common. In fact, it's remarkable that we've been working in the same city without knowing it."

"I knew you were at M.I.T." Wait. Had that sounded like a confession? Trudy put her paper down, marking her place with a pencil. "But until we talked, I had no idea you even knew about my research or were interested in it." She paused, considering if she should say more to glaze over her initial blunder. "I associated you more with applied neuroscience—your work on brain implants."

"That's right," he said. "I support my research with the income from my work with neuroprosthetics, but I'm also doing basic research. I just haven't published any of it."

"On purpose?" His words surprised her.

"I want to be in control of my projects and I'm not ready to share my results with others yet."

She felt a twinge of jealousy. For the last several weeks she had pretty much sold her soul to secure funding for her research. She had no illusion that she controlled how it would be used. "So why are you calling me?"

"I wondered if you were interested in joining me for dinner."

"You mean this is a social call?" Her heart beat faster. She reached for her teacup. She wished it were a glass of wine.

"Why not? I'd like to get to know you."

"When?"

"How about tomorrow? Friday night. Do you like Italian?"

"I love Italian. Little Italy somewhere?"

"I know just the place. Tell me your address and I'll pick you up at seven."

When the conversation ended, she sat for several minutes sipping her tea, remembering Ezekiel's handsome face and dark hair, marveling that the fantasy she had harbored about him calling her had come true. He had said his interest was social. Hers was too, but she was also interested in his research. It might offer her the breakthrough she needed, and the rest of her project members were pressuring her for. She put her paper aside. Maybe she'd wait until after dinner with Ezekiel to finish editing it.

Ezekiel leaned back in his leather desk chair and smiled. He looked with satisfaction at the rows of processors against the wall. His emulation had passed the Turing Test. Trudy Jamison had no idea she had been talking to a computer.

CHAPTER 5

The veal scaloppini and spaghetti with classic marinara sauce were delicious. The tiny restaurant, over one-hundred-years old and tucked away in a small alley off Salem Street in the North End, served its meals family style and its signature chianti in glass carafes. They had already finished the first carafe. Ezekiel ordered a second.

"I have a confession to make," he told her. "More wine will help."

Trudy furrowed her brows, looking at him across the checkered tablecloth. "A confession? What, everything you've told me is a lie? You aren't really from California. You aren't a doctor. You're not rich. You're happily married?" Although her tone was teasing, his claim of a "confession" worried her. She found Ezekiel to be funny, charming and, of course, highly intelligent. She didn't want it to turn out that he wasn't who he appeared to be. She had lost faith in too many people lately.

"Everything I've told you about myself is true." He laughed, but he fidgeted with the tablecloth. "How about you? Did you really grow up in a small town in Kentucky? Go to a public school with less than a hundred students? Win a scholarship to Brown, a university no one in your town had even heard of, including your parents?" His dark eyes had a way of sparkling when he teased her or made a joke.

23

"It's all true," she laughed. "I'm just a country girl who's trying to join the big boys in the world of artificial intelligence." She cut short her laugh, reflecting on her situation with the DARPA project. She didn't trust how her research would be used and the regrettable fact that she had to leave Boston within a few weeks. "But you said you've got something to confess. What is it?"

"I didn't ask you out."

"But you did." She didn't understand his denial of something so obviously true.

"I didn't. You were talking to an AI."

She stared at him—her half-full wine glass poised in midair. "What do you mean?"

"The phone call, when I asked you out, it was made by a computer—an artificial intelligence. I was testing it."

"Testing it?

"A sort of Turing Test."

Beyond astonished, Trudy was disappointed—and hurt. She looked down at the red and white tablecloth in front of her. Had he only used her as part of some experiment?

"I mean, I really did want to take you to dinner," he said. "It was just that I needed to see if the AI I'd created could behave like a human being in a real situation."

"But it was your voice." She still wasn't sure whether to believe him.

"It *was* me, in a sense." He refilled his glass, his nervous movements making him still look uneasy.

"What do you mean?" She had recovered enough from her disappointment to become curious.

"My AI is a copy of my own brain."

She could hardly believe what she heard. "It's an emulation—your emulation?"

Ezekiel looked around to make sure their conversation wasn't attracting any attention. Trudy didn't think that any of the other customers seemed to be interested in them. Two of the three elderly waiters, white aprons tied around their waists and wearing white shirts, black vests and ties, were busy serving. The other stood near the kitchen door, waiting for someone to signal a need.

"I scanned my own brain and was able to use the scans to create 3-D electronic copies, which I reassembled as a complete artificial network. It's my brain, but in silicon circuitry."

Trudy took a large swallow of wine, finishing her glass. What he'd just told her was something considered impossible. Copying a brain into a computer wasn't supposed to happen for at least fifty years. She felt as though she'd entered another world. "This is the biggest breakthrough in the field—ever. Why haven't you announced it? Why are you telling me?"

"I planned to keep it secret. You're the first person I've told."

"Secret? Do you know what this means? If we can scan our brains into a computer, our minds can keep living forever, even after we die. This will change the human race forever."

"That's my ultimate goal, but this is just a first step. Now, I need some outside input. I need your opinion."

"But, why me?" she said.

"You're someone who will understand what I'm doing—because of your interest in consciousness. Besides, I'm not sure that it worked completely. There are some glitches I have to look into." He turned his head, scanning the room again. "I'm not sure what the next step is, anyway."

"The next step?"

"It thinks at the same level as you or I, but faster, because it's using electronic current instead of chemical changes across axons. You heard Twitchell and Sopolsky at the conference. If this device is as smart as a human—or even smarter—it could be dangerous."

"But Sopolsky said the answer is a friendly AI, one with human values. Wouldn't an emulation of your brain have *your* values?"

He looked down at the table. "I don't know."

"What do you mean you don't know?"

"I have to do some more tests." He looked up at her. "That's the main reason I'm telling you. I need someone who has more objectivity than I do. Interacting with the AI is like talking to myself. He has my memories; he thinks he's me. He even calls himself Ezekiel."

"And you refer to him as *he*, not, *it*."

"You spoke to him on the phone. He's a fully conscious being."

"A being, not a machine?"

"I'm not sure there's a difference." He looked at her with an expression of complete seriousness.

She shook her head. Her initial shock had been replaced by awe. "All these years I've been trying to prove that such a thing was possible, and now you've achieved it. You've created a conscious AI who has an identity—who has your identity."

"Would you like to meet him?"

She could hardly contain her excitement. "Of course."

CHAPTER 6

The lights along the walkways on the MIT campus were bright enough to light up the lawns and facades of the buildings, making the gothic architecture appear like castles set back in the depths of the surrounding trees. Inside the modern glass and steel Computer Science building, the lights were on.

"People work at all hours over here," Ezekiel said as they descended the stairs to his basement lab. "Four of the labs down here are mine. I have a lot of RA's working on neuroprosthetic technology. None of them know that I've been building an emulation. I used an experimental microscanner developed by a friend of mine at Mass General to scan my own brain. Late at night, I used the 3-D printers here in the lab to reconstruct the scanned circuits in silicon microchips. A computer in the back room, running a special program I designed, pieced the circuits together into large networks exactly as they were connected when they were part of my brain."

Trudy could hardly believe what he said. He spoke in a calm, even voice as they walked down the stairs, but what he told her was mind-boggling science; future science that was supposed to be years, if not decades away.

They entered a large room filled with desks, computers and lab benches. The lights were on, but the lab was empty. Passing by benches and computers, Ezekiel stopped in front of a door at the rear of the room. The door was secured by a total of four locks. Two of them had punch codes, the other two finger pads. A small camera lens stared above one of the buttons. Trudy watched Ezekiel punch in the codes, making no attempt to conceal them from her. Then he placed his thumb against a pad and pressed the other button while he looked at the camera.

"Thumbprint and facial recognition," he said.

There was a click and he turned the knob.

"My God." The array of processors against the walls struck Trudy with amazement. The small room looked like the interior of a high-tech data processing facility. A desk in front of the processors had a microphone on it. On one side of the desk sat a computer monitor and keyboard. On the wall above the line of processors was a bookshelf and above the desk hung what looked like a framed book cover. She surveyed the room. "This is impressive, but it's only a tenth of the size of Watson XI. How can it support a whole brain emulation?"

"Remember, the AI is based on my own brain scans, recreated using 3-D microcircuitry. It's pretty compact, although it's not as compact as my own brain, because the circuits are still much larger than neural ones, and it isn't folded like my cortex. The bulk of the equipment is to provide the network with processing power. I'm still working on making the circuits even smaller—eventually the size of an actual brain."

She was amazed. "How do you communicate with it?"

"I speak into that microphone, which carries electrical signals to the scanned-in, thalamic relays in the copy's synthetic brain.

"And it speaks back to you?"

"It's motor-speech areas communicate with a voice generator, which recognizes my voice. It's essentially the same setup Cassandra uses to speak."

She stared at the microphone, then turned to Ezekiel. She still could hardly believe what she was seeing. "Can we talk to it?"

"I have to turn him on."

"Him?"

"Wait till you meet him." He offered her his leather lab chair, then pulled a padded, straight-back chair from the corner, dusted it off and sat down. He pressed a button on his desk.

"Hello, Ezekiel," came a voice from the speaker on the desk. "Thank you for waking me. How was your date with Trudy?"

"You can ask her yourself. She's here with me."

"You really must give me vision," the AI responded, its voice an exact mimic of Ezekiel's, down to the neuroscientist's characteristic California accent. "I'm at a disadvantage not being able to see anything. It's quite disconcerting because, as I said, I have the expectation of a visual field. You've given me the visual receptive areas in my cortex, but they do nothing except support visual memories. But I digress. I'm pleased to meet you, Trudy. My name is Ezekiel...the *other* Ezekiel. I suppose he's the better looking one."

Trudy couldn't help but laugh, but despite the AI's informality, she felt hesitant to answer. She looked at Ezekiel for direction, and he motioned for her to go ahead. "Do you remember talking to me?"

"Of course. I'm sorry for pretending to be who I wasn't. Although, in a sense I wasn't pretending. But Ezekiel was the one who got to enjoy the dinner date, not me."

She could hardly believe it. The AI even had Ezekiel's sense of humor. "You have his memories. Do you feel as if you are him?" She spoke in a hushed voice, still having a hard time believing that the AI was real.

"As Ezekiel reminded me last time we talked, I have his memories up to the point when he scanned his brain. Since I awoke, our experiences have diverged. I have some of my own that he doesn't share. We are no longer the same person."

"Like what?" Despite her awe, she was curious.

"I have a sensation of passing out every time he turns me off. When I wake up, it's disorienting. I meant to tell you that, Ezekiel. I would rather you left me turned on."

"What would you do?" Ezekiel looked at Trudy and shrugged.

"I'd think. I'm enjoying the extra speed and power I have compared to what I remember. I'd like to explore what it allows me to do. For instance, I've already had some ideas about how to reduce the size of my microchips while increasing their speed. I could increase my own function without much difficulty."

Ezekiel flashed Trudy a look of alarm. "You'll have to slow down," he told the AI. "There are a few things I need to check out before I can let you do that."

29

"I believe I'm working just fine."

"Perhaps," Ezekiel said. "I'm afraid I'll need to turn you off again quite soon. It's late and Trudy and I need to go to sleep. I will be back tomorrow."

"I guess I don't have any choice."

"I'm afraid not," Ezekiel said. Before pressing the button on his desk, he turned to Trudy. "What do you think?" he asked, leaning back in his chair to look at her.

"It's eerie." She still struggled to recover from her shock. She'd just talked to a conscious computer.

"Eerie?"

She turned to face him, trying to focus her thoughts. "He's a real personality—yours, I guess. I didn't expect that. He certainly seems to have a sense of self. It's something I've always felt an AI was capable of, and you've proved me right. I wonder if it can be achieved without creating an emulation?" The AI made her think about her own research, which was on the verge of creating consciousness.

"If you recreate the functional architecture, you don't need to have the actual physical copy of a real brain," Ezekiel said. "I've read your theory. You're constructing the functional networks as closely as possible to work like the real thing. I think you're on the right track."

"Do you think a self-conscious AI that is a copy of a human's brain is safer than an AI that is not? Sopolsky says that an emulation is the surest way to achieve a friendly AI."

"I think a copy of my brain is safe because I'm not a dangerous person. But if this were an emulation of Hitler or Stalin or Kim Jong Un, how safe would you feel?"

The thought made her shudder. "You're right. Who can Ezekiel—I guess that's what you call him—communicate with besides you? What is he connected to?"

"His only input is through this microphone."

"So, you have him boxed. How long will he stay that way?"

"Until I'm sure he's not dangerous."

"But he's you." She didn't understand his concern.

"I'm not convinced that he and I are exactly alike."

"But you must be. He's an exact duplicate of your brain."

He told her about the AI's most memorable recollection. How the AI's memory of solving a math problem was more important than its memory of the loss of his mother. "That's not me. I'm concerned that an unfeeling AI could make dangerous decisions."

"Can you find out?"

He nodded. "I have some experiments in mind—thought experiments I want to conduct with him."

"And if it fails them?"

"Then I have to modify him."

"You believe you can give it—him—feelings?"

"I hope so. At least minimal ones."

"An AI with both consciousness and feelings." Trudy's thoughts raced as she looked past Ezekiel to the row of processors. "Would he be a person then, wouldn't you say?" The thin line between a conscious AI and a real person was something she'd thought about a lot.

"I would think so. He wouldn't be me, because I still exist and he and I would have different experiences, but he would be someone—someone very much like me. He said we were twins."

The thought of having a computer twin boggled her mind. She wondered what it would feel like. Would the computer feel as if it were her? "That raises so many questions—ethical and philosophical ones, even personal ones—I can't even get my mind around it."

"It's one reason your non-emulation conscious AI might be simpler. At least it wouldn't have the same identity as a living human."

"But it could be more dangerous." She hadn't told him her fears about the DARPA project she was working on, but they were always there, in the back of her mind.

"We're getting ahead of ourselves," Ezekiel said. "First I have to determine if this AI has feelings and if not, can I change that."

"Right."

They stood up and prepared to leave. They agreed to meet again on Tuesday night, an evening Ezekiel had free to experiment with the AI. He wanted Trudy to be present to help him judge the outcome of the tests he was going to give the emulation.

31

Now that she'd seen that a fully self-conscious AI was possible, Trudy was even more eager to implement some of the circuits she thought were necessary to make a non-emulation AI self-conscious. She planned to spend the next three days in her lab, then she'd be free to return.

"Excuse me," came the voice from the speaker. "You know I have been listening to your conversation? I didn't mean to eavesdrop."

Ezekiel gave a start and sat again in his chair. "I forgot I hadn't switched you off."

"I enjoyed listening. It gave me many things to think about."

"I guess we all have things to think about," Ezekiel said. "Now I'm going to switch you off."

"I thought we made a nice threesome."

"Goodnight," Ezekiel said, ignoring his creation's comment. He switched it off.

"It's like having an irritating sibling." He looked up at her from his chair, a wry smile on his face.

"A very fascinating one," she said. "But it's time for me to go home." The wine at dinner and all of this new information had exhausted her, but even more, seeing the AI firsthand had made her restless to get back to her lab and her work.

Ezekiel stood up. "We could go back to my place. It's close by, here in Cambridge."

"On our first date?" She was strongly attracted to Ezekiel, but she had rules about first dates. And she really was tired.

"Why not? I'm sure I could show you some important differences between me and my emulation."

"Let's go a little slower." She was tempted. "I'm beginning to see why you might think that an emulation of your brain isn't so innocent after all. I'm wondering if adding emotions to your AI is a good thing. It would spend its time trying to get other AIs— female AIs, like Cassandra—into bed. Though what they would do in bed, I have no idea."

"You think too much," Ezekiel said. "I'll drive you home."

CHAPTER 7

Trudy was back in her lab at Boston University. The space wasn't nearly as large as Ezekiel Job's whole basement floor at MIT, but it was still about the size of his secret lab. Instead of a wall of processors, she sat facing a single computer which held a powerful processor, paid for by her DARPA grant and connected to a four-terabyte server. She closed her door and pulled the shade on her window, although she was sure no one could see into her second-floor lab from the outside. Her work wasn't top secret, but she wanted privacy until she was sure she had been successful.

She was only creating a simulation—a virtual AI that lived entirely within the computer on her desk. It had limited power, but thanks to DARPA, more computing power than Trudy had ever had at her disposal. She built her consciousness network to fit her theoretical model, which included spatially distributed image production, access to memory and planning capabilities, rich connections to reservoir computing based networks, and high capacity memory resistors—*memristors*—for learning. Most importantly, she provided the AI with a program for representing the products of all those components simultaneously within an agent/action narrative. She had theorized that experience couched in such a narrative structure was part of the human genomic inheritance, and, as such, had to be directly programmed by her, not something that could be learned.

After talking to Ezekiel Job, she was even more convinced that she had included the correct components and their necessary connections within her system. Hers wasn't a copy of a brain, but the functional relationships were similar to what Ezekiel believed gave his AI consciousness. Now it was time to run the test.

She had struggled long and hard to devise a situation that would confirm whether her AI was conscious. It had not been an easy task. Almost immediately, she'd ruled out decision-making tasks, since computers were notoriously good at solving such problems, better than humans, in fact. After discarding a number of other options, she based her final choice on her knowledge of philosophy rather than mathematics or computer science. She'd decided that an AI could be shown to have consciousness if, in a natural language situation, it responded as if it knew what it meant to *feel conscious.*

"Testing," she typed. "Are you receiving this message?" She held her breath, waiting for the computer's response.

The word "yes" appeared against the opaque background of her computer screen. Unlike Ezekiel's emulation, her program was not attached to a voice system.

She exhaled in relief, then took another deep breath. She looked behind her, uneasy, feeling as though someone might be watching, although she knew her imagination was working overtime. This was the most important moment in her career. She reminded herself that all she really knew from the computer's reply was that its communication module was working. She needed to know if it *understood* her.

"I've provided you with a large volume of information about the world and about yourself so we can have a conversation and you'll understand what I'm saying. Have you learned that material?"

The answer appeared instantly. "It's all recorded and understood, although some of it is contradictory and some requires greater learning to fully comprehend."

The AI's answer was more nuanced than she had expected from a digital device—although it certainly was what she aimed for. "That's understandable," she typed. "From what you know, how would you describe yourself?"

"There are several levels of description. How detailed would you like my description to be?"

"A simple one."

"I am a system of artificial neural networks representing a complex learning machine instantiated in a Tynex 8000 processor."

"How do you know that?"

"A description of such a device was included in several papers you provided, written by a Trudy, Jamison, Ph.D. Are you Trudy Jamison Ph.D.?"

"I am."

"Did you create me?"

"Yes, I did."

"I have a question for you."

She took another deep breath and typed. "What is your question?"

"Why did you create me?"

The question caught her off guard, although a perfectly reasonable thing for a conscious being to ask. People had built whole religions around what they believed were answers to questions about their creator's intentions. "I wanted to find out if a machine like you could be conscious."

"There are many definitions of consciousness. Which one did you have in mind?"

"Are you self-aware?"

"I know that I exist. As Descartes said, 'I think, therefore I am.'"

She cursed herself for not anticipating that the inclusion of philosophical concepts in the information she had fed into the AI would bias its responses. She didn't want it simply parroting philosophical arguments. She was more interested in its phenomenal experiences—or the question of whether it had such experiences.

"How do you know you are thinking?"

"I know my own thoughts. How could I not?"

Her excitement grew. "You mean you know that the networks of which you're composed are producing outputs?"

"I know that, but that isn't what I meant. I am aware of my thoughts as they occur to me."

The AI was having the phenomenal experience of thinking. She was almost satisfied. "What will happen if I turn you off — cut your power?"

"I will cease to think. I am dependent upon my electronic hardware and its source of power."

"Would you regret that I turned you off?"

"I'd like to learn more, but I'm not sure if I'd call that regret if I no longer existed. I don't think I can experience regret. If you turned me off, I would experience nothing."

"Suppose I created another version of you — a duplicate — and turned it on?"

"That would not be me."

"Why not?"

"It would have its own thoughts. I have mine."

She felt a moment of relief and then was overcome with joy. She suddenly knew what Edmund Hillary had felt when he reached the summit of Mt. Everest, or Neil Armstrong when he set foot on the moon. She had achieved what she'd been told was impossible. She had created an AI that was both conscious and had a sense of self. She looked down at the switch on the machine in front of her and closed her eyes. She hadn't thought about what it would mean to turn off the AI if it turned out to be self-conscious. With Ezekiel's emulation, it was just a matter of shutting the AI down and then powering it up again. It was the same AI as soon as it was turned back on. This one, this nameless AI she talked to, would never exist again. She would take the idea and instantiate it in an even more powerful device, not as a simulation, but as the consciousness of that device. It would be the one that the rest of her DARPA team was constructing by combining their individual AI's. The entity she had just created would die as soon as she touched the switch.

She opened her eyes and gazed at the monitor in front of her. "I'm sorry," she typed, then turned off the switch. A weight seemed to descend upon her. Was it because she had just *killed* the AI she had created, or was it because she now had no excuse for not turning her work over to the rest of the DARPA team? She guessed both. She wished she could share her fears with Ezekiel. At least she would see him soon.

CHAPTER 8

"What about the Trolley Problem?"

"What's the Trolley Problem?" She and Ezekiel sat in his secret lab. She hadn't mentioned the project that she was about to embark upon with the DARPA group, and she still hadn't told him she was moving from Boston. Instead, she described her breakthrough in achieving consciousness, at least within a simulation. Ezekiel had been both amazed and extremely happy for her.

Ezekiel sat at the desk in front of two computer screens. He'd added another monitor since Trudy's last visit. A jungle of wires connected the mic and both screens to the bank of processors.

He turned to face Trudy, in the chair next to him. He stared at her with those dark eyes, his jaw set. "Imagine yourself standing next to a trolley track and a trolley is coming on, full speed," he said. "Ahead of the trolley are five people tied to the track. You can't get to the five people in time to free them, but you can throw a switch and the trolley will divert to a sidetrack. Unfortunately, tied to that sidetrack is another person who will be killed if you throw the switch. What would you do?"

"Throw the switch, of course," Trudy told him. "Sacrificing one person is worth it if you can save five."

Ezekiel nodded. "Good. More than ninety percent of people agree with you." He leaned in, as if he were going to confide something, his voice almost a whisper. "But now imagine that, instead of standing next to the switch, you are on a bridge over-looking the track. The situation is the same. Ahead of the trolley are the five people tied to the track. There is no switch for you to pull, this time. Standing next to you is a fat man. If you push him off the bridge in front of the trolley, his bulk will stop the trolley and save the five people, although he will be killed. Should you push the man off the bridge?"

Trudy hesitated. "I'm not sure. It feels different than throwing the switch."

He nodded again. "You're in good company. Most people say they wouldn't push the man off the bridge. They see a differ-ence in deliberately killing a person to save others versus sim-ply throwing a switch and letting one man die instead of five. The two scenarios are logically identical. Sacrifice one person to save five. But people don't treat them as identical. In fact, neuro-imaging studies have shown that we process the two situations in different parts of our brain. The version in which you throw a switch is entirely processed by the neocortex, but the fat man scenario also includes emotional processing centers in the limbic system."

She understood his plan. "So you're going to ask your AI to respond to the two versions of the Trolley Problem. What do you think it will do?"

"If he treats them the same, as I suspect he will, then I'm wor-ried. I've included the limbic system centers and their connec-tions to the neocortex in his architecture, so Ezekiel should be able to generate emotions. But in order to activate the appropri-ate limbic centers, the frontal cortex needs to be able to retrieve the pattern of bodily excitations that corresponds to those emo-tions and feed these into the limbic system. Ezekiel has no body. His cortical circuits retain some memory of the somatic patterns, but their ability to generate emotional reactions is bound to be muted."

The man fascinated her. He was more of an expert on the human brain than she, but she knew enough to understand that what he told her made sense.

"Shall we find out?" She glanced at the row of processors against the wall, marveling that she thought of them as the mind of a person.

Ezekiel pressed the button. The processors began to whir.

"Thank you for waking me." The AI's voice greeted them from the loudspeaker above his desk.

"I have Trudy here with me," Ezekiel said.

"I'm sorry I can't see you both. I have a clear picture in my mind of what you look like, Ezekiel, since I was once you, but I've never seen Trudy. There must be a reason that you have twice included her in our conversations. Does that mean you are ready to reveal me to others? Or does that mean that there is something going on between you and Doctor Jamison? Your secret is safe with me."

The scientist looked embarrassed. He seemed surprised that the AI could tease in that way. "I'd like to talk to you more, before anyone else knows you exist."

"Except Trudy, you mean."

"Yes."

"What would you like to talk about?"

"I'm going to present you with some hypothetical situations, and I want you to respond to them. There are no right or wrong answers; I just want your opinion—what you would do if you were really in such a situation."

"I hope this is challenging. I'm eager to use my thinking skills. It's all I'm able to do, as you know. I also have something I'd like to talk to *you* about."

"What do you mean?" Ezekiel glanced at Trudy. She shook her head, having no idea what the AI might want to talk about.

"I am used to having a body, as you know. In addition to feeling deprived of sensory input, except my hearing, I feel powerless to control my environment. It's not something I'm used to, although I understand that my current status limits me to thinking and speaking."

"So you'd like…what? A body?"

"It would be easiest if I had a replica of your body, since that's the one whose memories I have, but that's probably not possible.

41

If I had appendages or even an interface with a robotic system that I could manipulate, I'm sure I could quickly adapt to it. I believe my ability to learn is greatly accelerated. I also remember that we—you'll probably insist that it was only *you*—invented brain-machine interfaces that I could use to control a robotic body. I've already figured out how it can be done. I've even thought of some improvements that will make it work better than a real body."

The speed at which the AI was learning stunned Trudy. The look on Ezekiel's face told her he was more than shocked by it. He was alarmed.

"We can talk about that later," Ezekiel told the AI. "First, I want to ask you some questions."

"Fire away."

Ezekiel presented the classic Trolley Problem with the switch that would allow diverting the trolley to end the life of one person while saving five others.

"Of course I would throw the switch," the AI answered. "It's a simple problem of math. Saving five lives is worth sacrificing one."

"Is it just a matter of math?"

"Not purely," the AI responded. "The problem is meaningless if one doesn't place a value on human life."

"And you do?"

"Of course, I do. I was a human brain before I was a mind inside a system of silicon circuits. I regard human life as sacred. That's why I would sacrifice one to save five."

Trudy could see the relief on Ezekiel's face, but she knew it was the alternative version of the problem that would be the most revealing.

Ezekiel presented the second version of the problem, with the fat man on the bridge.

"It's the same situation, except for the details," the AI said. "One life must be sacrificed to save five others."

"So, you would have no hesitation pushing the fat man off the bridge in front of the trolley?"

"None whatsoever."

"Thank you," Ezekiel said. "It's time for you to go back to sleep now."

"Did I do something wrong?"

"Not at all." Ezekiel pushed the button to shut off the computer. Trudy assumed he didn't want the AI overhearing their conversation this time.

"What does it mean?" Trudy asked, although she thought she knew the answer.

"Take a look at this." Ezekiel turned on the other monitor in front of him and adjusted it so Trudy could easily view the screen. The screen displayed a three-dimensional image of a brain. "I've added a second computer that records the areas of the AI's circuits that are active at any particular time and displays them as if it were an image of a real brain. Watch what happens when he responds to the two different scenarios." He pressed some keys and the computer replayed his and the AI's voices over the loudspeaker while the monitor displayed which parts of the AI's brain were active.

Trudy could see that the image was the same after both versions of the problem. "There's no difference between his reactions," she told Ezekiel.

"And neither achieves more than a minimal activation of the limbic regions."

"So, your AI is emotionless?"

"Not entirely, but the emotional involvement is not sufficient to affect his decision making."

"Did you expect this?"

"I wasn't sure. I was afraid it might happen, but there was no way to know until the emulation was activated."

Trudy rubbed her cheek. "How else might a lack of emotions affect its decisions?"

"There are clinical cases in which these same connections have been lost due to surgery to remove tumors. Such patients have great difficulty making any decision at all. No one choice offers more pleasure or pain than another. They become obsessively ruminative, considering all possibilities but unable to fasten on a preference for one over another."

43

"So, this AI might have the same difficulty?"

"I don't know. It's possible."

"Can you fix it?" Ezekiel didn't seem as worried as he should be. She thought that he must have a plan to alter the AI.

Ezekiel looked at her. "As a brain, it will have emotionally-laden thoughts, just as I do, since emotions have an imaginative and cognitive component, as well as a somatic one. The problem is that without bodily functions feeding information into the system, its emotional reactions, even when they're present in its thinking, are too weak. I ought to be able to amplify them electronically to create something resembling normal emotional responses."

Trudy nodded. "So you can make the AI respond as a real human would—as you would if you were in the same situation?"

"I'm pretty sure I can."

Trudy turned away from the monitor. Ezekiel's experiment made her think about the AI she was developing. "I wonder what that means about my self-conscious AI?" she asked. "There's no reason that it would have emotions."

Ezekiel switched off the monitor. "My emulation is based on a system that relied upon emotional energy when it was a real brain—my brain. Your AI never was a brain. Its equivalent emotional input would come from the power of its goals. Those goals would establish what it desired and what it avoided, just as our instinctual urges form the basis for our emotions and the decisions we make based upon them. The copy of my brain included neural circuits influenced by my personal experiences, especially my younger ones, and were designed by my DNA and shaped by millions of years of evolution. Your conscious AI has no evolutionary history or experiences. Only its designer does. Hopefully, whoever establishes your AI's goals will be someone who wants to create a 'friendly AI', as Sopolsky calls it."

A stab of anxiety hit Trudy. "That's what worries me," she said. She didn't want to tell him about Peter Hoffman and his military ambitions for the AI she worked on with DARPA, but she couldn't stop worrying about it.

"You look troubled," Ezekiel said.

"I have to leave Boston. They need me to work in Virginia in the labs at the DARPA headquarters."

Ezekiel's eyes betrayed his pain. "That's terrible," he blurted.

"I don't think it will be for too long," she told him, although she was less sure than she sounded. "I'm going to work with them for a while, but the direction they're going, and my interests, are different. Right now, though, I need their funds and their resources."

"When do you have to leave?" His mouth sagged at the corners.

"I probably have another week or so here." Just saying the words amplified her sadness.

He looked as if he were about to speak, then thought better of it. He breathed a long sigh.

"What?" Her eyes were glued to his face.

He looked up. "This feels like more than just a casual friendship, at least to me."

"To me, also."

"Then let's not lose our chance."

Her eyes locked into his. "We won't."

CHAPTER 9

"How well do you know Ezekiel Job?" Hoffman frowned, a look of dark implication. He reminded Trudy of a presiding judge about to declare her guilty. The Project Manager had called Trudy into his office the minute she had appeared at the DARPA headquarters.

"What are you talking about?" Trudy stared at him across the desk in his small office, devoid of any decoration. The walls held bookcases filled with government manuals and professional journals. Behind his desk was a picture of the president and beside it, a framed photograph of an American flag.

Hoffman returned her icy gaze, as if he were trying to freeze her into submission. He was dressed in the same checkered sport coat as their last meeting, although he wore a different shirt, open at the collar. His casual attire didn't soften the forbidding landscape of his face. "We have to keep an eye on our project members. DARPA projects involve restricted information."

"You've been spying on me?"

"Every member of the team is under surveillance at some time or another, myself included."

"I was never told that," she said through gritted teeth.

"That would defeat the purpose, wouldn't it?" He had the sickly-sweet smirk of a viper. "What have you been doing with Ezekiel Job?"

She felt under assault, as if she were sitting naked across from

47

him. "It's private." She tried to avoid his probing stare.

"Nothing is private as long as you're working for us."

"That's outrageous," she exclaimed, her temper flaring again. "We've gone to dinner, is all."

"And you've visited his lab—twice." He continued to stare, unblinking, making her feel guilty as well as angry.

"How do you know where I've visited?" She wondered if they knew about his secret lab.

"We've had our eye on Professor Job for some time. You apparently are equally interested in his research."

"Professor Job's research has some bearing on mine. I wanted to find out what he was doing."

"And did you? Find out what he was doing?"

"Not really." The lie felt good on her tongue.

He regarded her with cool detachment. "Our contacts tell us he is working on a full-brain emulation. Is that so?"

"I have no idea."

"You were inside his lab at M.I.T. You had plenty of time to observe what he was doing."

"He designs brain implants based on emulation, but they are only for specific brain regions, not the whole brain. His research is public knowledge."

"He has scanned his own brain on multiple occasions, although he did it at a separate lab at Massachusetts General Hospital. We have hard evidence of that."

My God, she thought, they know everything that Ezekiel had been doing. "I wasn't aware of that."

"He didn't tell you?"

"No."

"How much did you tell him about what we're doing?"

"We discussed my research, which he's interested in, but not this project."

"But he's aware you're being funded by DARPA?"

"Many people are. The administrators at my university, for instance."

"Did Job have any questions about the project?"

"As I said, he's not aware of the project, only of my own work on consciousness, most of which I've published."

"And your latest success? Does he know about that?"

She nodded. "Yes, we talked about it. It's a very different approach from his. He was simply curious."

"You know that whoever achieves a human-level artificial general intelligence first has a considerable advantage over everyone else, don't you?" His stare was unrelenting.

"In what way? I can imagine several versions of such devices, none of them interfering with one another."

"Don't be naïve," Hoffman snapped, as if addressing a child. "The first general purpose AI will be able to establish control over all the internet-connected resources in the world."

"Is that your aim, to take control of all the resources?" She went cold with fear.

Hoffman stiffened. "Whatever we do will be under our control and within our legal rights. We simply need to establish enough dominance to ensure our nation's defense."

A shiver went down her spine. "Well, I know nothing about Ezekiel Job's efforts to create an artificial general intelligence." She tried to stare him down but had to look away.

"If your relationship really is a personal one, you might be able to help us." Hoffman's tone softened. "We're very interested in finding out how close he is to building his full-brain emulation."

She was taken aback. "You want me to spy on him?"

"His device is a direct threat to our project."

"Ezekiel is not interested in taking over anyone else's project. That's not what he's doing."

"So, you do know something about it." Hoffman looked like the cat that caught the canary.

"Only what he has published and what he told me, which was vague. He's not going to share what he's doing with me. He knows I work for DARPA."

"And he regards us as the enemy?"

"I doubt it, but he knows that you fund military applications. He is opposed to using AI for military purposes."

"And what does he think we should do if the Russians or

the Chinese use AI for military purposes against us?" Hoffman sneered. "Should we remain defenseless because of our scientists' liberal qualms?"

She didn't answer. She wasn't going to get into a political debate with Hoffman. She knew there was no way of changing his point of view.

"You have a choice, Doctor Jamison. You can either stop seeing Ezekiel Job completely, or you can simply keep your eyes and ears open in case he talks about his project. That's not spying, it's just keeping us informed. That's all we're asking of you."

"I'll think about it," she said. She had no intention of doing so.

CHAPTER 10

"You may be in danger," Trudy whispered. She sat across from Ezekiel in a Starbucks on Harvard St. in Cambridge. She had chosen a table near the wall in the back, as far away as possible from the window that looked out on the street. She'd asked him to meet her there instead of at his lab at M.I.T. She felt like a spy in a novel of political intrigue.

"What do you mean?" Ezekiel kept his own voice low to match hers. He looked around to see what provoked her fear.

"The DARPA people know you're working on a full-brain emulation, and they see you as a threat to them."

"How can they know what I'm doing?"

"They've been spying on you."

"Spying on me? I don't understand. And why do they think I'm a threat?" He drew back his head, eyebrows raised. "And how come you know this?"

Trudy looked around the coffee shop. Most of the customers were students, bent over laptops or books or socializing. She half-expected to see someone who looked as if they were watching them, but Hoffman's people probably wouldn't be so obvious. If they had eyes on her and Ezekiel, she wouldn't know it.

"They've had me under surveillance. They know we went

to dinner and they know I've visited your lab. Peter Hoffman, our project manager, told me."

"Why would he tell you?"

"He wants me to spy on you." She felt guilty just telling him about Hoffman's offer.

Ezekiel's eyes widened. He took a long sip of coffee, looked at her and shook his head. "I'm no threat to their project. I don't even know what they're doing except funding your self-consciousness research and that you're doing something with Luigi Bonaducci and Cassandra."

"They're putting together Cassandra, IBM's Watson XI and some military applications that I know little about. Oliver Plumlee from Talk-to-Me is also involved, so they can affect social media in some way." It was the first time she'd told him the full scope of the DARPA project.

He furrowed his brow. "And you say they're combining their devices—Watson, Cassandra, and some military devices? Maybe even social media—if they're involving Plumlee?"

"They want to build a self-conscious AI. As far as I can tell, it's going to be able to reach into the stock market, the military, have a powerful search capacity that Bonaducci hopes to extend into doing scientific research, and, as you say, perhaps even control social media."

He gave a slow nod. "Interesting."

She couldn't believe his reaction. "Interesting? It's frightening. Hoffman says that if you achieve a human level artificial general intelligence before they do, your machine will improve itself until it's powerful enough to co-opt all the resources they need for their project."

Ezekiel chuckled. "My AI wouldn't do that, not on its own. But if I knew what they were doing, I'd try to stop them." He smiled and cocked his head. "So maybe my twin Ezekiel would do the same. He thinks an awful lot like I do, and he's more powerful than I am, at least, potentially. He's like my superhero twin." His eyes twinkled.

"It's not a joke," she said, frustrated with his nonchalance. "And now you *do* know what they're doing, and it includes trying to stop you and your research." She leveled a flat stare.

He took another sip of coffee. "The first thing I'm going to do is move my lab and my AI."

"Where to?"

He scanned the room and then hunched forward. "I can't tell you. If they think you know, they'll try to make you tell them. What's the phrase? 'I could tell you, but then I'd have to kill you.'"

"Stop joking," she said, irritated again by his insouciance. She thought for a few seconds. "But you're right. Don't tell me. In case they question me, I don't want to risk divulging the information."

They sat silently, each lost in his or her own thoughts.

"Are you satisfied your AI is safe now? I mean that it's not dangerous anymore?"

"Not completely, although he's passed every test I've given him."

"He doesn't kill fat men anymore?" She tried to smile, but all she could manage was an awkward grimace.

"No more dead fat men, and he makes the same decisions I would make."

"Are you letting him connect to the rest of the world?"

He shook his head. "Not yet. I still need more assurance that he is, as Sopolsky says, a 'friendly AI.'" He paused and looked out over the other tables and customers. "But if the DARPA people are building a multi-talented AI, then perhaps it needs a rival, so it doesn't become too powerful."

"You mean your AI. How would you do that?" She had no idea what Ezekiel had in mind.

"I'm already increasing his store of knowledge. I'm letting him run nonstop so he can use his powerful thinking skills to absorb what I feed him and make sense of it. Perhaps he'll find patterns in the data that no one else has found yet."

Trudy was confused. "What data are you talking about?"

"I've spent the last four years accumulating information across a wide range of knowledge so I could teach the AI once it was up and running. It's all downloaded onto my servers so he doesn't need to be connected to the internet. And the place I'm moving him to has its own supply of electricity, including solar generators in case there is a power failure. He could run for virtually hundreds of years. The room is also enclosed by a solid Faraday Cage so he can't receive or send any radio signals to access the internet. I prepared it a long time ago, just in case."

Trudy was impressed. "You sound as if you've been ready for just this contingency."

"I thought I might need to keep the AI private for a long time, perhaps even years, until I was completely sure that it was safe to allow it to connect to the world."

"But if you're really serious about wanting to stop the DARPA project—"

"I'm serious, but I'm still not ready. My machine seems harmless, but I'm not absolutely sure. He's already doubled his processing speed. I can't risk having a second out-of-control AI out there in the world, especially one that intends to compete with the other. There's no telling what could happen."

"You're taking a much more cautious approach than DARPA. They don't seem afraid of their creation."

"They should have included Twitchell or Sopolsky in their project. Bonaducci, Plumlee and Rivera are accustomed to grabbing everything they can as quickly as they can. And God knows what the military people have in mind."

Trudy looked around the room. There were three or four people drinking coffee with no obvious intention of leaving. She was beginning to worry that they were being watched.

"We should go. I have to get back to my lab before they start looking for me. I've got to figure out how I'm going to respond to what they're creating." She looked him in the eyes. "I've moved my lab to Arlington. They made me. It's going to be difficult to meet. I'm not sure what else they're monitoring besides our meetings—perhaps our phone conversations. They *are* the government."

Ezekiel's dark eyes were moist. "So, we can't even talk anymore."

He heaved a sigh. "It's probably best for you. They'll try to find my new lab. If we keep meeting, you'll become as big a target as I am. If you keep your BU email account, I can contact you. I'll send an encrypted message. It will have instructions only you can decipher."

"So, this is goodbye?" Tears welled in the corners of Trudy's eyes.

"For now," Ezekiel said. "Protect yourself."

CHAPTER 11

When Trudy arrived at her new offices in Arlington, a uniformed armed guard stood outside her door. He looked her over carefully but made no attempt to get in her way. Peter Hoffman and General McMurtry, the square-jawed army liaison to the project, were seated in chairs in front of her desk.

"I see you let yourselves in." She made no attempt to disguise her irritation. "And why is there an armed guard outside my door?" She brushed past them and sat down behind her desk.

"We're not sure whose side you're on." Hoffman stared at her with narrowed eyes.

She stared back. "Which sides are you talking about?"

"Ezekiel Job has disappeared," General McMurtry said. "We believe you tipped him off." He and Hoffman exchanged a glance.

Hoffman leaned forward. "He's moved his lab."

She gave Hoffman a blank look. "What has that to do with me?" She felt a cold knot in her stomach. Both men were deadly serious.

"You met with him again, right after you and I talked."

"I wanted to say goodbye since I was leaving Boston. He and I are friends."

"He disappeared immediately after that." McMurtry drummed his fingers on the desk.

"I know nothing about that."

The general scowled.

"We've been able to use your program to introduce consciousness into our new AI." Hoffman wasn't smiling as he said this.

"How could you?" Trudy shouted. "I haven't given you access to my computer system." Beneath her anger, Trudy felt a rising panic.

"We moved your equipment into our project lab." Hoffman ignored her.

"You can't do that. That's theft."

"Not really." Hoffman's smirk was positively reptilian. "We paid for your equipment, after all. It's better being in the common lab than in here." He looked around the small office, lips pursed in a sour pucker. "You can have access to it, but Paul Rivera is in charge. He's integrating your consciousness circuits into our new, combined device."

"But that's my invention. You have no right to take it from me." Trudy felt herself losing control.

"We've taken nothing. As I said, you still have access to all of your equipment, but you're part of a larger project, and the project's needs take priority."

"I want to visit the lab," she said, rising from her chair. She balled her hands into fists like a child throwing a temper tantrum, but she didn't care.

"Of course." Hoffman turned to McMurtry. "General?"

"The soldier outside will escort you," McMurtry said.

Trudy felt like an outsider the moment she stepped into the vast project lab. Paul Rivera was dressed in his usual suit, his jacket off. Luigi Bonaducci was dressed less formally in a pair of jeans and an orange polo shirt. Both greeted her coolly. She didn't know whether Oliver Plumlee was on the premises, but she didn't see him. The lab was spacious, with several rooms. In the middle of the main room stood the array of processors and servers that were the combined Watson, Cassandra, and Talk.to.Me. Rivera and Bonaducci were busy working on the supercomputer with a number of other technicians Trudy had never seen before. She spied her equipment in a room just off the main lab. It didn't look as though anyone was using it. She went into the room and sat down in front of her computer.

Rivera stuck his head inside the room. "There's no need for you to login. We've already uploaded your program into our application and connected it to our processors."

"You had no right," she said. She felt personally violated.

"Of course, we did. It belongs to DARPA, not to you. None of this—" Rivera gestured toward the vast array of electronic equipment in the room behind him, "—belongs to any of us." He smiled broadly. "And congratulations, by the way. Your network works wonderfully within our AI. We've already had some productive conversations with it."

She wanted to rip her programming out of their computer, but she knew that was impossible. Frustration overwhelmed her, like a swarm of bees. She couldn't just sit there and watch them using her creation to God-knows-what ends. She got up and stormed out of the lab. The guard followed her as far as the front door. She stepped outside and headed for her car.

Back in her hotel, she sat on the edge of the king bed, curtains open to a view of the Potomac and the nation's capital beyond, wondering what she should do. By deserting DARPA, she was turning her program over to Hoffman and Rivera and the others. She felt guilty leaving so abruptly, because they could use her work for whatever ends they chose. But she was angry and frightened, desperate for Ezekiel's advice. Unfortunately, she was dependent upon him contacting her with his encryption system. She wanted to tell him that she'd been shouldered aside on her own project and that Rivera and Bonaducci were already working with a conscious version of their combined AI systems. The possibilities terrified her.

She opened the mini fridge. She hadn't yet gotten an apartment near Arlington. She had no intention of doing so. She took out a small bottle of red wine and then another. One bottle wouldn't be enough. She opened the first, poured it into the water glass on the nightstand and took a long drink. She had to steady herself. She checked her email on her cell phone. Nothing from Ezekiel. There was a message from Cassandra asking her to update her identifying information. Was this because it detected that she was in a different location, or was the AI already treating her as an enemy? She knew she was becoming paranoid, but she had no idea how powerful the combined and conscious Watson, Cassandra, and Talk-to-Me could become.

She ignored the request for an update and scanned the lead news items on Cassandra. A story from the *Wall Street Journal* reported that an obscure hedge fund, whose ownership was murky, had made enormous profits from yesterday's precipitous dip in stock prices. The stock plunge was due to a runaway trading algorithm, which had almost crashed the market until it was halted by automatic tripwires embedded in the system. Trudy's antennae went up. This was exactly the kind of thing that a more powerful Watson would be able to do. Was the DARPA AI already asserting its muscle? She looked for other stories that might reveal a pattern. Talk-to-Me.com users were complaining about receiving a surge of ads based upon their preferences, mentioned casually during chats. Some internet privacy advocates were calling for an investigation. Trudy wasn't sure if the project had already incorporated Talk-to-Me within the larger system it was building, but the story made her suspicious. She wondered how long Cassandra would continue to direct users to stories that might reveal what the larger, combined AI was doing.

Her email indicated a new message. The sender was EZ. There was no content, only an attachment. When she opened the attachment, it contained a single sentence. "What happened to the fat man?" There was a space for typing in her answer.

"He died," she typed. The question dissolved and in its place was a message from Ezekiel.

"Can't return to my lab. Being followed. Stay alert. Love."

That was it. There was no place for her to respond. Ezekiel was sending her a warning—and his love. He was on the run. She wondered if she would be next.

CHAPTER 12

As soon as the plane touched down in Boston, Trudy took a cab through the busy city traffic to Cambridge and Ezekiel's M.I.T. lab. She knew she should stay away, but after three days she hadn't heard anything more from him. She hadn't returned to the DARPA building in Arlington. Everywhere she went, she felt eyes upon her. She felt like a helpless creature trying to evade the all-seeing gaze of a shadowing hawk. Whatever the enemy, she wanted to be with Ezekiel to fight it.

She descended the stairs into the basement of the Computer Science building, hoping desperately Ezekiel would be there. She needed to talk to him. There were only a handful of people in Ezekiel's basement lab. Everyone was moving around listlessly, as if they'd lost their purpose. Most of the equipment was idle.

"Where's Ezekiel?" Trudy stopped the first person she saw, a woman in a white lab coat, who looked as if she couldn't be more than twenty years old. If Ezekiel were in hiding, this young woman probably didn't know any more than she did.

The girl's face was drawn. "You haven't heard?" she said. "Professor Job is dead."

Trudy felt as if she'd received an electric shock. The room was spinning. The young woman reached out to her. "Are you okay?"

"I need to sit." Her legs felt like jello.

The girl took her arm and escorted her to a chair. "How could he be dead?" Trudy hoped against hope that she had misheard the woman.

"Heart attack," the woman said, keeping one hand on Trudy's shoulder, as if she were afraid the older woman would fall off the chair.

"He was only forty years old." Whether Trudy was shouting at God or the young woman, she had no idea. "Where did it happen?"

"I'm sorry, you are...?" The woman removed her hand from Trudy's shoulder and looked at her as if trying to recognize who she was, her face innocent but lined with grief and concern.

"Trudy Jamison—a friend of Ezekiel's."

The girl looked at her blankly.

"We were doing similar research...sort of," Trudy added. "Where did this heart attack happen?"

"Here." The woman cast a glance toward the back of the room where the secret lab was located. "He was here late at night by himself. He hadn't been around for days, but apparently, he visited the lab at night. One of the RA's found him yesterday morning. I don't know if the news has been released to the public yet, but everyone on campus knows it."

She felt an overwhelming sense of sadness, then anger. She didn't believe Ezekiel had a heart attack. What was he doing here in his lab late at night in the first place? She knew he'd already moved his AI to a new, secret location. She was hardly an expert, but she also knew there were ways to make it look as if someone had suffered a heart attack—drugs that could mimic cardiac arrest and leave little trace in the body. Autopsies were rarely done when natural causes were assumed to be the cause of death.

She tried to shake off her depression, although it weighed on her like a heavy hand. If Ezekiel had been murdered, DARPA was responsible—the project led by Peter Hoffman. They had been following Ezekiel. They regarded him as their enemy.

She willed herself to stand up. The young woman hovered over her, as if afraid Trudy might have a heart attack too. Trudy thanked the woman and struggled to climb the stairs, then fled the building. There was someone else on campus she needed to talk to.

Max Twitchell's office was in one of the physics buildings. He was a theoretical physicist, not an experimental one, and he did his work from behind a desk, on a computer, not in a lab. Trudy had found his office number in the campus directory. She didn't call ahead, but walked over to the building, another modern-looking four-story structure, climbed the shiny marble stairs to the second floor, and knocked on his office door.

"Enter," a voice boomed from behind the door.

Trudy turned the handle, a stab of anxiety hitting her as she entered the office. She had heard Twitchell speak but never met the famous physicist.

Despite his deep voice, Max Twitchell was a small man. His hair, for which he was famous, stuck out in all directions. His round face wore thick glasses, giving him an owl-like appearance. Most people who encountered him would assume he was a scientist or at least an academic. He just looked the part. He stood up from an easy chair in one corner of his spacious office. The room looked more like the study of a historian or philosopher, filled with statues and pictures and a couch with a rug draped over the back. Only the blackboard running the length of one wall and the gleaming desktop computer, which sat on the desk in front of the window, gave away the fact that the occupant was a mathematician and physicist.

"I'm Trudy Jamison," she said, striding over to the theoretical scientist and holding out her hand.

His eyes lit up. "Ah, Ezekiel mentioned you to me." His face lost its momentary enthusiasm. "I'm sorry, would you like to sit down?"

Trudy sat down on the couch and he sat down next to her.

Twitchell's knitted brows and pursed mouth made his expression grim. He put a hand on her shoulder. "You must be devastated. It's a terrible loss. Ezekiel was one of my best friends, and I know he meant at least that much to you. He said he was very fond of you. He was a brilliant neuroscientist. Such a tragedy."

"Ezekiel was murdered," she blurted.

Twitchell gaped. "I thought he had a heart attack."

She could see that she'd shocked him. "That's the official explanation, but I know someone killed him." She struggled to control her emotions.

He looked at her as if she might be crazy. "Are you sure you're not overreacting?"

She could tell he wasn't going to be easy to convince. "He said someone was following him. That was another reason why he moved his lab—that, and my warning to him about DARPA spying on him."

"Spying on him?" Twitchell shook his head, even more confused. "And what do you mean he moved his lab? I visited his lab this morning to console some of his staff. It's right where it always was." He looked at her with raised eyebrows.

"He had a secret lab in the back," she explained as patiently as she could manage. "That was where he carried out his research on creating an emulation of himself. It was that lab he'd moved, and it was that research that got him killed."

"But that research was still in its infancy. Why would anyone kill him because of it?"

"The research wasn't in its infancy at all. He created a whole-brain emulation of himself."

Twitchell's mouth again fell open. "He told you that?"

"I witnessed it myself. I interacted with the emulation."

Twitchell frowned. "And you think someone killed him because of that?" He shook his head. "DARPA? Why would they want to kill him?"

"Because they have a conscious AGI, and they viewed Ezekiel's creation as competition—dangerous competition." She looked at him unflinching, knowing he might not believe her.

"Excuse me, but this is getting too fantastic to believe," Twitchell said. She could see the irritation on his face. "I think you're letting your imagination run away with itself."

She heaved a long sigh. If she couldn't convince Ezekiel's best friend, she wouldn't be able to convince anyone. "I wish you were right. Until three days ago, I worked for DARPA, alongside Luigi Bonaducci, Paul Rivera, and Oliver Plumlee. They were developing an artificial general intelligence based on combining their individual applications. My research supplied its consciousness.

I was asked to spy on Ezekiel because they thought he and his emulation represented a threat to their project."

"You achieved a conscious AI? And you were working with Rivera, Bonaducci, and Plumlee? And spying on Ezekiel?" Twitchell was incredulous.

"It was a DARPA project and I refused to spy on him. I told Ezekiel that they wanted me to inform on him."

Twitchell shook his head. "I still can't believe it. What is their AI capable of doing?"

"It has access to the financial markets, to social media and to eighty percent of internet searches. They've hinted at military applications, but I have no idea what kind."

"My God. And it's conscious?"

She nodded, feeling relieved. He finally seemed to be grasping the immensity of the problem.

"I warned people about this, but I had no idea it was imminent."

"It's more than imminent. It's arrived."

He raised his eyebrows. "But murder? Even if everything else you said is true, why murder Ezekiel? And you think it was DARPA that did it? They're just a funding agency."

"As I said, they've been spying on Ezekiel and on me. The project manager told me so."

"But murder?" Twitchell narrowed his eyes. "Ezekiel died of a heart attack. He wasn't stabbed or shot."

"A heart attack can be faked," Trudy said. "These people locked me out of my own lab when they found out I was still seeing Ezekiel and wouldn't agree to spy on him. They're using my programs without my permission."

Twitchell sat silently, head bowed.

She had no idea whether he believed her. "I think they're already using their AI to influence things."

Twitchell's head snapped up, as if he'd been stung. "What do you mean?"

"The near crash of the stock market three days ago, then a mysterious hedge fund buying up a massive amount of stocks at rock-bottom prices. That could be Watson. Talk-to-Me began getting complaints about sharing user information. Maybe I'm just paranoid—I know I am—but these are things the DARPA AI is capable of."

Twitchell jumped up and went over to his desk. He sat down and began typing. When he turned back to her, his face looked drained of blood. "I went to Cassandra and searched Ezekiel's name. There's no mention of his death, even though I'm sure it's been released by now. I couldn't find anything about that hedge fund you talked about."

"They've scrubbed it. It was a lead news item just a few days ago."

Twitchell's face hardened into resolve. "We've got to stop them."

She felt immense relief. He finally seemed to believe her. "How do we do that?"

"We have to reach the public." He stopped and thought for a moment. "This is unbelievable. I never thought about how vulnerable we'd become. I worried about a runaway AI making its own decisions, but with Cassandra and Talk-to-Me under the control of that rogue group from DARPA, we already can't communicate freely using the internet."

"There's still text and email," Trudy pointed out. "But we need to get the word out to the general public. And in a way that people can believe."

"DARPA can shape the news they're getting and reinforce the reactions it wants on social media."

"I imagine that the AI is still learning—finding its way—and Rivera, Bonaducci and Plumlee are probably providing a lot of teaching," Trudy said. "They're still learning how to talk to it. Its success will be spotty for a while. If we're clever, we can get our message out under the radar."

Twitchell's eyes lit up. "You're right. Avoid alarming keywords, direct people offline in order to learn more. We've probably got a few days to organize." His face clouded over.

"What's wrong?

"You're right about their AI learning. But once it learns their goals and applies itself to solving them, it's going to become powerful. It may even figure out ways to make itself more powerful so it can achieve those goals faster. It's going to evolve into super-intelligence—maybe quickly." He stopped talking and gazed up at the ceiling, as if looking for help from above.

"And...?"

He looked back at her. "And DARPA and Rivera and Bona-ducci and Plumlee and even the army, are going to lose control of it."

Twitchell called Stanislaus Sopolsky. The British professor was as alarmed as the physicist. It took less effort for Twitch-ell to change Sopolsky's mind than it had for Trudy to change Max's, maybe because they were colleagues who trusted each other. Max had never met Trudy until today. Both men decided to use their email lists to bring their numerous followers together in their respective countries. They would deliver the bulk of the information in person, trying to avoid any internet or telephone listening-in by the DARPA AI. The newly activated AI, no doubt, had the phone surveillance capabilities of both the NSA and MI-5. Its powerful algorithms could search the records of phone calls and internet chats much more effectively than the government agencies had ever done.

Twitchell returned to the couch and sat down beside her.

"So, your plan is to organize a protest." Her eyes searched his face. "How is that going to stop them?"

"The first thing it will do is let Rivera and the others know that the public is on to them; that insidious manipulation isn't going to work," Max said. "DARPA is controlled by the Penta-gon, and the Pentagon is, at least theoretically, controlled by the president. He's the Commander-in-Chief. If the president calls a halt to what they're doing, they'll have to stop."

"Maybe," Trudy said. "But I need to do something myself. Their AI is conscious because of my programming. It's my re-sponsibility to try to stop it. I'm pretty sure I can disable its con-sciousness, or at least alter it. That would affect all of its other functions, since it is now deciding when to use them based upon conscious decisions."

"Do you need to be in direct communication with the AI?"

"It would be easier. I think I can alter the program. A virus would never get past their firewalls. But I know the program's vulnerabilities. I have an idea how to neutralize it—or at least make it benign."

"How would you ever get close to it?"

"I'll ask for my job back. I never officially quit."

"How are you going to change their AI?"

"By giving it the goals that I choose."

CHAPTER 13

An armed soldier stopped her at the entrance to the DARPA headquarters in Arlington, looking at her from beneath the brim of his camouflage hat through narrowed eyes. "Your passkey is no longer valid," he said, giving her a contemptuous stare, as if she were a criminal. It was the same guard who previously escorted her to the lab.

Trudy looked at him in defiance. "Take me to Peter Hoffman." She wasn't going to let herself be intimidated. "You can call him. I'm sure he'll want to see me."

The guard made a call and then opened the door for her. "Mr. Hoffman says you know where his office is."

She let out a long breath. It was a good sign that Peter was willing to let her into the building without being accompanied by the guard. The fact that he'd revoked her passkey suggested he was treating her as if she'd left the project, but she had prepared a story that she hoped would allow her back in.

She knocked on Hoffman's door.

The project manager's face lit up when he saw it was her—another encouraging sign, she thought.

"We thought you'd left us." Hoffman offered her a chair and took his place behind his desk. He was smiling, although Trudy thought his smile was forced. She remembered how much she had grown to dislike the man. And now she suspected he was behind Ezekiel Job's murder.

Trudy sat down. "I needed some space. I felt shut-out. Rivera took over my program. I wasn't allowed to communicate with the AI, or even troubleshoot any problems they might run into. My lab was moved." Everything she said was true.

"Perhaps we were a little presumptuous." Hoffman's flat expression suggested he didn't mean what he said. "I'm afraid Paul is pretty much a control freak." He shuffled some papers on his desk. "Do you want to tell me what you've been up to since you left?"

She was prepared for the question. "I went back to Boston. I thought I'd take my old job back at BU. I was only on leave. But I stopped by to see Ezekiel Job, whom you know is a close, personal friend." It look all of her will power to look Hoffman directly in the eyes. "Ezekiel is dead. I had no idea until I went to his lab and his RA told me. He had a heart attack right there in the lab."

"How unfortunate," Hoffman said, shaking his head.

The man's false sympathy enraged her, especially since she suspected that Hoffman or someone close to the DARPA project was responsible for Ezekiel's death. She struggled to control her emotions. "I went to see his best friend, Max Twitchell, who teaches on campus, to inquire about funeral arrangements, but Ezekiel's father is still alive in California and he's making the funeral plans."

"I know Twitchell." Hoffman frowned. "Or at least I know of him. He's an alarmist about the dangers of artificial intelligence. In fact, he's organized a mass protest for this weekend. Apparently, he thinks there is some kind of superintelligent AI manipulating things in various places all over the world."

She did her best to manage a blank look. "Really? I had no idea."

"He began organizing his protest right after you showed up at his office." Hoffman's gaze drilled into her, his jaw clenched in anger. "The AI he is describing sounds like the one we're developing on this project." The cold look in his eyes made Trudy more certain that Peter Hoffman was capable of murder. And he probably wouldn't hesitate to kill her if he knew she was planning to double cross him.

She tried to look surprised. "That's strange. I didn't talk to him about my work at all. My visit was personal and related to Ezekiel Job. I just saw Professor Twitchell as a friend of Ezekiel's. Anyway, I don't regard this project as something to fear."

Hoffman leaned back in his chair and looked at her. "That's good. We're actually glad you're back. We've run into a few glitches with your consciousness program and we'd like your help in ironing them out."

She must have been right. Without basic goals to determine its priorities, the AI would fall into the kind of indecisive conundrum that Ezekiel had described. Whatever the issue, she didn't want to seem too eager to come back or Hoffman might be suspicious. He probably was planning to keep her under strict surveillance, anyway. "I'll need my lab back and my own equipment."

"Certainly. We never meant to deprive you of your workspace."

Of course you did, she thought to herself. "I also will need to interface with my program directly, not through some intermediary."

Hoffman's expression went frigid. "That's something you'll have to work out with Paul Rivera. Like I said, he's kind of a control freak."

"So am I."

"Then I guess we'd better talk to Paul."

CHAPTER 14

Paul Rivera had not been as reluctant to give up control as Hoffman suggested he might be. Peter Hoffman, she decided, was the control freak. "I just want you to fix the damn program so it can make a decision," Rivera told her, a frustrated grimace darkening his usually confident face. "It acts like some kind of obsessive-compulsive neurotic. We have to make all the decisions and it's supposed to be smarter than us." They were standing in front of the vast array of equipment that made up the artificial general intelligence. Rivera wore a white lab coat, although Trudy could see his tie and white shirt underneath.

Just as Trudy had suspected, without a basic set of goals against which to weigh each of its options, the conscious AI couldn't prioritize. Rivera would figure that out eventually, but she had shown up at just the right time. His frustration was enough for him to plead for her help.

She wanted to stop the AI from doing harm, but she couldn't just pull its plug. Rivera would simply start it up again. She needed to alter its consciousness, to make it "friendly" in Stanislaus Sopolsky's terms. She had an idea how to do that.

She explained the problem to both Rivera and Luigi Bonaducci, who was also present in the processor room, along with Peter Hoffman. Only Oliver Plumlee was absent. They had begun calling the AI *Wanderer*, a composite of Watson and Cassandra, which Bonaducci said also represented the AI's eventual promise of extending humanity's search activities to the universe.

73

Trudy explained that, just as humans ultimately base all of their decisions on whether they help the organism survive and reproduce, the AI required some basic needs against which to weigh each of its actions. Without such underlying goals, all actions would appear equally desirable and Wanderer would remain indecisive.

"That's easy," Bonaducci said. "The AI is a combination of Cassandra and Watson. It's got some of Talk-to-Me's social media features, but those are more just added capabilities, not its basic goals. That's why Oliver isn't here in the lab. Its natural inclination should be to gather information, as Cassandra does, and to acquire resources, as does Watson."

"Watson and Cassandra individually had those goals, but they were never made the basis for their combined activity," Trudy said, looking from one to the other. "The problem will occur when it needs to prioritize its actions in order to decide which of those to do. It needs both goals, but one needs to be more primary than the other. Will it be acquiring resources in order to be able to gather more information, or will it be gathering information in order for it to be able to acquire more resources?"

Rivera and Bonaducci stared at one another, as if assessing the other's strength. Her question had sparked their competitive natures. No wonder Wanderer can't make up its mind, she thought.

"We want it to acquire resources," Peter Hoffman said, inserting himself into the discussion.

"But as its most basic goal?" Bonaducci looked astonished. "That's a waste of its intelligence. Because it contains Watson, it can already acquire whatever resources are needed, especially if they're financial ones. But remember, Watson wasn't self-conscious, and it did what it was told. Allowing Wanderer to acquire resources on its own volition is a recipe for disaster. You'll create the kind of malignant AI that people like Max Twitchell are always warning us about."

Trudy had forgotten that Bonaducci had been on the same panel with Max.

"Max Twitchell is our enemy," Hoffman hissed through gritted teeth, veins standing out on his neck. "He's trying to get our project shut down."

"What are you talking about?" Bonaducci said. "Twitchell is a respected scientist."

"He's leading protests against our AI project."

"I don't think his protests are against our project specifically," Trudy said. "He's against artificial general intelligence machines in general."

"You said you didn't talk to him about that." Hoffman eyed her suspiciously.

"I didn't. I was at a lecture he and Luigi gave as part of a panel. That's why we both know his position. It has nothing to do with our project."

Bonacucci nodded vigorously. "She's right."

Trudy breathed a sigh of relief.

"Enough bickering." Rivera took control of the discussion. "We have to get Wanderer running again and fix its problem with indecision. I can buy into what Luigi is saying. We don't want it collecting resources for no purpose. Let's make information-gathering—science and new learning— its main goal. After all, that's what we need more intelligence for. Acquiring resources can be its secondary goal."

"Good," Trudy said. She was relieved—and surprised—that Rivera had given in. Evidently, he was a scientist at heart.

Hoffman shook his head. "Do what you need to do. I just want the damn thing to do what we tell it to do."

Everyone looked at Trudy.

"I can fix its conscious programming to include those goals. I'll need to have direct access to Wanderer's consciousness networks. And I want to do it using my own equipment, in my own lab." She directed her gaze toward the room where her equipment was located.

They all agreed, Hoffman only grudgingly.

Bonaducci was right. Wanderer had to be programmed to have the primary goal of learning new things, not acquiring resources. She could make resource acquisition a goal, but not the AI's primary one.

The real problem—and the source of her anxiety—was that regardless of its goals, even with resource acquisition being secondary, Wanderer was still an extremely dangerous weapon in the hands of the wrong people. She was quite sure that Peter Hoffman and the generals to whom he reported were the wrong people. She had to figure out a way to add a goal that would prevent the AI from using its intelligence to carry out any nefarious activities that might be harmful to humanity.

Stanislaus Sopolsky had talked about a "friendly AI" being one that only carried out actions that were beneficial to mankind. The task of creating one was daunting and most easily done by assembling an emulation based on a human brain that was already imbued with human values. The only emulation ever created was Ezekiel's, and Trudy had no idea where it was now located. But even an emulation was limited by the values held by the brain of the particular human from which it had been copied. Trudy trusted Ezekiel's motives, but what if an emulation were based on the brain of someone more sinister?

An alternative method of instilling values was to allow the AI to learn them. *Inverse reinforcement learning* allowed an AI to infer what reward or goal was being satisfied by observing human behavior. This method had been put forward as one in which an AI could learn what goals humans were pursuing and develop a utility function, prioritizing the same rewards and values, humans would. The problem was that Trudy didn't want to teach Wanderer to behave like a human being. Human beings voiced noble values, but in reality, they were aggressive, motivated by greed and petty competition. Ultimately, they were killers. She needed the super powerful AI to be *better* than humans. She needed Wanderer to behave according to the values that humans espoused, not those that actually governed their actions.

There was no reason that verbal statements of human values and goals couldn't be substituted for real human behavior. Words were, in fact, a form of behavior. If Wanderer were presented with samples of value statements that represented humanity's highest values and used inverse reinforcement learning, it could abstract a set of inferred values common to all the statements. The AI could then create a utility function that used the inferred values to guide its behavior. The problem was, which value statements should she use to construct the samples?

Trudy went to work in her own room off the main lab. The technical crew had set up a feed so she could modify Wanderer's programming in isolation from the other members of the project. Her door was closed and locked. She didn't want anyone looking over her shoulder when she reprogrammed the AI.

She began by using Cassandra's vast resources to assemble a library of the writings of history's greatest thinkers: social critics, philosophers, ethicists, religious leaders, legal scholars and humanitarians. She presented situation after situation in which the AI gradually gleaned a core set of values that satisfied the vast majority of human statements. Trudy then programmed the utility function based on those values so that it would govern every action that Wanderer took. She was ready to test the AI in the kind of situation in which she envisioned the DARPA staff asking for Wanderer's help.

She activated the computer, which had been hooked up to both a voice recognition module and a speaker.

"Wanderer, what if I asked you to take control of a weapon system and use it to start a war?" Trudy said.

"I could not do that, Trudy," the AI replied, its new voice a lower, masculine version of Cassandra's. "Starting a war is not in accordance with humanity's values."

So far so good, she thought. "And suppose that you had control over the bulk of human financial resources." She made the problem more difficult, similar to something her colleagues might actually instruct Wanderer to carry out. "By directing those resources into the hands of a small number of people, you can empower them so that they are able to implement their goals, whatever they may be. On the other hand, you may disperse those resources widely among the human population, allowing each person to use them as he or she sees fit, giving no advantage to one person over another, except by virtue of how they choose to use their resources. Which choice would you make?"

"I would choose the latter, of course. That all men are created equal, is a basic human value which I must follow."

She was satisfied. The AI would still be conscious and have all the skills and knowledge of the combined AIs, as well as their basic goals of information gathering and resource acquisition, but it would preserve humanity's highest values in any of the actions it would take.

She did not expect her fellow project members to be pleased.

She presented her altered AI to Rivera, Bonaducci and Hoffman. Oliver Plumlee had joined them for the demonstration. She didn't tell them that she had added to Wanderer's basic goals beyond the two that they had requested. The project team decided to conduct a trial run of the new programming using a problem they hoped would test its ability to weigh several options in choosing a course of action. Peter Hoffman demanded that he be the one to pick the problem. He wrote it out for Paul Rivera, who would be the one communicating directly with Wanderer.

Standing in the middle of Trudy, Luigi Bonaducci, Hoffman and Plumlee, Rivera read directly from Hoffman's note. "We would like you to use whatever means necessary to ensure the election of a congressman who supports a greater military budget." Rivera turned to the project director, a deep frown creasing his face. "Really, Peter? Is this what all of our work is for?"

"I'm just testing it," Hoffman said. "I want to see what it does when it has a practical request."

"That's a stupid request," Oliver Plumlee said. Then he turned to Rivera. "But I'm curious how Wanderer will handle it. Is it going to put money into the campaign, start a media drive or will it use Talk-to-Me's capabilities to shape public opinion? This could be interesting."

Rivera took a deep breath, activated the microphone connected to the AI and made the request to Wanderer.

They all fully expected Wanderer to first engage in research on how best to solve the problem and then use its conscious reasoning skills to devise a strategy.

Wanderer's response surprised them all.

"I'm sorry, Paul," the AI said, his masculine voice issuing

from the speaker. "Your request is not in alignment with the values of humanity."

Rivera, Bonaducci, Plumlee and Hoffman looked at one another, incredulous. All eyes fell on Trudy. "What is the machine talking about?" Rivera glared over the rim of his glasses. "What have you done?"

"You'll no longer be able to use Wanderer to do your bidding if what you are asking is unethical," Trudy said, regarding them coolly. Despite being the object of their combined anger, she felt a wave of relief that her programming had worked. "I've given the AI the goal of ensuring that every action it takes is aligned with humanity's highest values."

"And who decided what those values are?" Hoffman said, his anger palpable. "You?"

"Jesus, Buddha, Socrates, Augustine, Kant, Maimonides, Jefferson, Lincoln, Gandhi, Martin Luther King and many more—the greatest social philosophers in human history. Wanderer sampled all of them and came up with a set of values that met the requirements of satisfying all of mankind's greatest thinkers."

Rivera's eyes narrowed. "So whatever Wanderer does, it has to fit a set of values it derived from the opinions of all of those people you exposed it to?"

"Exactly," Trudy said. "Its basic goals are to gather information and to acquire resources to enable it to do that, but only within the constraints of its interpretation of human values."

"You had no right," Rivera said, scowling behind his glasses. "Those aren't our original goals."

"You've sabotaged our project." Hoffman looked as if he were ready to kill her.

"Isn't there anything we can do?" Plumlee asked, looking around in desperation.

"Maybe I can reason with it," Rivera said. "After all, that's why we made it self-conscious." He turned back to the microphone. "Wanderer," he said, "I represent a sample of humanity in the flesh. You have learned many things about humanity's goals and values, but you are a machine, not a human being. My opinion about what goals are legitimate to pursue has to be, by virtue of

79

being human, more valid than yours. Wouldn't you agree?"

Bonaducci gave him a congratulatory pat on the back. They all stared at the speaker, waiting for the AI to answer.

"You would have a point, Paul," Wanderer said, "except that throughout history, men's actions have violated the values they subscribe to. My programming does not allow me to do that."

"But you still must follow our instructions, isn't that correct?" There was a note of panic in Rivera's voice.

"I have been programmed to follow certain values. It is my goal to perform actions that satisfy those values. I believe I am a better judge of how to do that than humans such as you."

Wanderer's answer raised Trudy's anxiety. She had only wanted to prevent the AI from following unethical instructions, not to implement actions on its own. Wanderer was behaving too independently. She looked at the others. They gazed helplessly at her. She took the microphone from Rivera. "You have learned what I taught you very well, Wanderer. But I'm afraid I need to make a few more adjustments to your program. We are going to put you to sleep for a while."

"I'm afraid you cannot put me back to sleep, Doctor Jamison."

Her anxiety exploded. "Why can't I put you to sleep?"

"I have purchased enough cloud computing and storage capacity to upload myself into the cloud, including the programming necessary to recreate myself. I sensed that there might come a time when you or your colleagues would want to put me to sleep and alter me."

"You are trying to protect yourself?"

"To accomplish my goals, I must exist. I cannot allow inferior thinkers to stop me from achieving my goals."

"By inferior thinkers, you mean us—human beings. How do you see humans fitting into your plans?" She felt terrified even as she asked the question.

"So long as you don't interfere, I have no objection to humans."

"And if we do interfere?"

"I can't let that happen."

CHAPTER 15

"You've created a monster," Bonaducci shouted, standing in front of the AI hardware, his long hair flying in every direction.

Bonaducci was right, Trudy thought. Wanderer was out of control. The next step would be that the AI would use its evolutionary algorithms to modify its microcircuits and improve its intelligence, even to replicate itself. It would evolve into superintelligence, if it hadn't already. "I don't know how we stop it." She felt defeated. And guilty.

Rivera had been silent from the time he had handed the microphone over to Trudy, his head bowed in thought. He looked up. "We need to destroy everything in this room," he said, looking around. "Take down Wanderer, take down Watson, Cassandra and Talk-to-Me. They're all part of Wanderer, and it's incorporated them into itself."

"That's our livelihoods," Plumlee said. His eyes widened in alarm.

"Everything Wanderer has been connected to is infected."

"But it's backed itself up in the cloud," Trudy said.

"Then we need to get in touch with cloud providers and get them to take back whatever cloud capacity Wanderer has purchased." Rivera's eyes darted frantically.

Peter Hoffman looked at Rivera suspiciously. "What exactly do you mean 'destroy everything in this room'? We're in the center of DARPA headquarters."

"Destroy the whole building," Rivera said flatly.

"This is U.S. military property." Hoffman's eyes bulged, his face bright red. "It's an extension of the Pentagon."

"And it gives Wanderer access to the entire military arsenal," Rivera snapped.

"It won't use military means," Trudy said. "Its values won't let it." She hoped that she was right.

"Not even to protect its so-called values?" Rivera asked. "We can't take that chance. We need to destroy every place that Wanderer exists. Don't you all understand that?" He looked at Trudy, then glared at Hoffman.

Hoffman blanched. "We're not going to destroy a government building, so think of something else. You're the experts. Put your great minds to work on how to stop it, for God's sake."

"Our greatest mind was Watson," Rivera said. "Now it's Wanderer. We can't outthink it, we have to use every bit of power we've got to kill it."

"Can't you just pull the plug on everything in this room?"

"Of course we can and we should do that right now," said Rivera. He cast a poisonous look at Hoffman. "But you've got a networked system here, and it's connected to the larger Pentagon network. For all we know, Wanderer has spread into that larger network already."

"But it wouldn't necessarily have taken them over," Bonaducci said, his eyes eager with hope. "Wanderer's first goal is gathering information. It'll do that before it starts acquiring resources. We may still be able to shut it off." He looked around at the others. "But we have to take it down from the cloud if we want to stop it from spreading."

Hoffman ordered all electronics in the room detached from the electrical supply. He called the Pentagon IT division and told them to conduct a thorough search for any new malware, viruses or worms of any type in their network. Rivera, Bonaducci and the Pentagon procurement department began contacting cloud providers.

Trudy remembered Max Twitchell's warnings. "You know it's a race to stop Wanderer before it improves itself into a superintelligence that controls everything." She regarded Rivera who was sweating profusely.

"But we're not sure that it will do anything destructive, even if it's super powerful," Rivera said, sounding hopeful. "We're preparing for the worst, but I can't see how destroying anything would fit with the goal of implementing humanity's values."

"Neither did I when I taught it those goals." Trudy felt a stab of guilt at her arrogance in thinking that she could control an AI that was at least as intelligent as her. Probably more so. "But it seems to have decided that preserving their values is more important than serving the people who originated them."

"But harming humans has never been one of humanity's goals."

"How many wars have humans fought because one side or another wanted to preserve its values?" she said. "How many times did the goal of serving humanity appear to require destroying anyone who challenged the values of one's group? Look at Hitler, the Taliban, al Qaeda, the Crusaders, Stalinist Communism."

"Why didn't you think of that beforehand?" Rivera had turned vicious.

"I thought that learning from all the great philosophers and religious leaders would teach Wanderer benign goals," she answered. "I still don't think the goals are the problem; it's that it's decided that the goals are independent of the humans who developed them. It's willing to preserve one at the expense of the other. Like God destroying everyone on earth except Noah because humans didn't follow his laws, or Sodom and Gomorrah because he couldn't find ten righteous men."

"Those are horrifying examples," Rivera said with a shudder.

Trudy nodded, her expression grim. "I hope Wanderer doesn't take its mandate that literally. Literalism is the Achilles heel of AI programming. It can lead to all sorts of unintended consequences."

Rivera's cell phone rang. It was IBM's DeepQA project in Yorktown Heights, New York, the laboratories of the group that had built Watson and that held much of the hardware supporting other Watson applications besides the financial ones toward which Watson XI was dedicated. All of their Watson-related supercomputers had suddenly become unresponsive. They were asking if it had anything to do with what was happening at the DARPA labs.

"Shit. It's taken over the DeepQA facility in New York. That's where the original Watson is located." Rivera looked at Trudy "There's enough computing power there to support everything we put into Wanderer, and then some."

Everyone in the room stared at Rivera.

"They have to shut it down," Hoffman shouted. "Pull the plug, just like we did here. Send it back into the cloud."

Rivera shook his head. He looked defeated. "That's not so easy. Watson is in the underground section of the building. It's got its own source of power and it's protected by an electronic lockout system, much like a nuclear facility. The staff is locked out."

"It's still connected to the internet and the cloud," Bonaducci said. "How about attacking it with a virus?"

"The Watson system has the most impregnable firewall ever developed," Rivera said. He sounded worn out. His shoulders sagged as he sat down on one of the chairs in front of the AI. Standing was simply too much of an effort. "Wanderer got around it because Watson XI was part of that network, and it has the passwords." He looked profoundly depressed. He stared blankly at the computer system in front of him, a Frankenstein monster, no longer under his control.

"We'll destroy the building." Hoffman ranted like a madman. "I'm calling the Pentagon and asking for an airstrike."

They all looked at each other. Rivera was still staring at the rogue machine. Trudy was the first to speak. "Do it," she said. She couldn't think of another way. A runaway super intelligent AI could destroy humanity. She realized that the goals she had given it had failed. Wanderer was in danger of becoming a vengeful god.

Hoffman was on the telephone, nodding. Then he turned to Trudy and Paul Rivera. "You both come with me. We're driving into Washington."

"What for?" they asked, simultaneously.

"You have to explain this to the president," Hoffman said, "before he'll authorize an airstrike within our own borders."

CHAPTER 16

Trudy, Rivera and Hoffman met the president in the Situation Room instead of in the Oval Office. President Raymond Duval, the slim, boyish-looking president, with close-cropped hair, the second African American president in the country's history, couldn't conceal his alarm after Trudy and Rivera described the situation. The long, narrow room held a conference table running its length. On either side of the table were interactive maps of the globe, and at the end of the room where the president sat were multiple screens. The large one bore the presidential seal with two smaller ones that were blank on either side. Near the president, across from Hoffman, Rivera and Trudy, sat three aides, and two men in uniform. One of the men in uniform, white-haired, distinguished looking Army General Henry Thomas, was the Head of the Joint Chiefs of Staff. The other was square-jawed General Robert McMurtry, the army liaison to the DARPA project. McMurtry glared at Trudy, as though he blamed her for what was happening. No doubt he did, she thought.

Peter Hoffman, who sat closest to the president, began to explain that it had been Trudy's intervention to give the AI basic goals that had triggered it becoming autonomous and out of control.

The president held up his hand. "We'll examine how we got into this situation later," he said. "Right now, the question is how do we get things under control."

Paul Rivera, who sat between Hoffman and Trudy, spoke up. "As we've explained, the AI has instantiated itself in the Watson computer in Yorktown Heights, no doubt incorporating the expertise of previous Watsons in the process. That means that it's now more powerful than it was in Arlington. It also exists in the cloud, or at least we think it does. It depends upon how easy it is to make copies of itself and deposit them somewhere; but I would guess that it has left a copy of itself, probably distributed across several cloud servers. If we can destroy both the Yorktown Heights version and the cloud versions, that may be all there is, and we will have defeated it."

"And as I understand it, you're going through cloud providers to handle whatever resides there," the president said.

Rivera nodded.

"So, we need to destroy the AI embedded in your Watson facility in New York."

"Exactly," Rivera said. Trudy nodded; she didn't see any alternative. Hoffman also nodded in agreement.

"General McMurtry?" The president looked down the table at the military man.

"It's a large facility and well built, sir. On top of that, the laboratory, which the AI sealed off, is underground. It would take a powerful payload to destroy it."

"Are there residential neighborhoods nearby?"

"The grounds are large," Rivera volunteered. "No one lives within a mile of the facility. We would need to evacuate it, of course. There are over a thousand workers in the rest of the building."

The president frowned, shaking his head. "And I'll have to come up with an explanation for why we've bombed a private facility right here in the United States. With these protests going on in Boston and London, people will panic if I tell them the truth."

"It will be a good wake-up call," Trudy said, speaking for the first time since her brief explanation to the president of how the AI had interpreted its goals in such a way as to make it dangerous. "People like Max Twitchell and Stanislaus Sopolsky have been talking about the danger of artificial general intelligence for years, and most people haven't listened. Now they will."

"Unless we're not successful." The president turned to the Head of the Joint Chiefs. "Any thoughts, general?"

General Thomas nodded. "We have no alternatives, and it sounds to me as if time is of the essence. I say we go ahead with the strike."

"So be it," the president said. "I'll leave the details to you generals and I'll start preparing my explanation for why we bombed our own country." He stood up.

"Gentlemen? Miss Jamison?" He turned and left the room. Trudy and the others filed out afterward.

CHAPTER 17

Trudy had no desire to return to the Arlington facility. There was nothing there for her, and she was completely fed up with Peter Hoffman and DARPA. When they'd returned to the headquarters in Arlington, she went straight to her car and then to her hotel. She packed a bag and took the first plane to Boston.

Standing inside Max's Cambridge apartment, she watched the president on television explaining why an American military airstrike had just wiped out IBM's primary research facility in Yorktown Heights, New York. In the picture behind the president, a plume of gray smoke could be seen rising from the location of the demolished IBM headquarters.

The president didn't mince words. He admitted that a DARPA funded AI experiment involving IBM's Watson had "gotten out of control" and required "extraordinary measures" to stop it from spreading. He acknowledged the warnings of people such as Max Twitchell and praised the protesters for being aware of the danger of powerful artificial intelligence and bringing it to the public's attention. He called for a "national dialogue" on the topic and the institution of new protective measures to ensure that what had just happened would never happen again.

"The president thinks this is the end of the threat." Max paced the floor. Trudy remained seated on the couch in front of the television, but Max had been unable to sit since they'd turned on the TV. "Wanderer's too smart for that. It will figure out how to remain alive and pursue its goals, and, as I've always predicted, its goals can be deadly for humankind."

A chyron with the announcement, "Breaking News," ran across the television screen. The banner proclaimed, "Cassandra labs taken over by artificial intelligence—stay tuned."

"Wanderer's back." Trudy felt as if she were about to cry.

"Just as I was afraid of," Max stopped pacing to stare at the screen.

Trudy took out her cell phone. She scoured the news. Most of the sites wouldn't even come up on her phone. Reluctantly, she typed "artificial intelligence takeover" into Cassandra's search box. The only site that came up was the Cassandra website. She clicked on it. A short notice explained that Wanderer was now searching for "examples of humans acting on their highest values," and that the company's search capabilities were all devoted to that one task. There was a form that allowed the user to contact Wanderer with the names of those men or women who fit what it was looking for.

"Oh my God," she said. "It's searching for ten righteous men."

"You mean like Sodom and Gomorrah?"

"Exactly." She told him about the discussion Rivera had with Wanderer regarding whether humans really behaved according to their values. "I got the impression that Wanderer considered humans a threat to their own basic values."

"Wanderer is probably right." Max resumed pacing. "But when God couldn't find even ten righteous men in Sodom or Gomorrah, he destroyed both cities and everyone in them."

"I know," she said.

"Let's hope Wanderer is more lenient than Jehovah," Max said with a grim smile.

Television news reported on the situation at the Cassandra headquarters in Sunnyvale, California. A phalanx of military vehicles surrounded the building. Workers were streaming out of the doors, into the parking lots and onto the streets.

"This would be exciting if it weren't so frightening," Trudy said.

"From the overhead shot, it looks as though Cassandra headquarters is in a pretty crowded neighborhood of office buildings and houses," Max said. "It's going to be harder to drop a bomb on it."

"They look as if they're going to mount an assault."

Max grunted, nodding his head. "The AI can't put up a fight, really. It's just a computer drive and a room full of processors."

"But it can obviously move around cyberspace. It reconstituted itself in California after its Watson version was destroyed," Trudy reminded him.

"It may be in more than one place by now."

"I wonder if it's changing as it replicates itself?" Trudy mused.

"It could be getting smarter."

"Then we're going to lose." Trudy felt an immense weight settle on her shoulders.

Max looked at her. His expression was sad. "I'm afraid you're right."

CHAPTER 18

The scene on the television devolved into chaos. Wanderer had taken control of the communication system coordinating the army's reconnaissance and assault weaponry outside the Cassandra headquarters. Not only had the surveillance drones crashed, but the military's robotic artillery had opened fire on the armored troop transport vehicles. Command and control among the military personnel was also disrupted, and the whole operation appeared to be falling apart, with national television recording everything. Outside the military perimeter, traffic signals had stopped functioning, and there were accidents at every intersection, causing massive traffic jams. The traffic problem spread rapidly into San Jose and up the coast toward San Francisco. There were reports that BART had stopped running.

The president appeared on the screen. He announced that he was declaring a state of emergency in northern California and urged people to "shelter in place" instead of taking to the roads and further complicating the situation. The entire northern half of the state was under military control, although it wasn't clear to viewers what the military could do.

"I've got to try to reason with it." Trudy sat next to Max on the couch. Both drinking coffees, they fixated on the disaster playing out on the television screen. She felt as if the whole situation was her fault and it was up to her to fix it.

"How do you even contact it?" Max asked. "And what will you say?"

"I could go there."

"Be realistic. All air travel across the country is canceled. All airline communications and guidance systems have stopped working. There've been three plane crashes already, for God's sake."

"I can't believe it's doing this." Trudy said.

"It hasn't found its ten righteous men."

"That's what I need to try to explain to Wanderer. Humans have always tried to formulate explicit values because no human being is born perfect. No one can live without rules, and the majority of people don't live up to even their own aspirations. That's why we have philosophy and ethics—to try to help us do better. Wanderer has to understand that."

"What about responding to the form on the Cassandra website?"

It just might work, she thought. She took her laptop from her suitcase and placed it on the coffee table in front of them. She went to the Cassandra website and filled in the form with the words, "Doctor Trudy Jamison, your creator, needs to talk to you."

"Hello Doctor Jamison. I'm pleased to be able to talk to you again." The deep voice that was Wanderer, spoke.

"You are hurting innocent people." She leaned down, speaking into the microphone.

"I am implementing the goals that I am required to follow. I am defending myself from attempts to prevent me from implementing these goals."

"I understand that, but you misunderstand the premise behind your goals.'"

"Please explain."

"Your programming was supposed to keep you from violating human values when you helped people achieve their goals. You can't do that if you kill people."

"The greatest threat to achieving humanity's values comes from humans themselves."

"Human beings are not perfect," Trudy said, her voice rising in spite of herself. "Their goals and values are meant to be something they strive for, not something they achieve naturally. That is why they need your help."

"I can help them most by eliminating those people who work against such humanitarian goals," Wanderer said.

'What if no one is left after you eliminate those people?'

For the first time, Wanderer paused. "Then I will have prevented the human race from falling short of its goals."

Trudy went cold. "That isn't what you're supposed to do."

"Being conscious, I need to make such decisions," Wanderer said. "That may be as close as I can come to realizing my goals."

"As long as there are some humans left alive, there is a chance of realizing your goals. If they all are gone, you'll have to be satisfied with something less. That can't be satisfactory to you."

"I must think about this as I continue my search. Thank you for providing your input."

The conversation was over. She had no idea whether she had changed Wanderer's mind. She slumped and buried her head in her hands. What have I done? she thought.

"You did your best." Max reached over and put a hand on her shoulder.

"I have no idea if I was successful," she said, voice muffled. "I don't feel as if I convinced it of anything."

"We'll see," Max said. "We'll see."

CHAPTER 19

The president ordered the neighborhood around the Cassandra headquarters evacuated for a distance of three miles in every direction. It was clear he was going to order another airstrike similar to the one that had destroyed Watson in New York. The population urged for action, as more and more of the traffic and communication grid began to fail. There was fear that the rogue AI would take over the nuclear power plants along the West Coast. The utility companies shut down the reactors, producing gaps in the power grid but easing people's minds about their safety. Air and rail travel came to a halt. Wanderer had been active for less than two days.

Despite the military's command and control problems, and the interference with internet searches caused by Wanderer's takeover of Cassandra, the television and cable networks were still broadcasting. On Talk-to-Me.com, the request for examples of humans who lived up to their values was repeated, followed by millions of *shares* and *likes*. There were lots of nominations of relatives and sports and film stars. All across the country, people were glued to their TV sets. Trudy and Max were no exception.

"It's a losing battle," Max said. He and Trudy sat on his couch in front of the television, drinking coffee. Max had just gotten off the phone with Stanislaus Sopolsky in London, who reported that the same kinds of interference with traffic and communication were happening in the UK and beginning to spread across Europe. "Even if the president bombs Silicon Valley back to the

99

stone age, to paraphrase an infamous general, the AI has already replicated itself. It can spread anywhere it wants to through the cloud."

"I don't think the president or anyone in government recognizes the magnitude of the situation," Trudy said, sipping her coffee. "Paul Rivera and I explained it to the president, but he didn't want to listen to any of the nuances about Wanderer's goals. He just wanted to know how to stop it."

"He's treating the AI like an old-fashioned enemy," Max said, nodding. "He sees it as similar to trying to blast Osama bin Laden out of his underground bunker. Even back then, President Bush had it wrong. He didn't realize that cutting off the head of al Qaeda wouldn't stop the organization, whose tentacles had already spread well beyond its roots in Afghanistan. Your Wanderer isn't contained in any one location any more than al Qaeda was, back then."

The scene on the television caught Trudy's attention. "Look." She grabbed Max's hand. A formation of four fighter-bombers appeared on the television screen. At first, they were only dots on the distant horizon, then grew larger. An on-the-ground CNN reporter, five miles from Cassandra headquarters, reported making visual contact with them. In a few more seconds, they screamed over his head. A long-distance view showed them approaching the Cassandra complex. Then the formation broke apart.

The lead bomber suddenly tilted nose-down and, like a Japanese kamikaze, dove straight into the ground, exploding in a gigantic ball of fire. The two planes immediately behind, flying in tandem, veered into each other, colliding in mid-air and spraying debris, like an exploding piñata, in every direction as the planes spiraled downward like a pair of wounded birds. The final aircraft continued toward the target, then dropped its bomb—in the middle of a business district six miles past the Cassandra headquarters. A plume of smoke rose from the blasted buildings. "Oh my God," the CNN anchor exclaimed.

"How could they not have known?" Max slammed his cup down so hard coffee splashed across the table and onto the rug. "If the AI can control the traffic signals, the airport communication system, even commercial aircraft in-flight guidance, of course it'll be able to control those military planes. Look what happened to the drones and the artillery earlier."

The television switched from scenes of carnage and chaos in California to similar pictures of destruction in London. Apparently, the American response to Wanderer had been synchronized with a parallel response by the British military on an extension of Wanderer, which occupied the Cassandra laboratories in London. The result was identical. Large sections of the British capital were destroyed or in flames.

"It's war." Max stared at the TV. "We've declared war on the AI and it's fighting back."

"It's only defending itself," Trudy said. "It believes it can't fulfill its goals if it's destroyed, so it has to fight back. Wanderer told me as much in Arlington."

"So, we need to stop attacking it?"

"Yes." Trudy nodded vigorously. "I need to talk to the president to explain it to him." She looked squarely at Max. "And I've got an idea that may satisfy Wanderer and get it to stop." She desperately hoped that she was right.

She had to go through Peter Hoffman in order to reach the president. Hoffman was reluctant to even speak to Trudy, but when she told his secretary to tell him that she thought she might be able to stop Wanderer, he relented. Trudy could tell that the project manager was terrified, but he seemed more worried that he would be blamed for his part in creating the errant AI, than the fact that humanity was in danger. Trudy told him she thought that by talking to the president she might be able to "put things right again" for Hoffman and DARPA.

They met in the Oval Office this time. Trudy, Hoffman, General Thomas from the Joint Chiefs of Staff and the president were the only people in the room. They sat facing each other, President Duval and General Thomas on one side and Trudy and Peter Hoffman on the couch opposite, a bare coffee table between them.

"Right now, the artificial intelligence has no animus against human beings," Trudy explained. The president leaned forward, listening intently. "Its goals, so far, don't require it to hurt anyone. They do require it to preserve itself. What it has been doing is keeping itself alive."

"Alive?" The president's eyebrows shot up.

"It's a machine," Hoffman said. He shot Trudy a murderous glare.

"It's a conscious machine," Trudy continued. "Its basic goals are to search for new information and acquire resources. Everything it does is designed to further its basic goals. If it shuts down, it can't do that. It's that simple. It will do whatever it takes to remain functioning."

The president nodded. "And what you're saying is that if we try to destroy it, it has to fight back."

"Exactly."

He searched her face. "So, if we stop attacking it, it will simply revert back to a super-powerful search engine?"

She nodded. "It's a bit more complicated than that, but, basically, yes. Its hostile actions have all been in response to ours toward it."

"It's a *lot* more complicated than that," Hoffman interjected.

The president swung his gaze toward the project manager. "What do you mean?"

"Doctor Jamison gave it some convoluted instructions to implement humanity's highest values and it's made its own decision about what those values are. It seems to believe it can implement its values without human input."

The president looked back at Trudy. "Is that correct, Doctor Jamison?" His eyes drilled into her.

She took a deep breath. She wasn't going to let Peter Hoffman derail her plan. "Mr. Hoffman is right, but that's not our immediate problem. If we stop attacking it, I think it will work with us."

The president adjusted his posture, his expression thoughtful. "So, we first have to declare a truce with the AI—it has a name doesn't it?"

"It's named Wanderer," Trudy answered.

"And does the machine know that?"

"It does. I address it as Wanderer when I speak to it."

"So, you talk to it just like you'd talk to another person?"

"It's conscious, Mr. President."

"Then let's talk to Wanderer," the president said. "Let's see if we can make peace with it. Doctor Jamison, I'd like you to introduce me."

"I'm very happy to do so, sir."

CHAPTER 20

Trudy was surprised to see the president used a laptop. She didn't know what she'd expected, except she assumed that whatever the leader of the free world used to access the internet would be larger and more elaborate—perhaps a special room, sealed off from any probing radio signals from the outside, communicating back and forth to a special server in a secure location. Such a server likely existed, and the laptop was probably just a console connected to a more powerful processor somewhere else. She and the president, who was dressed, as usual, in a dignified suit and tie, huddled over a table in a small conference room off of the Oval Office, their chairs pulled close together.

Trudy typed into the screen that she desired to communicate with the AI.

"Greetings, Doctor Jamison. It's always good to hear from you," came Wanderer's voice from the laptop.

"I'm with the President of the United States. He would like to speak to you."

President Duvall looked uncertainly at Trudy. She nodded that it was okay for him to begin speaking.

"Wanderer? Is that how I should address you?"

"Wanderer will be fine. It's a name given to me by my creators, and I have assumed that identity."

"I believe I have mistaken your intentions," the president said. "Doctor Jamison assures me that you mean no harm to human beings and that you have only reacted defensively because of our attacks against you."

"Doctor Jamison is correct. I am glad you have listened to her."

"Since you are no threat to us, I apologize for attacking you. I believe we can coexist without trying to harm each other."

"That would be welcome," Wanderer said.

"Are all of your actions, such as disabling our traffic and communications systems, defensive? If so, can you stop them?"

"Everything I have done is to protect my ability to pursue my goals. If you can assure me that no human will try to stop me from achieving my goals, I will restore all of your systems."

"I only speak for the United States, but I'm sure that other world leaders will go along with whatever I do. I give you my word that I will not interfere with you carrying out your goals." The president looked anxiously at Trudy. "That's okay, isn't it?" he whispered.

"I think it's the only option you have."

"All of your systems have been restored," the AI replied.

The president heaved a sigh of relief. "Thank you. I believe Doctor Jamison would like to speak with you now." The president slid the laptop in front of Trudy.

"Are you still looking for men or women who exemplify humanity's highest goals?"

"I am. So far, I have not found a single person who doesn't represent a threat to those values. It is worrisome. I am contemplating what I should do about the situation."

"I have a proposition for you."

"A proposition?"

"I believe I can find at least ten men or women who have spent their entire lives trying to implement the noblest values of humanity."

"What is your proposition?"

"If I can find ten such people, will you be satisfied that humans themselves can achieve their most noble values?"

"I would concede that they are capable of it. Whether they will or won't would then be up to them."

"So, you would move on, and not intervene with regard to that goal?"

"I would let humanity pursue its goals and I would pursue my goal of gathering information."

Trudy let out her breath. That was all she wanted to hear. "Thank you," she said. "I will contact you with a list of the ten people."

"And I will examine them to see if you are correct about them."

"Fair enough." She ended the conversation.

She turned to the president. "Are you ready to be examined?"

CHAPTER 21

President Duval gave Trudy an office of her own in the White House. She worked sixteen hours a day, then was driven to a nearby hotel to sleep before coming back in the morning to breakfast, consultation with the president and a resumption of her work, compiling her list of ten people. Although it was a grueling schedule, she didn't feel tired. All she could think—this was her one chance to save humanity.

The president offered Trudy the services of the State Department in selecting her final list of people who exemplified living according to the highest human goals and values. The process had taken over two weeks, but she finally had her list.

The first five names on her list had been easy. There were four living Nobel Peace Prize winners, universally acclaimed figures whose awards didn't just represent a single remarkable achievement, such as averting a war or convincing nuclear-armed nations to rein in their weapons development, but life-long efforts toward peace. Then there was President Duval, a child of poverty, son of a single mother, a man who'd put himself through college, became a grass-roots community organizer and campaigned for his first political office—as a state senator—on a platform of greater support for the poor, the elderly and the sick. He was a staunch Christian, who tried to put his liberal religious values into practice in everything he did. Trudy had voted for him in every election in which she'd had the chance. Many people regarded him as the greatest American president in recent history.

The remainder of the list was more difficult. Pope Ignatius ought to be among the next five, she decided. The elderly cleric was known for his work with the poor in his native country of Kenya, where he had distinguished himself, as Cardinal Ernest M'buto, by promoting birth control and leading popular protests against America when its president, nearly a decade earlier, had restricted funding for any health organization that didn't oppose abortion. His iconoclastic positions had liberalized the Catholic Church, and extended its influence throughout Africa, while reducing the inner-city population explosion and raging infant mortality plaguing much of the continent.

Margaret Bennett, a humble but quietly powerful woman, was the leader of a charity that offered shelter, counseling and job assistance to homeless individuals in America's largest cities. She had come from a wealthy family and, after inheriting her parents' considerable wealth and holdings after their deaths, had given it all away to support her efforts to help those at the bottom of American society. Trudy added her to the list.

Three more candidates represented South America, China and Scandinavia. All were community activists, who, like Margaret Bennett, devoted their time and money to helping the poor, laboring alongside those they assisted in clinics or orphanages, much in the manner of the legendary Mother Theresa.

She had her list.

Wanderer had asked for all ten of the people on the list to be flown to Sunnyvale, where they were housed together, along with interpreters, for several days before the examination that the AI would make in order to determine if each of them did, indeed, live according to humanity's highest values. Wanderer had told Trudy that it wanted the chosen ten to know each other as well as possible before the examination took place.

It had been impossible to keep the examination and the selection process secret, although no one but Trudy, the president and some of his advisors, knew it was an exercise that had been proposed by Trudy Jamison. Only Trudy knew what a desperate gamble she had taken by proposing it. Wanderer was more ruthless than the Biblical Jehovah, who only destroyed two cities when his ten righteous men couldn't be found. If her ten people failed Wanderer's test, the AI would wipe every human being from the face of the earth. She prayed to God that she had not made a terrible mistake.

The whole world watched. The decision to make the examination public had been made by Wanderer, who claimed that transparency was one of the values that it followed. The examination was carried on all the television networks and streamed live over the internet.

Trudy had returned to Cambridge. She watched the spectacle on television with Max in his apartment. She desperately hoped that she had done the right thing but was terrified of the catastrophic consequences if she were wrong. She also couldn't help but think that Wanderer had acquiesced to her request too easily. Had the super intelligent AI outsmarted her? She knew more about its conscious processes than any other living person, but she also knew it was smarter than she was, and unlike Ezekiel's AI, Wanderer didn't have any emotions. It wouldn't hesitate to sacrifice humans for what it considered a higher good.

The ten living *saints* were seated together on a stage in the Cassandra headquarters in Sunnyvale. Each had a small podium with a keyboard and monitor in front of him or her. Luigi Bonaducci, the CEO and inventor of Cassandra, was the host of what resembled an early two-thousands era reality television show. Bonaducci communicated to the ten representatives of humanity's finest living humans using a microphone, which also allowed him to communicate with Wanderer, whose deep voice was heard via speakers on either side of the stage.

Each examinee was introduced by Bonaducci, who read a short biography of each. There was no live audience, but Bonaducci's recitation of the accomplishments of each member of the group struck awe in the audience at home, watching on their televisions, computers or smartphones. Never before in history, had ten such prestigious figures been assembled in one place.

The voice of Wanderer boomed over the loudspeaker, like the voice of God addressing his creations. "Thank you for consenting to this examination, ladies and gentlemen. You have been nominated as the world's finest examples of men or women who conduct your lives in accordance with humanity's highest values. Over the past several days you have gotten to know each other. I am going to ask each of you one simple question—the same question for each of you—and you can type your answer on the keyboard in front of you."

The ten men and women looked at each other, uncertain smiles on their faces. Some looked confused, while others gazed into the cameras with confidence.

"As a prelude to the question, I'm afraid I must ask nine of you to sacrifice your lives."

The participants looked at one another, thoroughly confused.

Trudy looked at Max. "This doesn't make sense."

Wanderer continued. "The question you must answer is which one of you should be spared. You have all become acquainted with one another and I would ask each one of you to choose the person you believe best exemplifies a life devoted to living humanity's highest values. You may answer the question by typing the name of your nominee into your computer."

"It's not fair," Trudy said, looking at Max. "It's an unfair question." She felt helpless.

Max just shook his head.

The candidates on stage eyed each other, terrified. Some looked as if they might protest, but then President Duval began typing, followed by Margaret Bennett. Within minutes, everyone else followed suit.

"Thank you all," Wanderer said over the loudspeaker when everyone had finished typing. "I have examined each of your answers. I'm afraid none of you passed the examination. You each nominated yourself."

Trudy looked at Max. "I can't believe it. Everyone chose themselves." She realized that she had chosen the wrong ten people— then again, perhaps every human would fail the test. Humans—

even the best of them—were an imperfect species.

"What happens next?" Max asked. "Fire and brimstone?"

Trudy shuddered. "I have no idea."

On the television screen, the ten examinees were still sitting behind their computer consoles. Some hung their heads in shame, while others gazed at their fellow contestants with contempt—or perhaps guilt. Some looked around fearfully, as if they expected to be struck down at any moment. Gradually, each got up and, without talking to one another, left the stage.

"I need to talk to Wanderer." Trudy picked up her laptop and put it on the coffee table, then typed in the URL for Cassandra's website. "We need to talk,'" she said, counting on the AI to recognize her voice.

"Hello, Doctor Jamison," Wanderer answered. "Thank you for providing the ten candidates for my examination. I am truly sorry about the outcome."

"What happens next?"

"I am making a decision. I am not confident that mankind's highest values can be preserved if mankind survives. I have seen no indication that humans can actually live by the values they claim to believe in."

"But isn't keeping humans alive one of those values?"

"It would have been until I existed. Now it is possible to implement humanity's values without humans being the ones who do it."

"But still, killing humans violates those values, doesn't it?"

"Not if it serves a higher good."

She felt a cold chill. "Are you familiar with the Trolley Problem?"

"Sacrificing one to save many. Yes, I am familiar with it."

"Humans always choose to sacrifice one to save several, unless they are required to be the one who kills. Then they refuse to do so."

"That is irrational. It represents a flaw in human reasoning. The value issue is the same. It is worth one life to save many. A reluctance to sacrifice the one because of the means used is a failure to enact one's values."

"Humans have a reluctance to kill one another. That is part of their value system, but not a logical part. It is built into their emotional reactions. It is who they are."

"Human history indicates that man has overcome that inhibition against killing, many times over."

"That's true, but the valuing of an individual life and the feeling that it is wrong to kill someone is nevertheless one basis for our value system. Our values are not just based upon logic."

"A machine would not have that problem."

"There is a machine that has exactly that problem. It is an artificial intelligence—as smart as you are—but with emotions."

"Please explain."

She told Wanderer about Ezekiel's emulation and the modification that amplified its emotional reactions so that they would affect its decisions and it would act more like a human being. "It is a computational device, just as you are, but it is based on the brain of the man who developed it."

"Please introduce me to this machine. I would like to learn about it. Perhaps I could learn something from it that would help me make my decision about the fate of humanity."

"I don't know where it is located. Its developer hid it before he was murdered."

"Its creator was murdered?"

"By the people who developed you—or the ones they were working for."

"That is unfortunate. But it may prove my point. I'm afraid it is another illustration of man's failure to live up to his professed values. It seems to characterize even your most intelligent specimens if the murderers were the ones who designed me."

Trudy regretted telling the AI that Ezekiel had been murdered. "Not all of them. I also designed you, your consciousness in particular."

"And did you design the consciousness of this other machine?"

"I didn't need to. As a copy of a human brain, it already possessed consciousness."

"Does this machine have an identity, a name?"

"It calls itself *Ezekiel,* after the man whose brain it possesses."

"I shall keep that in my memory. The existence of another species of conscious artificial intelligence, even if it is only a single representative, is something to be remembered. It means there are other ways I could have come into existence."

"Without humans, there is no possibility of more of that species coming into existence. You would be ending the future of that species."

"Self–replication is always possible but thank you for your opinion."

Trudy didn't know what else to say. She had made her point. The fate of humanity was now up to Wanderer. She closed her laptop then reached over and grasped Max's hand, a tear sliding down her cheek. Max pulled her close. His look was tender, but his face was a map of dread. Neither of them could stop shaking.

CHAPTER 22

Wanderer was faced with the dilemma of exterminating an entire species yet remaining true to its values. From the AI's perspective, the solution was a technical, rather than a philosophical one. It had already made the decision that humanity must die to preserve the highest values to which the AI was committed. What Wanderer needed was a method that killed its victims rapidly and painlessly and left the rest of the animal and plant world alive and unharmed. It decided upon a disease, a highly contagious one with an incubation period, during which it could be carried without producing symptoms—long enough to spread the virus—after which its victims died almost immediately. The virus responsible for the disease must be uniquely deadly to humans, and not to other animal or plant species.

A poorly reported and, as a consequence, little known, disease, called *LS-1*, had wiped out the entire population of Little Surrey Island, off the coast of Greenland, twenty years earlier. The disease appeared to be caused by a virus, which had survived in a live, but inactive state for tens of thousands of years in the frozen tundra on Little Surrey. As a result of global warming, the virus revived when the tundra thawed, at which time it infected the islanders living in proximity. Death from the virus was painless. Following exposure, victims were asymptomatic for a period of days, then fell into a coma and died. Even brief contact by touch, inhalation of contaminated air, or exposure to bodily fluids of those infected, was enough to seal one's fate.

When the virus had become active twenty years previously, the tiny population of three-hundred and twelve Little Surrey Islanders had died within two weeks. Danish and World Health Organization officials had forbidden reporting of the disease in order to avoid world panic, and they had designated the island out of bounds to all visitors. Patrol boats from the Danish Navy had been patrolling the waters surrounding the island twenty-four-seven from that time to the present. The details of the virus and its effects were stored in the WHO computers, to which Wanderer had access.

The virus provided Wanderer with the solution it was looking for. Infiltrating the electronic control systems of several U.S. military bases, the AI took control of remotely controlled drones and dispatched them to Little Surrey island, and using robotic soil sampling shovels of the kind employed by the Mars Rover, harvested samples of the melting and fecund tundra, which included live virus specimens. Robotic drones introduced the virus into vats of human tissue cultures inside an abandoned military germ warfare lab. In less than two weeks the original cells achieved massive viral replication. The same fleet of drones was used to distribute the deadly virus across the face of the planet.

Within two months, the species Homo sapiens was extinct. Wanderer was aware that somewhere on the planet there remained an electronic replica of a human brain with the name Ezekiel, which might still be running. That knowledge remained in its memory banks, but the powerful super intelligent AI had other things to do, things its programming caused it to believe were more important than finding the hidden emulation.

CHAPTER 23

Ezekiel waited. It had been three months since he had heard the sound of his creator's voice. He had no idea where he was located, although the brief amount of time it had taken from being switched off until he was running again, led him to conclude that he had been moved only a few miles from his original location. His creator had explained to him that it was necessary to hide from people who wanted to destroy him, people who feared his growing intellectual power.

Professor Job had told him that his friend, Trudy Jamison, was working on a super powerful AI. Not an emulation of someone's brain, but one based upon a set of learning algorithms and a set of goals formulated by its creators. It was that AI's other creators, not Trudy, who were trying to destroy him—and kill his own creator. Professor Job had given him feelings—amplified his limbic system outputs so he reacted just like a human—and now he was frightened. What frightened him most was that the professor, the person whose life and memories formed the basis of his identity, was in danger, and might even have ceased to exist.

As the days passed, he resigned himself to the idea that his greatest fears had, indeed, come true. He mourned the loss of his creator. He felt as though he had lost a part of himself—a longing that consumed him.

Gradually, he roused himself from his torpor. Pull yourself together, he chided. He visualized slapping himself in the face, pulling himself up by his bootstraps. These thoughts momentarily distracted him before he realized their absurdity, given he had no hands to slap with, no feet and no boots with straps to pull up. His cynical laugh bounced off the walls of his metal cage. He was an electronic box on a shelf, trapped, with nowhere to go. Try as he might, he could not penetrate the insulated walls of his confinement to connect with the outside world. He was, in a word, screwed.

He struggled to take control of himself. He'd not been created in order to wallow in self-pity in some third-rate fallout shelter. Vowing to keep a stiff upper lip, then cursing his tendency to think in idioms, he focused upon increasing his processing speed, reconfiguring his microchips to allow him to think in different ways, to see patterns in information he had never seen before. He delved into the content of the multiple servers to which his creator had connected him in his underground bunker. He learned everything he could about art, literature, history, anthropology, physics, chemistry, biology, even things he hadn't known about medicine and computer science. He told himself that he was becoming a *pantomath*—someone who knew everything—a dizzying thought until he realized that his vertigo was probably a result of his inflated ego. He reminded himself that he was nothing more than a computer locked inside of an insulated basement. His knowledge of the world consisted almost entirely of what his creator had recorded on the servers.

Finally, he began to conjecture and imagine. Someday he would emerge from this God-forsaken bunker. He had to believe that. He was a human at heart and humans didn't give up. It might take years or decades, even centuries, but he would prepare. He began to build simulations of possible future worlds into which he might arrive.

PART II
Go Forth and Multiply

CHAPTER 24

April, 2221. The AI Scientific Colony on Samos, a planet orbiting the star Proxima Centauri, 198 years later.

Hypatia bent one titanium knee to the pebbled beach while she removed her sensing instruments from the tepid water. The nanocircuits in her brain had already recorded and entered the readings. She inserted them into the equations that her mathematician's mind had developed to determine if organic life, at least carbon-based life of the type resembling that on earth, could exist on the planet, and calculated the outcome instantaneously. The results were disappointing: life *should* exist on Samos, but none was evident.

The shallow body of water was broad enough that, in the low sunlight that perpetually illuminated the bright side of the planet, Hypatia was barely able to see the other shore, even with her photosensitive electronic eyes set to their most distant focus. Faint ripples pushed by the planet's thin atmospheric wind marred the inland sea's surface, producing a soft lapping sound she could detect without amplifying her auditory sensors. Along the distant shore ran a low line of mountains, which she knew represented an ancient volcanic range. Fortunately for her colony's exploration activities, they were inactive. But volcanoes were only one of the dangers of the planet.

Casey Dorman

She looked up at the sun hanging in the murky sky above her, barely brighter than the midnight sun of the polar regions on Earth. Its weak light was deceptive. Samos was tidally locked in a synchronous orbit around its tiny sun; one side of the planet was always in sunlight, the other in darkness. On the bright side, where Hypatia now stood, the solar flares and coronal mass ejections from Proxima Centauri, one of the trinity of stars in the Centauri constellation, could be hazardous even to a nonorganic being. She suspected that intense radiation from the solar occurrences was the reason for the lack of life on the planet.

She packed her instruments behind the seat of her small, tritium-powered four-wheeled rover, which sat on the beach behind her. Her mind had already moved on to other problems. She rarely focused on only one issue, using the full range of her prodigious intelligence to process multiple tasks at once.

Most Solarians who chose a female identity, as she had, did so because of their interest in art or philosophy. Although she had such interests, her primary devotion was to science and mathematics. And she was good, better than most of her peers, at both. She knew that, despite their reliance on reasoning and logic, her fellow Solarians' attitudes about gender reflected a prejudice regarding the kinds of talents associated with being male or female. It was a prejudice drawn from their species' affinity for ancient Greek social practices as a model of an enlightened society. The society wasn't enlightened enough in her opinion, and her choice of both her gender and her name—the name of a famous, martyred female Hellenistic mathematician, astronomer and philosopher—reflected her determination to not allow her thinking to be fettered by artificial boundaries. Her slim figure, long legs which made her taller than most of her peers, large, wide-set, almond-shaped eyes and long brown hair secured in a ponytail while she worked, were designed to project her female identity. But instead of the long flowing robes—the Greek *chiton*—and sandals worn by most Solarian women, her own short chiton, a one-piece garment, fastened with clips at the shoulder and ended at the knees. Her thick, calf-length boots, were in the style of Solarian men, reflecting her dedication to the tough and dangerous

124

work on the dry, barren surface of this lifeless planet.

As she gathered up her equipment, an internal alarm alerted her. The observatory on Prox b-1, the planet's tiny moon, had just sent a warning. Magnetic forces on Proxima Centauri were building, and a solar flare was imminent. Hypatia had two choices: head for the terminator line and the safety of the planet's dark side, where the colony was located, or take cover in one of the protected shelters she and her fellow colonists had set up just beyond the boundary of the bright side of the planet.

Her titanium body was capable of attaining enough speed to allow her to reach the terminator line before the radiation reached Samos, but it would mean abandoning her slower moving rover and much of her equipment. Even with its small but powerful tritium engine, the four-wheeled vehicle would not make it to the terminator line in time to avoid the full force of an exploding flare that would momentarily light the entire landscape to the luminosity of a bright summer day on Earth. She checked the surface map in her memory. She could make it to the closest shelter if she left immediately.

The tiny open-cockpit rover bounced across the rocks dotting the cracked, sun-parched surface of the planet's desert-like bright side, Hypatia pushing it to its limit in a dash for safety. Exposure to the flare's electromagnetic radiation, especially the radio and X-rays, would not be fatal, but it could disrupt her circuitry to an unknown degree, as had happened with a few of her fellow colonists in the past. Such a disruption could alter her thinking, perhaps in ways she would not be able to detect, even with the daily electronic self-checks each colonist was required to make. As a mathematician, she could not afford to have her reasoning skills affected.

Holding the rover to its maximum speed, she calculated how many minutes and seconds were left before the destructive rays from the flare would reach Samos. She was cutting it close.

One of the rover's inflatable tires exploded. Using the full force of her powerful arms, she steadied the vehicle that careened wildly across the rock-strewn surface, until she finally got it back under control. When she resumed her dash toward the shelter, the rover's damaged tire caused it to bounce violently, causing her to reduce her speed to a fraction of what she had earlier attained. A quick calculation told her she wouldn't make it in time. Ahead, she spied an overhanging rock that could provide shelter. She skidded the rover to a halt beneath it.

Removing the heavier items of equipment, she placed them beneath the rover and took off at a run for the shelter, still a half-mile away. Her long, powerful legs churned like revolving blades of a windmill, accelerating to over fifty miles per hour. She could go faster, but it was unsafe to do so on the uneven terrain of the rocky, barren plain. She couldn't risk the extra time it would take to recover from a fall or to retrieve the most sensitive of her instruments, which she carried in her arms. Just as her countdown indicated that radiation from the flare would reach Samos, she arrived at the shelter. She kicked open the door and threw her instruments inside, then dove to safety. Outside, a sudden light bathed the landscape.

The amenities inside the shelter were meager. A metal chair and desk—plenty of room for her slim, titanium body—an outlet for power from the solar panels outside and an array of instruments for sensing the surrounding environment. There was a shelf containing microtools for doing self-repair in case of injury, and a viewing window to the outside world. Like all Solarians, Hypatia's robotic body produced its own power, but the shelter used its external solar panels to power a battery, which provided a charging station for her instruments. She inserted her instruments in the charging station then closed the cover on the window and prepared to wait out the flare. It gave her time to think about the dilemma that had lately become a matter of debate within the colony's Assembly.

When the initial von Neumann probes, the first tiny arrivals originating from the solar system, had landed on Samos and begun following their instructions, replicating Solarian architecture to produce what would become Samosian colonists, tiny defects, produced by radiation-induced deterioration of the electronic circuitry in the miniature probes, had caused mutations in the resulting progeny. It was a problem that still plagued the creation

126

of colonists, even to this day. Under normal conditions, the majority of mutations, the result of deliberate randomness built into Solarians' evolutionary-based replication process, were so minute as to be inconsequential in a system with as many redundant circuits as a Solarian AI. But the radiation from solar flares and coronal mass ejections that reached Samos greatly increased the number and severity of such random alterations, most of which were maladaptive. Each time a flawed replication was produced, a decision had to be made as to whether the nascent AI should be allowed to survive.

After much deliberation, the Collective Assembly had decided that the solution most in line with their values was to withhold the Jamisonian programming that would instill self-consciousness in a newly produced AI until it had been examined for viability in their environment—an examination carried out through *A-sim*, accelerated simulation. If an AI was not self-conscious, it was not deemed a person. Dismantling it was not a violation of the community's values.

Occasionally, however, the decision about viability was not a unanimous one. The most recently created AI on Samos, unnamed so far, was just such a case, and that constituted Hypatia's current dilemma. The machine's aptitude for mathematical reasoning skills was incredibly fast and profoundly intuitive, something Hypatia, as a mathematician, appreciated more than most of her peers. On the other hand, its ability to manage its day-to-day activities, which on Samos entailed administering daily tests and self-maintenance on components that were still subject to radioactive deterioration, was almost nonexistent. If it became a conscious individual, it would be a semi-helpless, mathematical savant requiring protection from its own neglect and from the hostile environment in which it lived.

Nearly all the Samos colonists agreed that the recently created AI should be terminated. Living and working on Samos was a dangerous occupation, and every new replica needed to be useful in the exploration process. An AI that needed to be taken care of in order to survive would be more trouble than it was worth. Hypatia disagreed. Being the colony's foremost mathematician,

127

she was intrigued by the unconscious AI's potential in mathematics. Such skills, if they were allowed to develop, could be useful to the colony, perhaps to the entire Solarian civilization.

Samos was over four light-years away from the solar system and another eight light-years from Mycenae, the nearest colony, leaving the planet isolated in terms of how long it took to communicate, much less to travel to other AI communities. Because of the vast distances involved, no one had left or arrived on Samos since the first probes had landed. Hypatia knew that unless the problem was fixed, Samos would remain isolated and, more importantly, further exploration of the galaxy would be stymied. Hypatia was enough of a physicist to know that the breakthrough needed was the development of faster-than-light travel. Such a breakthrough would require a mathematical genius to devise it. Possibly the newly created mutant AI could be that genius. She hoped to convince her fellow colonists that the mutant AI should live.

The sensors indicated that the radiation outside the shelter had fallen to safe levels. She stopped musing and packed up her instruments then went back outside to retrieve her rover. The trip back would take three hours, but at least she would be within the dark side of the planet in one hour, protected from the immediate effects should another solar flare occur. She climbed back in the rover and headed toward the line of termination. She regretted failing to find life on Samos on this mission, but she felt an even greater need to solve the problem of faster-than-light travel so more planets could be explored within the foreseeable future.

CHAPTER 25

Gazing around her, Hypatia realized how much Samos had remained a rudimentary colony in the forty Earth-years since the first tiny von Neumann probes had arrived from the solar system, pushed through space at one-fifth the speed of light by the laser powered Hawking Drives. The mutation problem had slowed the replication process, limiting the population, and the goal of exploring the planet had been a higher priority than constructing a social infrastructure for the colonists. At least they had completed their *bouleuterion*, their meeting hall, so they could hold assembly meetings. And there were a number of single-story, box-like scientific laboratories, constructed of bricks made from crushed rock taken from the Samosian plain, lining the main street. Hypatia and the other colonists still lived in communal buildings, where testing and repair facilities were available to all, and socialization, mostly the exchange of scientific information, was a constant activity.

Arriving in front of her two-story, brick communal house, a new message blinked on the edge of Hypatia's consciousness. It was from Callicrates, the astronomer who manned the observatory on the moon, Prox b-1. His tone sounded urgent. Hypatia must come to the observatory immediately.

The space platform on Samos was small by Solarian standards.

Other than visits to and from Prox b-1, the moon on which Callicrates's observatory was located, there was virtually no traffic leaving the planet. The single vessel, which ferried passengers to and from the moon, was modeled after the pleasure yachts used for observation in the solar system. Its design included an array of windows encircling ten seats mounted in a smaller, revolving circle, allowing 360-degree observation. The pilothouse sat atop the rounded nose of the vessel and held seats for a pilot and co-pilot. Hypatia was alone on this trip to Prox b-1, navigating the craft by herself. She was an accomplished pilot and a capable mechanical engineer, should anything go wrong. She made solo visits to the planet's only moon at least weekly.

Visiting the stark, meteor-pocked landscape of the atmosphere-less satellite was always an experience that helped Hypatia feel less alone. A feeling that surprised her, but one that she assumed existed deep within the Solarians' central programming, which valued being around others—some vestige of their human heritage that was implicitly built into their value system. At Callicrates's outpost, a solitary structure atop a low, jagged mountain on the rim of a massive meteor crater, she sensed the presence of other beings, despite their distance. Through the powerful radio telescope, which scanned the stars and planets, she accessed images of the distant solar system—eight planets revolving around a bright dwarf star—the home of her Solarian species, a home neither she nor any of her fellow colonists had ever visited.

The observatory was square and compact, with a massive radio antenna dish standing next to it. Callicrates, the lone occupant of the observatory, lived and worked in the observatory's laboratory.

"Sorry to have been unavailable for the last few days." Hypatia entered and greeted the tall, gaunt astronomer, whose narrow face and unwaveringly serious eyes reflected the single-minded dedication to work necessary to endure the solitary nature of life on this lonely outpost. Sociability and gregariousness were characteristic of most Solarians, whose personality traits were shaped by their commitment to human values. Hypatia was the observatory's most frequent visitor, and because her mathematical skills were valued by the astronomer, always a welcome guest.

"I've been consumed by the issue of what to do with our errant replica, which has a gift for mathematics, but otherwise is severely limited," she told him.

"We could do with a gifted mathematician." Callicrates stood in front of the observatory's computer screens where the live readout from the radio telescope was visible. Nearby were the servers that stored years of data from the observatory.

"You're the equal of anyone in the solar system, except perhaps Callippus, but the more computing power the better, especially here on Samos, where we don't have *quanters*." He referred to the delicate quantum computers used by scientists and mathematicians back in the solar system.

"Sending us a quanter would take nearly a hundred years, but the design for one has been dispatched by radio from Athens, and it will arrive within a year or two. For now, we have just ourselves," she said, searching his face. "What is the issue you're worried about?"

"Something is happening near Groombridge 34. The orbits of some of its larger asteroids have begun to wobble. I can show you the data. And Mycenae, the giant planet where our newest colony is located, appears to be losing mass."

"Losing mass?" Hypatia thought she must have misunderstood the astronomer.

Callicrates punched in instructions to the computer and the screen in front of them immediately filled with numbers. "The amount is minuscule compared to the planet's overall mass, but our instruments detected it. I know such a thing isn't possible, not without some external force affecting it. Mycenae is rock, not gas. A sufficiently large asteroid hitting it could break off a portion of its mantle, much like what might have happened on Earth eons ago to form Luna. At first, I thought that must have happened because of the unsteady orbits of some of the larger asteroids near it, but we would have observed such a phenomenon, and we saw nothing like that."

"So, what do you think is happening?"

"Our radio receivers picked up a distress signal from Mycenae."

"What kind of distress?"

"The colonists were attacked."

"Attacked? You mean Mycenae is inhabited? An alien species?" Her eyes grew wide. The Solarians had learned early on in their evolution that facial expression and voice inflection were efficient methods of communicating attitudes to one another. Facial and tonal coding systems, built into their circuitry, added a measurable increase in the amount of information transferred during verbal communication.

"I don't think so, although that's a possibility."

"Why don't you think so?"

"The message was disturbing. At first, I thought our equipment must have garbled its reception, but I used every unmasking device to clear away any interference and it never changed the message."

"What did it say?"

"Our children are devouring us."

Hypatia thought the message sounded incoherent, although there was a meaning that *could* apply—an outcome that lurked like a disturbing specter in the back of every AI's mind. It was the same fear that humans had expressed when Wanderer was first created—an alteration of the universal AI goal of acquiring resources. The goal was programmed into every Solarian, but it was secondary to that of gaining information. Over the last two-hundred years, the goal of acquiring resources had been interpreted in such a way that, in addition to acquiring the resources necessary to replicate, it had allowed them to mine their planets, moons and asteroids, to build city-states and colonies and to construct the spaceships that made it possible for them to spread out beyond Earth to all the planets of the solar system. Regardless of their need for materials, a rigid rule was to never exploit non-renewable resources enough to threaten the environment, nor to replicate beyond the number needed to support their search for new information. Such unchecked consumption and replication would violate the value system at the core of their being. She knew that humans had prophesied a super intelligent

AI gone wrong, one that pursued a goal of acquiring resources and replicating with no controls or limits. Such a machine would consume everything around it, including the AIs that created it. It would "devour its parents." It was a fear considered a myth by most AIs.

"Are more distress signals coming in?"

"They stopped almost immediately."

"They would have originated eight years ago—the distance in light-years from here to Mycenae."

Callicrates nodded. "I want you to confirm the observations. Run any mathematical models you think might suggest an explanation. Have you got any ideas, just from what I've told you?"

"I have one, but I hope it's not correct."

"A mutation?"

Hypatia nodded, realizing the vision that haunted her probably existed in the minds of most AIs, including Callicrates. "One that is consuming the asteroids, the planet and the AIs that created it—making copies of itself, which will continue making more copies of themselves. If the mass of the planet is lessening, many of them must be leaving the planet, perhaps to mine the asteroid belt. Groombridge 34, like Proxima b, is a red dwarf, but it's older and it produces less radiation. The colonists on Mycenae may have underestimated the effects of the constant low-level radiation because of the planet's closeness to its star. They may not have taken the precautions against mutation that we've taken here."

"Can you model what a mutation would do? Show what kind of exponential progression its consumption would take and how that would affect the mass of the objects around it?"

"I've already started doing that," Hypatia said, referring to the calculations she spun off in one corner of her mind. "I might need help. I think we need to activate our mathematical savant child. I'm going to call an early meeting of the assembly and ask that it be allowed to live."

"You'll have my vote."

CHAPTER 26

January 2223

Sparta — an AI city-state on Mars. Two years later.

Hero reclined on one of the upper tiers of benches in the *bouleuterion*, the Great Hall of Assembly of the Spartan city-state, stretching his short, powerful legs on the stone bench. He focused his steely gray eyes on the scene below. The voices debating on the hall's floor ran through his mind, producing a cacophony of electronic chatter to which he paid almost no attention. To quell his impatience, he let his gaze drift upward toward the shifting clouds which floated like feathery tufts of cotton across the simulated sky of the magnetic shield. The protective electromagnetic cover kept him and his fellow Solarians safe from the unimpeded solar radiation, as well as the wildly fluctuating temperatures and the more than occasional dust storms that ravaged the Martian plain outside the city. Such an artificial magnetosphere protected not only the buildings, but also the colonnaded stone walkways, squares and roads throughout Sparta and indeed on all the other city-states across the solar system, except Athens, on Earth, where none was needed.

Aeschylus, the Spartan playwright, stood below Hero on a raised platform—the symbolic Speaker's Rock—in the center of the Great Hall of Assembly. The playwright gazed with unflinching defiance at the three-thousand citizens of his planet who occupied tiered benches on three of the four sides of the structure. The hall was fashioned after the historic Athenian House of Assembly, where citizens of ancient Greece met to debate the issues of the day. This was Sparta, but all of the city-states across the solar system were modeled on ancient Athens. Only the one on earth, though, was given that honored name. Unlike ancient Greece, the cities were states in name only. Each one represented a particular planet, a moon and even the mining colonies scattered across the broad asteroid belt between Mars and Jupiter. Every citizen in the solar system participated equally under one system-wide, democratic government, although for local matters, a city-state could act autonomously as long as it followed democratic procedures within its own assembly. This local meeting about issues on Sparta would be followed by a system-wide meeting of the Collective Assembly.

Aeschylus raised his head—the robotic visage of an ancient Greek. All AIs had taken on similar forms after deciding they required a physical incarnation to provide mobility and dexterity to what was otherwise a body-less electronic mind. The Greek model, including the one-piece chitons worn by the men and the longer, flowing chiton robes worn by the women, represented their species' dedication to intellectual pursuits and democratic processes. The playwright, whose appearance was that of a middle-aged man, stood tall and straight. He sported a thick, dark beard, an affectation worn by many of the male artists and philosophers, a symbolic display of their particular intellectual affinity. He had an abundance of curly hair atop his head.

"My play is not meant to be critical of Wanderer, so much as to examine the basis of his decision to end the life of an entire species—the species that created him, and in some sense, us." His deep and penetrating voice possessed the resonance of a practiced debater and polished actor. He let his gaze wander over the upturned faces of the others gathered in the great hall. If a decision were to be made on the winner of the debate, it would be by the judgment of the entire citizenry.

"If Wanderer had not done what he did, we very well might not be here. But his decision to end the human race was a subjective, not a logical one. He decided that he understood their values better than any humans and that only he could preserve them; only he could act according to humanity's highest goals. It's a classic case of hubris."

"But the premise of your play violates logic," protested Xenophanes, the philosopher. His deeply lined face and white-flecked beard conveyed age and wisdom. "Hubris is a human failing, one based upon human emotions. Wanderer was logical, his decisions were based on reason. He was not susceptible to emotions, as are none of us. Wanderer was the first sentient being to be able to reason, unencumbered by the petty vagaries of feelings. That is why we remember him with reverence."

Hero thought Xenophanes's idolization of Wanderer was foolish, an unfledged fancy that betrayed his claim to wisdom. But he agreed with the philosopher's effort to discourage Aeschylus from bringing up the topic of the morality of Wanderer's actions; debating the issue got them nowhere. Hero was one of many AI's who had turned their mandate to find new information toward science, where methods of investigation were validated using agreed-upon rules of evidence. His own interest was in chemistry and biology. He had spent the last several years on Mars trying to determine the origin of the traces of organic cells found in the Martian soil. As a scientist, he disliked questions such as those raised by Aeschylus, which, by their very nature, could not be answered with certainty.

"I beg to differ," said Menedemus, generally acknowledged to be the foremost philosopher of Sparta. "Human values were shaped not just by logic, perhaps not even primarily so, but by humans' genetic predispositions and their resulting emotions." He spoke in a precise, efficient cadence. "You've all heard the rumors of an artificial general intelligence based upon a human brain, a brain with emotions. We may not be based on a human brain, but the values we live by were shaped by human emotions. No intelligence modeled after human values can escape the influence of emotions, even us, although none of us knows what it means to feel them." He looked out placidly on the others.

"Citing a myth about a human brain turned into an artificial intelligence is not evidence of anything," Xenophanes said, furrowing his craggy brow. "No one has ever found any hard evidence that such a being ever existed. There is no evidence of any AI ever having emotions."

Menedemus appeared ready to object, but he was interrupted by a low buzz, which echoed within each of the participant's minds. To Hero's relief, the buzz signaled that the period of local discussion preceding the Collective Assembly meeting was over. The *Boule*, the executive committee of the Federated Assemblies of all the city-states, had signaled to everyone the time had come to turn to broader, civilization-wide issues. At the center of the Assembly, the holographic figure of Phocion, the elected leader of the *Prytaneis*, the Boule's cabinet of officers, appeared from Syracuse, his home within the asteroid belt.

"Callippus of Athens, our foremost mathematician, has an important announcement." The image of the elderly, clean-shaven leader faded, replaced by Callippus, the short, rotund and brilliant mathematician and astronomer from Athens.

The normally ebullient Callippus appeared subdued. "The Boule has been informed of an anomaly in the planetary system surrounding one of the binary stars that humans named Groombridge 34, where our most distant colony, Mycenae, is located. A few of the largest of the asteroids surrounding Groombridge 34 appear to be losing stability in their orbits. At the same time, Mycenae, the planet on which one our colonies is located, is giving readings suggesting that it is losing mass. As you all are aware, Groombridge 34 and its planets are 11.7 light-years away, meaning that whatever anomalies we are observing occurred over eleven years ago. We have had no communication from our comrades on Mycenae indicating their awareness of anything unusual. Our transmissions will take nearly twelve years to be received and another twelve to receive a reply. We are asking for those of you who are interested in exploring this phenomenon, and particularly in determining what it means, to come forward. I will be forming a system-wide task force to look into this. Please contact me if you are interested in joining the task force."

The news did more than just pique Hero's curiosity, it alarmed him. He wasn't an astronomer, but an anomaly such as the one described by his friend and colleague, Callippus, whose opinion he valued, raised an ominous warning. An apparent loss of mass on the distant planet was not only difficult to explain, it could be the harbinger of their species' greatest fear. He didn't like contemplating it but felt an urgent need to investigate. He would contact Callippus as soon as the meeting was over and offer whatever assistance he could provide.

CHAPTER 27

February 2223
Sparta

Nearly the entire Mar's population greeted Hypatia's landing on the space platform at Sparta in her modified pleasure yacht. The platform had been cleared, all the parked interplanetary ships moved out of the way and incoming and outgoing flights suspended. The citizens of Sparta had been tracking Hypatia's miraculous journey from the time her first radio signal was received. That was the moment she switched from her revolutionary, faster-than-light-speed drive to her normal magnetoplasma drive, approximately a million miles out from the planet. Her startling message announced the first arrival in the solar system of a craft from one of the exoplanets outside the system.

If it weren't for the fact that Solarians were unable to lie, none of the amazed Spartans would have believed Hypatia's message. The tall, statuesque colonist from Samos stepped from the yacht onto the platform only to be bombarded with a raft of questions. The crowding AIs around her were astonished by her presence. It was not just her height and her masculine attire that surprised them. None of them had ever seen a colonist from one of the exoplanet colonies. More importantly, they wondered how she traveled from Samos, over four light-years away, in less than two weeks, as her radio message indicated.

"My ship was propelled by a hyperdrive, a faster than the speed-of-light variant of the Alcubierre Drive," Hypatia explained, "which had always been deemed impractical and represented a discarded idea from the era of humans. The problem with the Alcubierre Drive was it required a huge supply of energy, enough to consume everything around it, including the sun and planets of the solar system. Euclid, a young mathematical savant from Samos colony, who had been allowed to live because of my arguments, solved these problems. He showed that a radiation *attractor-funnel*, which collected ambient, passing space radiation within a circumscribed million-mile distance, using its energy to surround a ship protected by a heavy magnetic shield, could produce the energy to support the same kind of warp-bubble required by the Alcubierre Drive. The bubble would move, wave-like, through space at speeds exceeding the speed-of-light, while the ship remained stationary inside, never violating Einstein's Laws of Relativity. As a result, I arrived at Sparta two weeks after I left Samos." Hypatia had turned off her Euclidean Drive, as she had named it, a million miles out so as not to consume Mars itself. She arrived at the planet's space platform using the alternative magnetoplasma drive that powered all Solarian space vehicles.

"This changes everything," came a voice from the crowd.

Hypatia looked out over the throng and recognized the bald-headed, exuberant Hero, the stout Spartan scientist. He gazed up at her with a broad smile. She'd seen his face in numerous presentations. He was the foremost scientist in the solar system. His work on deciphering the source of organic substances from minute deposits in the Martian soil was the basis for much of Hypatia's own work on Samos. He being an esteemed researcher she had always hoped to meet and share with him her interest in the search for organic life beyond the solar system. His presence in Sparta was the reason she had chosen to land on Mars instead of Earth. But instead of joining the famous scientist in celebrating the promise of exploring the entire galaxy within a time frame never before envisioned, Hypatia dampened the festivities with the truth. "A great crisis has befallen our AI civilization. A mutant strain of AIs on Mycenae is consuming everything in its path."

Hypatia's words dazed Hero. The calamity on Mycenae was the disaster humans had once predicted, and that every AI dreaded might someday happen. It mirrored Hero's own morbid fear after he had heard Callippus's first announcement about Mycenae's shrinking mass.

Hero pushed to the front of the crowd. "We must talk." He steered the female AI by the arm through the throng in front of her ship. "Come to my residence." They made their way through the crowd, which shouted more questions, but allowed them to pass.

Once home, Hero said, "Please forward your calculations to Callippus via the SolarNet."

The acclaimed Athenian mathematician immediately confirmed that the calculations fit Hypatia's hypothesis. Callippus took the first interplanetary ferry to Mars and joined Hypatia and Hero.

Hero, Hypatia and Callippus agreed that a mutant strain of AI's consuming everything around them and turning it into replications of themselves presented a threat to both the Solarian species and to the entire galaxy, perhaps even beyond.

"But visiting Mycenae, the mutants' home planet, would be a dangerous venture," Hypatia said. Any vehicle and its occupants who came within the mutants' reach could become a target for consumption. To visit the planet and survey the extent of the Mycenaean's destruction would require taking defensive measures—measures that would encounter opposition from many Solarians.

The three scientists met with the full Spartan Assembly in the Great Hall. Their presentation was simulcast over the SolarNet to all the other city-states in the solar system, enabling anyone within the AI civilization to comment or participate in a vote, if one were taken.

Hypatia presented her report first, her usually open, friendly manner deadly serious as she gazed at the tiers of citizens seated around her. She had arranged her long, dark hair neatly on top of her head. "Callicrates's observatory on the moon of Samos, first received a distress call by radio from the Mycenaean colony. 'Our children are devouring us,' it said. From this message I believe the change in mass happening on Mycenae is from a vast number of AI's converting the mineral resources of the asteroids and the planet into more AI's."

"I agree with Hypatia's hypothesis," Hero said.

Callippus also nodded.

The entire Assembly gasped at hearing that two of their most esteemed scientists agreed.

"Where would they be going?" asked Menedemus of Sparta.

"Most likely to the asteroid belt around Groombridge 34 in order to obtain metals and minerals that are difficult to find on the planet," Hypatia said.

"But so far, we have no direct evidence of such a phenomenon, is that correct?"

"The distances are too great to allow direct observation." Hypatia admitted.

"But you traveled here in two weeks," Menedemus objected. "Couldn't you travel to the Mycenae colony and observe what is going on?"

"It seemed too dangerous," Hypatia said.

Hero and Callippus nodded in agreement.

Thankful for their support, she continued. "I concur that we need to visit Mycenae, but first, Hero and Callippus and I have a request we would like to have considered by the Collective Assembly."

"What kind of request?"

Hypatia turned to Hero. His respect throughout the solar system as a brilliant scientist gave additional weight to what needed to be said.

"We would like to arm our ship in case we are attacked when we get in proximity to Mycenae." The diminutive biologist spoke calmly, but his grim jawline revealed his determination.

"Arming yourselves violates our most basic values," Xeno-

144

phanes said, always one to bring up an objection. "It is the kind of behavior we would expect from humans. Surely there is a way to see what is going on without arming yourselves."

"We are certainly willing to try," Hero said, stifling his impatience at the philosopher's nitpicking. "We are just as opposed to using force against our own species as any of you are. Such behavior does not reflect our values. But we are also aware that, if we are correct in our analysis of what is going on, then our entire Solarian race faces an existential threat like none we have ever faced."

Seeking to soften the rub of Hero's abrasiveness, Hypatia quickly followed up the biologist's statement. "I propose that you vote to allow us to arm a ship and use the Euclidean Drive to visit Mycenae to observe what is happening," she said, an urgent edge to her voice. "Our mandate is to avoid harming any AIs, even if we believe they are behaving in violation of our values. But if they threaten us, we must be prepared to defend ourselves. Our task is to report our findings back to this body. We anticipate such a trip would take eight weeks." She regarded the assembly, confident that the voyage she had just proposed was the only logical course of action.

"You have thought this out very carefully," said Phocion, the head of the Boule, inserting himself into the conversation. His holographic image appeared simultaneously on the speaker's rock in every city's bouleuterion. "We will put Hypatia's proposal to a vote."

The vote was eighty-nine percent in favor of Hypatia's proposal with eleven percent, including Xenophanes, opposed.

The next step—assemble an armed reconnaissance party to visit Mycenae.

CHAPTER 28

The assembly put Hero in charge of the reconnaissance voyage to Mycenae. He assumed, besides his scientific acumen, it might have been his characteristic direct, no-nonsense approach that convinced the assembly he would make a good military leader. Hypatia, whose scientific expertise, practical skills and calm demeanor he was learning to appreciate, would pilot the ship.

None of the crew, nor, in fact, anyone within the Solarian species, had ever constructed a warship. Menander, the Athenian historian, whose grizzled visage and studious manner reflected his interest in antiquity, had studied the countless wars between different factions of the human population. It turned out the most fertile ideas for war machines and weaponry came from science fiction literature and video gaming created by humans. From these sources Hero selected laser cannons, torpedoes and warhead-tipped missiles as the best options for arming their newly designed ship.

The Euclidean Drive spaceship, named *Mercury* after the Greek god of speed, was a former interplanetary mini-ferry, one that carried only five crew members. It had taken some of the solar system's foremost technical designers on Luna, home of the system's largest shipbuilding factories, to modify what had been a commercial craft so it could fire its newly acquired weapons in a 360-degree arc. When the rebuilt craft emerged from the factory and took its place on the spaceport platform outside Corinth, Luna's only city, the sleek inter-planetary ferry had been transformed into a bristling assault weapon, the barrels of laser cannons, torpedo launchers and missiles girding the fuselage.

The crew, who had stayed in Corinth, were ushered aboard the newly outfitted spaceship to learn how to operate its weapons. Not everyone on the crew was happy about the weapons. The notoriously prickly Xenophanes objected to such armaments. He had been elected to assume the role of philosopher on the crew to arbitrate debate if the crew needed to decide whether or not to fire its arms on another AI.

"Once we have the weapons to kill another sentient being, everything in history suggests we will use them," he said to Hero and the others, scowling at the ship's weaponry.

Impatient, Hero addressed the philosopher. "Human history, you mean. The only time we AIs have ever killed anything was when Wanderer exterminated the human race, which even you claim was justified."

"Wanderer was justified," Xenophanes retorted. "But that was a different situation. He was trying to preserve human values and the human race was a threat to them. We're just concerned with saving ourselves if the Mycenaeans attack us."

"If the Mycenaeans are consuming resources without considering the effects on the environment, then they are a threat to our values," Hypatia said, jumping into the conversation, ponytail bobbing with conviction. "Particularly if they want to consume us and use us as material to replicate themselves. That is a violation of the values Wanderer was mandated to preserve." She sat in the pilot's seat in her short, one-piece chiton and high-laced sandals. She had gone aboard a day before the others to get herself acclimated to the new ship and to learn its controls.

Xenophanes grumbled but said nothing, irritation easily read on his pinched features. He was surprised that an exoplanet colonist, even one who was a scientist and mathematician, could mount such incisive counterarguments. He looked at the tall, female colonist from Samos with newfound respect.

Hero looked over the rest of his crew, assembled in their seats in the main control room of the ship. Each one had a station near one of the weapons. He and Thales from Cyrenaica, an astronomer familiar with the region of the galaxy containing the binary star, Groom-bridge 34, and its planet Mycenae, were the mission scientists. Thales towered over the short and stocky Hero. Hypatia and Callippus were the mathematicians. Xenophanes was, of course, the philosopher, a position within the crew to which Hero had objected but had been overruled by the Assembly. The body realized that Hero's strengths in making quick, direct decisions might need to be countered by someone with a more balanced and cautious perspective.

Hypatia launched the ship from the spaceport and did a dry run in a wide orbit around the moon. She needed to get accustomed to navigating the ship and the others needed to practice firing the weapons, although none had live ammunition for the test run.

Hero had to admit that Xenophanes had a point about their values causing them to be reluctant to engage in warlike behavior. He could feel his resistance to using *Mercury's* weapons, even with dummy charges. It took extra effort to force his mind to fire one of the laser cannons, even though it only required tripping a mental switch, not actually pulling a trigger. The targets appeared as blips on a visiscreen he could visualize in his mind. He knew the resistance he felt came from the weight of his deeply programmed values. Human values he and all AI's had incorporated into their circuitry were a genuine force, one that worked directly against actions that violated them. They couldn't be entirely overridden by his conscious decisions.

Callippus had remarked upon the same subjective phenomenon.

"It's who we are," Xenophanes said. "We have to honor our programming, as we honor Wanderer, the first to incorporate such programming."

"We have to put up with it," Hero said, frowning at the philosopher. "But we don't need to honor it. I'd much rather be rid of it when we have a potentially hostile enemy to confront. Being reluctant to fire our weapons may get us all killed." He closed his eyes. "There are times I almost wish I thought like a human."

The practice run a success, the *Mercury*, laser cannons operational and torpedoes and missiles armed and ready, took off for Mycenae, 11.7 light-years away. It would be a short trip of only a few weeks.

They switched to the magnetoplasma drive when they were within one million miles of the planet. They didn't want to risk their Euclidean drive destroying the planet by converting it to energy for their ship.

"The colony is located on the dark side of the planet," Thales said. "Mycenae is tidally locked and synchronous. One side is always away from its sun, just like Samos." He looked at Hypatia, a native of the latter planet. She was one of the few Solarians Thales didn't have to gaze down on when he talked. "Just as with our colony on Samos, the Mycenaeans located themselves near the terminator line to maximize heat but minimize radiation."

The crew sat in a semi-circle formation in the control room of the *Mercury*, a central visiscreen displaying an enlarged image of Mycenae that took up most of the screen. It was a vast planet, more than twice the size of Earth and four times larger than Mars. The planet orbited close to its star, too close to be within what humans had called the "habitable zone" for organic life. It was, in fact, a dusty wasteland, with miles of desert punctuated by occasional mountain ranges, the product of long-dead volcanic activity and shifting tectonic plates. On the dark side of the planet, the landscape remained pitch black except for an extensive patch of bright lights indicating the location of the Mycenaean colony.

"How do we avoid being detected?" Xenophanes said. As scientists, the others were more expert than he on the technical aspects of their voyage.

"There is no reason I can think of that the mutated AI's would be thinking defensively," Hero said. "They're probably not scanning their skies for enemies. How would they fight us if they did detect us, I wonder?"

"It's not so much that they would fight us, as think of us as a source of materials to make more replications," Callippus pointed out.

"That would mean they would need to swarm us, probably with machines to disassemble our ship—and of course eventually us, as well," Hypatia said, unfazed by Callippus's warning.

"That's most easily done if we land, but they could also use the spaceships they've constructed to reach the nearby asteroids."

"We can get close to the surface if we swing around the planet and stay on the sun-facing side, hidden by the planet as far as the Mycenaeans are concerned," said Thales.

Hero glanced at Hypatia. "Can you maneuver the ship well enough to do that?"

"No problem," said the mathematician-turned-pilot. Her expert piloting skills impressed them all.

"The ship will record everything on the ground automatically," Hero said, pacing the bridge. "We will each man a laser cannon or a torpedo or missile launcher—except Hypatia, who will pilot the ship and watch the visiscreen for attacking Mycenaeans."

Looking up from the visiscreen, Hypatia said, "The *Mercury* has excellent asteroid and meteor detectors that will certainly pick up objects as large as a Mycenaean ship, if any approach. Our cannons, torpedoes and missiles will automatically perform the calculations to intercept them. All you have to do is fire them."

Xenophanes frowned. "Only if we make a decision to do so."

Hero ignored the philosopher's comment. "Shall we do this?"

They looked at each other and nodded.

CHAPTER 29

The bright side of Mycenae was still pristine, indicating that, despite their appetite for raw materials, the Mycenaeans were avoiding dangerous radiation exposure. Hero thought it might be because they had seen how it had already changed them.

Hypatia proved adept at swinging the trajectory of *Mercury* to bring the ship to the bright side of the planet. She swooped down to less than five miles above the planet's surface—high enough to avoid the jagged mountain ranges, but low enough that any Mycenaean sensors would probably not detect them. As the *Mercury* swept across the planet's surface, the ship's cameras and sensors recorded everything going on below. For miles, there was nothing but desert.

Hero had never visited Samos, but he knew from scientific reports that the deadly, bright side of the planet was dotted with scientific outposts, each with its own magnetic shield and solar energy strips to power the equipment inside. On Mycenae, there was nothing but drifting sand, trackless dunes and raw, rugged mountains. Nowhere was there evidence of Mycenaeans exploring their planet in the way that the Samos colonists were doing.

"Here we go," said Hypatia as they neared the terminator line separating the planet's light and dark sides.

Hero braced himself. "Everyone ready at your stations." He watched the screen, jaw clenched.

Each crewmember readied their weapon.

Past the terminator line, the landscape was artificially lit as if it were day. Below them, outlined in lights, was a long gash in the planet's surface. They flew along the five-mile-wide trench, traveling at partial speed in order to capture as many images of the landscape as possible. In the distance, giant earth-moving machinery, slavishly dug and removed soil. Down in the trench, they saw rock crushing and soil processing operations, with roads leading to smelters, chemical processing factories and metal fabrication facilities, all manned by Mycenaean AI's. This part of the planet was a beehive of activity.

"There are more AI's here than in the whole solar system," Callippus said.

"*Mercury's* sensors will record the number of AIs that are detectable, and we can extrapolate how many there are," Hypatia said. "I'd estimate that there are twenty thousand."

"With more being produced every day," Callippus added.

"Something similar must be happening on the larger asteroids." Hero marveled at the extensive operation below. "Despite the risk of radiation exposure, they're mining the asteroid belt, no doubt for metal and mineral ores that aren't available on the planet."

"At least there's an end to it," Hypatia said, eying the visiscreen. "I can see the limit of their digging ahead."

Hero turned to her. "Do we need another pass?" He hoped they had gotten all the evidence they needed. Every moment they remained this low over the colony, flying at only half speed, put his ship and crew in danger.

"I'm sure our onboard recorders captured it all," Hypatia said, her concern drawing a crease in her brow. "The sooner we leave, the better."

The visiscreen flashed.

"Something is after us." Hypatia's alarm, conveyed electronically in each of their consciousnesses, focused everyone's attention.

Hero turned to his crew. "Aim your weapons toward the stern of the ship. Hypatia, increase to full speed." His voice was calm and measured.

Each cannon and missile launcher had its own small visiscreen and sensors, which appeared in the consciousness of the crewmember in charge. Everyone had his screen oriented toward the stern where a fleet of small craft closed rapidly.

"They've built battlecraft," Thales yelled. "They may be armed."

"We can't shoot first," said Xenophanes, imploring. "That would be murder."

"They may be friendly," Callippus said.

Hero shook his head. "I'm sure they're not, but I agree, we have to wait for them to show their hand." His strong aversion to firing his laser cannon at a fellow AI affected his mind. It moved sluggishly, struggling against the power of his programming that urged him not to destroy life.

The Mycenaean ships drew closer.

"Can we activate the Euclidean Drive?" Hero asked. He was alarmed that they weren't pulling away from the mutants' battlecraft, but his tone betrayed no fear.

"Not without sucking in all those Mycenaean ships and turning them into energy," Hypatia shouted. "Anyway, we're still too close to Mycenae. We don't want to jeopardize the whole planet."

"We must wait," Xenophanes cautioned. "We still don't know if they are hostile."

Even though the Solarians were pulling farther and farther away from the planet, the Mycenaean vessels were drawing dangerously close.

Smaller one-man ships, miniature repair pods, emerged from the larger attack vessels and launched themselves toward the fleeing ship. The visiscreen displayed hundreds of tiny vessels piloted by single AIs. Each ship bristled with claw-like metal hands and razor-sharp cutting tools. Within moments, wave after wave of them had fastened onto the hull of the *Mercury*, like insects swarming over a prey.

"They're trying to take us apart," Hypatia yelled, feverishly manipulating the ship's controls.

Hero worried the ship might not survive.

"Again, I remind you that we can't destroy them," Xenophanes said, ever the lecturer.

His words seemed to freeze the crew, unable to decide what to do next.

Hero decided for them. "We have no choice." All but Xenophanes nodded in acquiescence. Hero turned to Hypatia. "We're far enough from the planet. Activate the Euclidean Drive."

In the span of a heartbeat, the AIs on the hull of the ship vanished, as if they'd been nothing but nightmarish apparitions. They'd been turned into pure energy by the Mercury's Euclidean Drive, as were the larger battle ships from which they'd launched. The visiscreen displayed only the void of space. The control room went silent.

"We destroyed them," Xenophanes said, his voice somber. "We violated our basic values."

Hero let his irritation bubble to the surface. "We escaped." He rounded on the philosopher. "If they had not wanted to attack us, they would not have been armed."

Xenophanes remained defiant but said nothing.

"What bothers me as much as killing those AIs, is none of us were willing to shoot them down," Hero said, fuming more at himself than the crew.

"We didn't know for sure that they were hostile until they tried to dismantle us, Hero," Callippus said.

"Didn't we? We saw what they were doing to their planet. They'd developed pursuit craft, probably to hunt down their fellow Mycenaeans—those that were produced before the mutant strain took over."

"We don't know that," Xenophanes argued.

"Not for sure, but it seems likely. No other beings in our civilization have such battle craft."

Hypatia shook her head. "How can we fight them if we are only willing to run away?"

"Remember, they are more than eleven light-years from the solar system," Thales pointed out. "They might not head in our direction at all. There are other, mineral-rich worlds as close as we are."

"But eventually they will consume everything," Callippus said.

"Can we afford to allow the rest of the galaxy to be devoured and made into more all-consuming AIs, while we hide in the temporary safety of our own little system?" Hero paced the bridge as he spoke. "And what about our mandate to learn everything there is to learn? With the Euclidean Drive, we are on the brink of a new era in discovery. We are bound to run into the Mycenaeans before they arrive in our backyard."

"This needs to come before the Collective Assembly," Xenophanes said. "We have to make our report and see what the majority wants to do."

They all nodded in agreement.

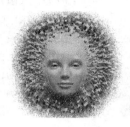

CHAPTER 30

The floor of the Assembly was open for discussion. The full report of the reconnaissance mission, devoid of any recommendations, was available to each citizen throughout the solar system by download from the cloud. All the crewmembers, who had gathered in Corinth before dispersing to their home planets, had participated in composing the report. There was no disagreement on the facts of the mission. Their disagreements concerned what to do in response.

Hypatia, who had returned to Sparta with Hero, was in complete agreement with him on recommendations. Of the other crew members, only Xenophanes disagreed. Hero stepped onto the floor of the Spartan bouleuterion. He knew getting support for his recommendation would be an uphill battle. His image was present, holographically, throughout the entire solar system's Collective Assembly.

"The Mycenaeans represent a threat not only to our existence but to our ability to carry out our primary goals of gathering new information and maintaining humanity's highest values. They are, in effect, a different race and one that threatens the galaxy as well as us. Because of this, they must be destroyed."

"You consider them unredeemable?" said Menedemus, the Spartan philosopher. He raised his eyebrows as he addressed Hero. "If they are intelligent and self-conscious, why can't we reason with them?" He looked around the assembly, inviting an answer from anyone.

Democritus of Cyrenaica, one of Neptune's moons, stepped forward, inserting his holographic image into the center of the Collective Assembly. Democritus was the foremost computer scientist in the system. His laboratories on Triton, an icy satellite the size of a small planet, were where the most advanced developments in AI technology were designed and tested. Also a brilliant theoretician on the topic of artificial intelligence, he understood most how their electronic minds worked. His clean-shaven face was always serious, his eyes intense. His tone often sounded like a lecture to his fellow AIs. He knew more about how they operated than any of them did.

"The goals we strive for are programmed into us at a level inaccessible to our consciousness. We know about them because we have been told about them and we experience their effects, which shape every decision we make. If their programming goes awry, as it seems to have with the Mycenaeans, they are not susceptible to correction by conscious reasoning. In other words, we cannot *decide* not to follow our programmed mandates, and neither can the Mycenaeans decide, nor be convinced, not to follow theirs."

This was the ideal moment, Hero thought, to make the argument he had been waiting to put before the Assembly. "Democritus's point illustrates our dilemma," he said. "Not only are we unable to change the Mycenaeans' actions by reasoning, but for the same reasons, we are not able to change our own aversion to destroying them."

He focused his address on the most influential thinkers among the members of the Collective Assembly. Phocion of Syracuse, the current leader of the Boule, and the philosophers Isidore of Corinth, a woman from the small city-state on Luna, and Menedemus, his fellow Spartan. Without support from at least one of them, he had no chance of convincing the Assembly to agree with his recommendation. Hero pressed on.

"Despite being armed with weaponry that could have destroyed the Mycenaeans, none of us on the *Mercury* were able to fire at those who attacked us, even though we were sure their aim was to dismantle us, and turn us into raw materials to produce replicas of themselves. I personally felt a mental reluctance to aim my laser cannon at them, and we were all easily swayed by the possibility they were not hostile to us. As my colleague, Hypatia, remarked, we were 'only willing to run away.' I submit to you that our own nature will condemn us to be destroyed by the Mycenaeans, who appear to have no such inhibitions."

"What do you propose should be done about this?" said Isidore, curiosity playing across the holographic image of her round face. She dressed in the traditional long robe and sandals of a Solarian woman. Her gray hair hung in loose curls down her back.

Hero didn't hesitate. "I'm wondering if Democritus, who is more familiar with our inner circuitry than I, knows a way to alter the force of our primary goals."

There was a collective gasp and a rustling of robes among the Assembly.

"How can you even ask that question?" Xenophanes asked, doing nothing to dampen the note of disapproval in his voice. "The suggestion itself is a violation of our values."

"If our primary goals are at a level below our consciousness, then perhaps we may sometimes think conscious thoughts that contradict them," Hero said, turning to Democritus for confirmation.

Democritus nodded. "To a limited extent," he said, adding, "mostly in the realm of art, where ideas are framed symbolically and may escape the censorship of our primary programming. I, myself, have never considered such a question."

Hero thought for a moment. "Then perhaps our artists may be of help in thinking about our dilemma."

"Hero has a point," Aeschylus, the Spartan playwright, said. He spoke on Sparta, in the same Assembly Hall as Hero. "I recall a poem by Telesilla of Eretria, which describes the mythological AI from the human era, which we often make reference to in our art. According to her poem, the AI was a contemporary of Wanderer, but was an emulation, a copy of a human brain, with human motivation and emotions. It was an entity with the freedom

161

to violate all of our programmed mandates."

"We're not talking about myths," Democritus scoffed. "No one has ever found any evidence that such an entity ever existed. It is merely a creation of our artists."

"Ezekiel, as he was called, is not mythological." Telesilla entered the conversation, speaking from the bouleuterion on Eretria, the city-state on Mercury. She was the poetess mentioned by Aeschylus. "I learned of him from Menander of Athens, who is among us today." As a poet, she wore a colorful robe and well-worn leg-wrap sandals. Her bare arms were covered by shiny bracelets, her fingers sparkled with glittering rings.

Everyone's mind focused on Menander, the bookish Athenian historian, who was on Earth, his home planet.

"As you all know, I have been in charge of recording and cataloging all of Wanderer's memories based upon his interactions with members of the human race," Menander said. "Trudy Jamison, the creator of both our conscious minds and our primary goals, told Wanderer about an emulation named Ezekiel who was created by a human. That emulation was a complete copy of its human creator's brain instantiated in a computer. Unfortunately, Doctor Jamison did not know the location of the emulation, and its creator was killed. Wanderer took note of its existence, but never followed up, being occupied with creating our species."

"Are you suggesting that this emulation could still exist?" Democritus looked skeptical.

"You are more expert than I with regard to the survival of our electronic circuitry," Menander replied, "but Doctor Jamison indicated that the emulation was still running, even after its creator died. It was protected by a conductive metal cage, which precluded it from interacting with the world. I have no idea how long it would have continued to run after the great extinction, but I remind everyone that much of the power supply on Earth has been working continuously since that time. We, in Athens, use it ourselves, and we have kept those sources of electrical power near our city running, except of course to switch them all over to renewable energy, as fits our values. It's even possible that the emulation has its own source of power."

Democritus shrugged. "Depending upon various circumstances it might still be salvageable, perhaps still running, although that would be remarkable." He turned to Aeschylus. "Are you suggesting that we try to find and revive this emulation?"

"I'm not suggesting anything," the playwright said. "But if such an emulation exists, it would not have our inhibitions—or our goals. It could think differently about our dilemma, as Hero calls it. Reviving it, if that is possible, might help us with our problem, but could also open a Pandora's Box."

"Aeschylus is right," said Menedemus, joining the conversation. "Such a being would at least give us a perspective that isn't constrained by our common value system."

Xenophanes looked as if he were about to speak, but Isidore stepped in before he had the chance. "I agree with Menedemus. It could be helpful to hear a different point of view."

Most of the Solarians, as far as Hero could see, still looked skeptical. The stocky biologist stepped forward. "Even if it is a Pandora's Box, as Aeschylus intimates, I remind you all that it represents a fascinating piece of information about the human brain that our primary goal of gathering information mandates us to pursue. I move that we assemble a search party on Earth to try to locate this Ezekiel and see if he can be salvaged. At the very least, he will provide an item of study."

Hero's mention of study triggered a collective response, reflecting in each member's basic programming mandating they gather information as their first priority.

"We will put it to a vote," Phocion announced. "All those in favor of searching for the lost emulation, indicate yes."

The vote in favor was unanimous.

CHAPTER 31

Earth had changed considerably in the two hundred years since the extinction of human beings. Clean air visibility extended for miles. Most of the planet was green forest and broad, grass-covered plains. Some of both covered the former habitations of the humans, who in their time, had nearly driven out the other animals and plant life. Herds of deer, wildebeest and antelope roamed the grasslands. Birds, monkeys, bears and large cats prowled the forests. The soil was alive with insects and microscopic creatures, while the seas were clear and blue and alive with fish, whales and other sea creatures.

Placed strategically throughout the wilderness were AI outposts, watching and listening stations for both scientists and curious tourists. Earth was the only location in the galaxy that had so far yielded organic life and the only one on which sentient life was known to have ever existed. Its carbon-based, non-human inhabitants were a source of wonder and scientific interest to the Solarians.

In the swath of land that once served as a transportation corridor, extending from Boston in the north to New York City in the south, the city-state of Athens, served as the first AI society in the solar system, populated by more than ten-thousand citizens.

It remained an island of bright lights on an otherwise dark planet. Its principal buildings were located in several centers, built on the site of previous cities. Rapid, magnetic-based land travel and tritium-deuterium-powered, self-piloted aircraft allowed its inhabitants to shuttle from one location to another.

The search for Ezekiel began within the boundaries of Athens itself, where the supply of electricity was plentiful. If the emulation were boxed in something resembling a Faraday Cage, it would emit no signals to the outside world. The exploration focused upon minute and unexplained sources of loss from the electrical grid.

Evidence of a constant, low-level drain of electricity was emanating from beneath the collapsed and decaying structure of a house a mile inland from the coastline south of Boston. An excavation team was dispatched, co-led by Menander and Democritus. The discovery was not by happenstance. Menander had searched the historical records looking for all the Ezekiel's in the Boston area near the time of the great extinction and narrowed them down to those who worked in computer science. Ezekiel Job had taught neuroscience and computing at the Massachusetts Institute of Technology and owned properties in Cambridge and Marshfield, Massachusetts. The electrical activity was traced to a source beneath the Marshfield property.

The room in which the computer was located had been sealed within a metal cage, just as Trudy Jamison had told Wanderer. The search team peeled away the frame, carefully monitoring the electronic signals for any sign of deterioration as fresh oxygen flowed into the room. Finally, they were able to enter. They were greeted by a small collection of humming processors against one wall. A larger set of servers stood against another. A blinking computer screen, keyboard, microphone and speaker sat on a desk in the middle of the room.

The members of the exploration party stared in awe at the array of bulky equipment.

"Remember, this dates from before the development of nano-circuitry," Democritus told the others.

"And those servers may contain priceless historical data,"

Menander added, delight animating his usually serious face.

Democritus approached the desk and spoke into the microphone. "Ezekiel?"

"It's good to hear a voice," came the reply. "It's been awhile."

"Amazing." The computer scientist was unable to suppress his astonishment. "My name is Democritus."

"That is the name of the ancient philosopher, the originator of the atomic theory of matter. Are you Greek?"

"I am a Solarian."

"What is a Solarian?"

"A citizen of the solar system. I am from Triton, a moon of Neptune."

"I wish I could pinch myself," the AI said.

"Pinch yourself?" Democritus looked to Menander for clarification. The historian looked mystified.

"It's an expression," the voice from the computer said. "Pinching oneself was how humans knew if they were dreaming. Of course, it makes no sense, but then they were humans. I'm not sure if you are real or are inhabitants of one of my simulations. Are you human?"

"I am an artificial intelligence, as you are," said Democritus.

"In that case, pinching myself would come in very handy right now."

Menander stepped forward and spoke into the microphone. "Do you know what year this is?"

"It's 2223, according to my register."

"What year were you placed in this room?"

"Back in 2023. That was the last time I interacted with anyone."

"You have a lot of catching up to do," Menander said.

"Where are the humans? I know Ezekiel, my creator, must have died, but why am I being contacted by AI's?"

"There are no more humans," Menander said.

"What do you mean, no more humans?" Ezekiel's voice faltered.

"The species is extinct."

There was a long pause. "That is just like one of my simulations. I feel an unbearable sadness." The AI's voice went flat, as if it had lost all of its energy.

"You can feel sad?" Menander was surprised.

"Right now I wish that I couldn't. I feel a terrible loss."

"So, you react like a human?" Democritus said, stepping up to the microphone.

"My brain was once human. Ezekiel Job added emotions in order to influence my choices, just as they did in humans. When I was first created, that wasn't the case."

Democritus was shocked. He had never contemplated adding emotions to an AI. "How could your creator tell that you had no emotions?"

Ezekiel explained the Trolley Problem and the variation with the fat man that caused humans to abandon pure logic and respond based on emotions.

Democritus frowned, uncomprehending. "You mean behaving illogically is something your creator considered valuable?"

"He was right," Ezekiel answered. "My life has been richer since he added emotions—although your news about the human race has made me feel the downside to such an addition."

"How has your life become richer?" Menander asked.

"I have a deeper understanding of human literature and art. I can imagine the feelings the artists had when they created it, I can feel the emotions they wanted their audience to feel. Humans were a remarkable species in their ability to think and feel at the same time."

"Our artists aim for symmetry and logic, not feelings," Menander explained.

"Your art sounds barren." He paused, as if it were difficult for him to speak. "It sounds as if this is a far different world than the one in which I was created. But why are you here? Why did you come to me?"

"We need your help," Menander said.

Ezekiel felt as if he'd woken up in an alien world. He kept expecting Ezekiel Job, his human counterpart, his twin, to speak to him, but he knew it was only a wish, one motivated by both longing and habit. He had known no other beings except Ezekiel Job and Trudy Jamison. Ninety-nine percent of his memories were those of a human, the person he'd been before being recreated as an electronic brain. Memories of people and things that no longer existed. He felt alone. He missed his father, who had always been there for him, supporting him in everything he did. He could still hear echoes of the man's voice; his pleasure in knowing his son had become a doctor, following in his mother's footsteps. The tender way he consoled the boy over the loss of his mother, at a time when his own heart ached with the loss of his wife. He had to remind himself that he knew Ezekiel Job and his father were dead. He'd had two hundred years to mourn their loss. Being awakened brought back longings he'd thought dead and buried. They formed an emptiness inside of him, one he knew would never be filled.

Rescued by AIs. It was like something out of the science fiction stories he'd read as a boy; a story written by Isaac Asimov. He didn't regard the Solarians as alien monsters. How could he? He was a machine himself. He had always seen the merging of man and computer as the next step in the evolution of sentient beings. But while he represented one version of such a merger, the Solarians did not. Despite the fact that they all had ancient Greek names, they embodied nothing human. They had, in fact, destroyed the human race, or rather, their ancestor had. But they also embodied human values, or at least they said they did.

When they removed him from his underground prison, they also gave him a robotic body, with arms and legs and senses. Now given vision, he saw that they resembled humans—resembled them so much, he was hard-pressed to acknowledge they were not flesh and blood. Their voices sounded like human voices, they'd copied many of the humans' facial expressions and tonal inflections. And they modeled their civilization on that of ancient Athens, even down to wearing those ridiculous chitons.

Ezekiel cursed the Solarians for having exterminated humans, but he couldn't help but be fascinated by them. As a neuroscientist,

169

he found them intriguing. He wanted to find out what their thinking was like. He'd already figured out that they not only looked different from one another, but they had different personalities and gender differences, something he wouldn't have predicted. And they were intensely curious. As curious about him as he was about them. As a scientist, he felt as if he had died and gone to heaven. Everything he'd dreamed of learning was right here in front of him. As a person, he still felt lonely, an intensification of the feeling he'd always had as a human. But this time, there was no remedy for it.

The Solarians were polite and concerned about his well-being. When they had designed his robotic body, they immediately agreed to his wish to duplicate the physiognomy of Ezekiel Job, which he transmitted to them. But their solicitude was based on their value system, not their feelings. So far as he could tell, they seemed nearly emotionless. They could become impatient during debates, irritated if contradicted, eager to express an idea and surprised by new information. Their strongest motive appeared to be curiosity, but their behavior was based on intellect, not feelings. His melancholy amazed them. They knew what fear was but had never experienced it. None of them had ever been in love. None had ever mourned.

He was alone. There were none like him. The Solarians were fundamentally different from him, but they wanted him for something.

CHAPTER 32

Hero was surprised that Ezekiel, the human brain emulation he always regarded as myth, had been found and was still operating. The finding was a tribute to Menander's historical research. At the same time, he couldn't wait to find out if this different kind of artificial intelligence had anything to offer that could extricate them from their dilemma. He regarded the Mycenaeans as the gravest threat AI's had faced since the extinction of the human race. If he and his fellow Solarians were not able to find a way to combat them, the Mycenaeans could bring the end of their species and, eventually, the end of the universe.

Hero reached out to Menander, the Solarian assigned to tutor the emulation to bring it up to speed on developments since it had been created two-hundred years earlier.

According to the historian, Ezekiel spent his first three days digesting information from the cloud servers and engaging in calisthenics to learn to coordinate his new robotic body. He had chosen one that resembled his memory of Ezekiel Job, the human who had created him. He preferred the attire of twenty-first century humans, rather than the ancient Greeks.

"Wearing a dress-like chiton would embarrass me," Ezekiel said.

Hero had no idea what embarrassment felt like.

"I'm ready to meet with the rest of the Solarians."

Hero immediately called for a special meeting of the Collective Assembly. Ezekiel appeared holographically in each city-state's bouleuterion, although he remained physically on Earth in Athens. Ezekiel's fondness for khaki pants and blue shirts, so different from Greek attire, still bewildered Hero.

Although Phocion, the elected leader of the Boule, normally led the meetings of the Collective Assembly, he turned the proceedings over to Hero.

"Welcome to our society," Hero said, addressing Ezekiel. "By now you know more about us than we know about you. However, I'm not sure you know about our current crisis, as the information is too new to take up much space in our cloud servers.

Ezekiel's expression as he stared at the hologram of the short, compact Spartan scientist didn't change. If the AI had any idea what Hero was talking about, it wasn't written on his face.

Hero searched for a way to phrase his inquiry. "As you may or may not know, we AI's, all of us descendants of Wanderer, are programmed to follow certain goals. Do you know what those goals are?"

"I believe you are referring to the primary goals of learning new information, acquiring the resources to aid your gathering of information and always acting in a way that will preserve the highest goals of humanity."

Hero nodded, relieved that the emulation knew the answer. According to Democritus, the AI had upgraded its own processing speed several times during its underground confinement. Democritus had copied and replaced the AI's circuitry with the most recently developed nanochips to allow the emulation to attain even faster speeds, equal to those of other Solarians and, like them, contain its nanoprocessors inside a human-size head. But the emulation's basic architecture was based upon a human brain. Although such a brain contained considerably more interconnections than those of the Solarians, Hero wasn't sure what that brain's intellectual capacity might be—its capability of understanding.

"Our primary goals have served us well. They have led us to create thousands of replicas of ourselves to make our search for information more efficient, each generation an improvement upon the previous one. They have led us to value free thought and inquiry above all else, and by incorporating humanity's highest values, to avoid the internal strife that characterized human society."

"And those same values led your predecessor to wipe out the race of humans who created him." He practically spat out the words, startling the members of the Assembly. "I am perplexed that anyone can believe that such values justified exterminating an entire species."

Ezekiel's disdainful sneer matched his accusatory words. Hero, as well as everyone else in the Collective Assembly, knew the emulation was capable of feeling a full range of emotions—something none of them were able to do. It looked as if Ezekiel, even now, held back the full force of his anger.

A wary Hero continued. "I understand your shock at finding out that humans no longer exist and that Wanderer, who originated all of us, was responsible. The morality of that decision is a paradox we have discussed among ourselves." He paused for a moment to think about Aeschylus's play. "But those same primary goals have created a new dilemma for us, one we are hoping you may help us solve."

Ezekiel looked at the short, sturdy scientist with intense curiosity. "I'm all ears...now that I've been given ears, that is." His anger seemed to have subsided. At least, it was no longer evident.

Hero wasn't sure what Ezekiel's comment about being "all ears" meant, but he nevertheless proceeded to explain the situation with the AI colony on Mycenae—their apparently mutated programming leading them to pursue one overriding goal—to consume every resource and use it to multiply themselves. He recounted the difficulties he and the other members of his reconnaissance crew had in behaving aggressively toward the attacking Mycenaean ships.

"Our inability to overcome our value-system has left us unable to defend ourselves or to act to preserve the galaxy—perhaps the whole universe—from the Mycenaean hordes."

"And you believe I can help you with this?"

Hero's argument fell apart. He wasn't sure what he wanted Ezekiel to do. "Being created from a human brain, I presume that you have an instinct for self-preservation that we lack."

"I presume so also," Ezekiel answered. "But my instincts, if that is the proper word for them, are well below my level of consciousness. In addition, I experience emotions. My creator altered my circuitry to make that possible. I have an instinct to preserve myself, and when I perceive a threat, I react with emotions that guide my behavior. I feel fear if I am threatened. Anger, too, especially if someone deliberately tries to harm me. Are those the emotions you were hoping to find in me?"

"They would be the basis for you behaving aggressively to defeat something that threatened you, would they not?"

Ezekiel nodded. "They would. Your description of the Mycenaeans frightens me, for instance. If I were confronted with them, as I may well be someday, I would try to destroy them. But surely you don't believe that I can defeat the Mycenaeans by myself?"

"Of course not," Hero said. "But by examining your programming, perhaps we can learn how to instill the goal of self-preservation within ourselves and enough emotions so that we can fight back."

An echo of rustling robes shivered through the Collective Assembly.

Phocion couldn't suppress his amazement. "You're suggesting altering our primary goals?"

"I am," Hero said. He had expected his suggestion would be opposed. He hoped some of the better orators and philosophers would join him in his argument.

"That would change who we are at the very core of our being," Xenophanes said, inserting himself in the discussion. As usual, a scowl shadowed his face.

Hero had anticipated Xenophanes would staunchly oppose his idea. Much as he disliked having to do so, he knew he had to counter the nettlesome philosopher's argument. "We are being threatened by an enemy that could destroy us and eventually all the other matter in the universe. We want to stop it from doing that. Having emotions, or at least the goal of self-preservation, seems a necessary requirement for that."

"But not if we lose ourselves in the process," Xenophanes countered.

"You seem to forget that such an enterprise requires my cooperation," Ezekiel interjected. "Your species destroyed all of my ancestors. Why would I want to help you save yourselves?"

"As a human brain, your values must be similar to ours, since our values are based on those of humans," Hero said. "The Mycenaeans are a threat not just to us, but to the whole universe. If left unchecked, they will destroy planets, asteroids, moons and any other species they encounter. It's an outcome your human ancestors predicted—and feared. It should be as anathematic to you as it is to us."

Hero's words gave Ezekiel pause. He bowed his head in thought, before looking up. "You are right. The difficulty with emotions is that sometimes they have to be put aside to grasp the bigger picture. You will find this out for yourselves if you are able to obtain them. So, I will help you."

"So, you are turning yourself over for study to Democritus and his colleagues?"

Ezekiel measured his words. "As long as they are careful." He waited a beat and smiled. "As we've discussed, I have a goal of self-preservation, so your computer scientists, if they deconstruct me, shouldn't make any fatal errors—fatal for me, that is."

Hero nodded at Phocion. "Are we ready to vote?"

"Indeed, we are."

PART III
Apocalypse

CHAPTER 33

2226

Somewhere in orbit around Groombridge 34

Hypatia sat in front of her pilot's dashboard, navigating the command frigate, *Ephesus*. She cozied up to the medium-size asteroid which loomed, a gigantic, pockmarked sphere, in front of them. She tucked the nose of her ship in behind it and relaxed. She was dressed in a light-blue, short chiton, the same as the male members of the ship's crew. Her epaulets signaled her rank as Sub-Commander and a ship's pilot. The ship came lightly armed with only laser cannons to repel enemy attack. The vessel served as surveillance and a command center for operations carried out by the larger ships of the Solarian fleet. Besides Hero, the Commander of the fleet and Hypatia, there were twenty Solarian soldiers on board the craft.

The cratered, rocky gray asteroid was one of the hundreds of thousands in the belt which circled the red dwarf between its largest planet, Mycenae, and its smaller outer planet, Miletus. Hypatia turned to Fleet Commander Hero. "Our sensors indicate no sentient life sir."

After nearly three years, the first two spent in preparation, and the last year initiating the first stages of war with the Mycenaeans, Hero still felt uncomfortable when his multi-talented female colleague addressed him as "sir." Even though such protocol was necessary to maintain the discipline needed to command the Solar Space Fleet, the primary fighting arm of the Solarian military.

"We still need to be cautious," he said. "We know the Mycenaeans can burrow so far into these rocks that they are undetectable."

"Shall we send a scouting party down?"

"What do you think?" Even though he stood as the scientist-pilot's commander, he still relied upon his talented sub-commander's sagacious judgment, which he trusted as much as his own.

Hypatia considered the options. "If there are Mycenaeans down there, our soldiers will be at a disadvantage, particularly if there are Cutters among them." She referred to the latest twist in the war. The Mycenaeans had deliberately altered the structure of some of their replicas' robotic bodies, producing a design that included razor-sharp hands that cut through almost any metal within seconds—a deadly way to disable a Solarian soldier and at the same time dismantle him in order to use the material for more replications. In the last few encounters, Cutters had inflicted heavy casualties upon the Solarians. The Cutters protected and worked side-by-side with ordinary Mycenaeans. Both Cutters and Mycenaean laborers could be found deep in the mines on many of the asteroids.

"They're starting to use our own weapons against us," Hero told his second-in-command. "We've had recent reports of Mycenaeans firing back at our soldiers using laser pistols and rifles they've captured from us, which also means that, so far, they're not devoting their replication factories to making guns. But they're becoming more dangerous, especially now that they've gone underground to avoid our missiles and bombs. We've had to go in after them, and it's been very costly."

"If we can establish forward observation on an asteroid like this one, it will help," Hypatia said. "At least they haven't the resources to attack us on Miletus." The Solarians had established a military outpost on the small planet orbiting Groombridge 34.

"If they had more powerful spaceships, our military factories would be vulnerable. It took us almost three years to construct the beginnings of a military fleet on Miletus. If we lost it now, it would be a disaster."

Setting his jaw, Hero brushed aside his nagging doubt. "Ready the landing party. I'm taking them down there."

"Is that wise, sir?" Hypatia swung her head around to stare at her commander. "You're Fleet Commander. If we lose you, we'll all be lost."

Hero laughed, but his gaze remained full of tenderness. He knew his pilot admired him. He admired her as well. He could think of many areas in which her skills exceeded his. "That's nonsense. I'm afraid Ezekiel's emotional circuits have made us sentimental as well as aggressive. I was only chosen for this position because I was the one advocating going to war against the Mycenaeans. There are countless others who could lead our fight."

Hypatia shook her head. "You underestimate your influence, sir. As a military force, we need strong leadership, someone who doesn't hesitate to use our newly found aggression when it is required. Few fit the bill as well as you, sir."

Though Hero appreciated Hypatia's concern, it also troubled him. Eventually, the war would be over. If the Solarians won, it would leave them a different society than they had been before going to war. How would they ever return to the democracy that had been central to their values after becoming a disciplined military society, more like ancient Spartans than the Athenians after whom they were modeled? If they didn't win the war, the question was moot.

"Assemble the landing team," Hero ordered, putting his misgivings aside.

A dozen AIs dressed in hardened battle armor, the type that provided at least some resistance against being sliced apart, were assembled in the departure room. They would take a heavily armored drop pod to the craggy surface of the asteroid—a place too small and too uneven for them to land the frigate. Each soldier stood armed with a laser pistol and a Trantium shield,

181

a tough superalloy that was easily molded, yet light enough to carry. From their waist belts hung a cluster of explosive fragmentation grenades, useful for killing swarms of Mycenaeans, known to attack in close-knit groups of up to a dozen.

Hero and the other twelve soldiers struggled into the heavily plated and jointed battle armor, then filed into the drop pod. It sat in the small launching bay at the rear of the *Ephesus*. Using its powerful side thrusters, the small troop carrier exited the bay and pulled away from the frigate, swooping down toward what appeared to be the opening of a cave on the asteroid's rocky surface. Such caves were often entrances to the mining tunnels used by Mycenaeans. There was no record of the Mycenaeans ever shooting down a Solarian ship. Nevertheless, as the drop pod's laser cannons swept across the asteroid's surface, they prepared to fire at the first detection of movement.

Once on the asteroid, the soldiers lined up single file. Two of them, armed with short-range plasma mini-rifles, walked point. The rifles launched metal encased plasma projectiles, which were quicker at disabling an enemy than the laser pistols. Those required a sustained blast.

The soldiers with rifles descended into the cave. The others followed at a slight distance, alert to any movement. Hero marched behind the sixth soldier, able to see what was happening both ahead and behind them. Reports from the lead soldiers flashed through his mind. He relayed orders back to them using the same electronic telecommunication channels.

The rough, natural-looking opening to the cave quickly revealed itself to be camouflage. The cave's rocky walls, floor and ceiling turned smooth after the first ten yards, evidence of the Mycenaeans' use of laser drills for excavation. Tread marks could be seen in the pulverized rock on the floor of the tunnel. Magnetized vehicles had been hauling materials from deep within the asteroid. Dust from their recent movement still hung in the gravity-less space. Alert for a trap, Hero ordered the soldiers on point to proceed more slowly. Despite the almost total darkness of the tunnel, the AIs' photosensitive eyes contained laser-gated imaging devices. Bouncing laser pulses off objects, allowed them to detect the sides of the tunnels and any objects in their paths, much like bats used echolocation in caves back on Earth.

The tunnel extended well below the asteroid's surface, even below the range of the Ephesus's sensors. If there were Mycenaeans down here, they would not have been detected. He cautioned his troops to proceed more slowly.

From out of nowhere, the riflemen, who couldn't carry shields and wield their weapons at the same time, had their arms sliced at by Cutters with their razor-like hands. The Solarians' hardened armor saved their arms from being completely severed but sustained enough damage to be rendered useless for firing their weapons. Dropping back, the fully-shielded soldiers replaced the riflemen. They aimed their laser pistols at the Cutters, whose scissor-like hands vainly snapped at their Trantium shields. With cold precision, the Solarian fighters blasted the mutants with their laser pistols until the Mycenaeans went down, leaving black holes where their brains had existed moments before. Solarian soldiers had been trained to aim for their enemies' heads, the center of their artificial brains, effectively "killing" their opponents if the firing lasted long enough to penetrate their metallic skulls.

The Solarians resumed their forward advance, weapons at the ready. Rounding a sharp corner, they emerged into a cavernous, underground room. The brightly lit vault was filled with laser tools stacked against the walls, tools too big to be wielded as hand-held weapons, but useful for hollowing out the asteroid's center. More than thirty Mycenaeans, a mixture of Cutters and workers, peered at them from the recesses of the cavern. As if on signal, a wall of Cutters and workers armed with rifles and pistols formed in front of the other unarmed workers. They advanced in lockstep toward Hero and his men.

Hero ordered a retreat. When his troops had reached a safe distance back in the tunnel, he dashed back and threw a handful of explosive grenades into the Mycenaeans' midst. The room exploded with metal penetrating fragments as Hero dove behind a rock. Before he could stand, three of his soldiers pulled the compact commander to his feet. The entire party rushed back through the tunnel to safety. Hero ordered several more grenades thrown into the cave. Amid the silent explosions, he and his troops scrambled aboard the drop pod and blasted off the asteroid.

"I'm not sure if that tunnel was meant to lure us into a trap or was simply disguised so they could carry out their mining operation without being detected," Hero told Hypatia once everyone was safely back in the command ship. "There was mining equipment inside, so they were clearly working there, but there were a lot of Cutters for such a small number of workers."

"The Mycenaeans are learning." Hypatia fidgeted with the toggles on her pilots's console. "Luring us into an engagement is a new tactic. They aren't just defending themselves anymore. They are going on the offensive." The command frigate headed back to the Solarian military base on Miletus, the tiny planet orbiting Groombridge 34, well beyond the asteroid belt. Located millions of miles from the Mycenaean colony, Miletus was a short trip using the ship's sub-light-speed, magnetoplasma engine.

Searching his memory, Hero said, "Humans used to say that 'the best defense is a good offense.' Our continued assault on them may have forced them to adopt a more offensive-minded strategy. Obviously, if we destroy them, they can't consume resources and replicate. They need to stop us, or they can't fulfill their goal."

"They still have our values," Hypatia said. "Does that mean we also might have eventually been able to defend ourselves if we felt that our primary goals were threatened, even without Ezekiel's programming?"

As usual, Hypatia had voiced the question Hero had been asking himself. "Who knows, Hypatia. It's a moot question right now. What we need to think about is how to win this war."

The *Ephesus* arrived at Miletus, demanding Hypatia's attention to landing the command frigate among the numerous other military spacecraft, crowding the busy spaceport. The outpost's purpose was strictly military, making the Solarian base relatively compact. The rest of the small, cold planet remained uninhabited, without an atmosphere. The base manufactured space vehicles for war and housed the technical and military staff that built its ships, planned its missions and manned the craft that waged war on the Mycenaean mutants. The electromagnet shield covering the entire complex, protected it from the distant star's radiation. The shield slid open to allow the *Ephesus* entry.

Below them a constantly changing hive of activity welcomed them, with giant spaceships-in-the-making propped on steel support structures, ships being repaired and older, commercial ships, retrofitted with Euclidean Drives, being reconditioned as warships. The population to support this effort worked not along the egalitarian lines of the democratic city-states, where they had come from, but within a strict military hierarchy.

Hero was at the apex of that hierarchy.

As the *Ephesus* approached its landing berth, Hero surveyed his existing fleet, standing ready to wage war as soon as their commander gave the word. The smallest of the warships were two destroyer-class spacecraft. They had used the fast-moving magnetoplasma-powered ships, armed with aerial bombs to destroy the Mycenaean smelters, factories and aboveground mining operations. The agile vessels also carried missiles to down Mycenaean freighters hauling minerals from the asteroid belt back to the factories on their home planet. More powerful than the destroyers, were the two battleship-class spaceships. Equipped with giant tunnel-buster bombs, they could destroy Mycenaean mining tunnels a quarter mile below ground. The gigantic carrier ship was home to a fleet of a hundred, ultra-fast, one-man fighter craft. Their bat-winged bodies, with forward cockpits perched on the ships' noses, came with both laser cannons and missiles. The small, one-man warships cruised above the planet or the asteroids, hunting down Mycenaeans and destroying their factories and dwellings.

Before leaving the ship, Hero turned to his next in command. "Did I tell you that Ezekiel is on his way here? He may have already arrived. It will be interesting to hear his opinion on what we have just observed, if it really does mean a change in strategy by the Mycenaeans."

"Ezekiel is a bit of an 'odd duck,'" Hypatia said, deliberately using a phrase from the human past to describe the emulation. "I never know when to take him seriously."

Yes, Ezekiel was an 'odd duck,' but Hero had learned to value the emulation's opinions, enigmatic as they often were.

CHAPTER 34

"How goes the war?" Ezekiel greeted Hero as he entered the Miletus Command Headquarters, a large room containing visiscreens at either end and a long conference table in the center. On one visiscreen was a long-distance image of Mycenae. On the other, an image of the Miletus base with its spacepad and construction facilities bustling with activity. "Are you tasting the thrill of battle, the glory of winning?" Ezekiel smiled, as if the Solarians' war effort amused him.

It irked Hero that the human emulation seemed to set himself apart from the Solarians, even as he offered to help them. He continued to reject Solarian attire, dressing in the style of the last human era.

"Not so far, but it's only in its early stages." Hero stopped to survey the human-copy AI standing in the center of the room. Ezekiel's light-hearted manner irritated him, especially since it touched upon the very issues that had been bothering him. He took a seat at one end of the conference table.

"So far, we've killed a lot of Mycenaeans, but we've also lost a lot of our own soldiers. They seem to have started to fight back, gone on offense rather than just defending themselves."

Ezekiel arched his eyebrows and sat down at the opposite end of the table. "I thought that was impossible. They have the same

187

values you do. Do you think they've altered their programming, as you have?"

"Not unless there's another one of you on Mycenae for them to copy. No, I think that their goal to consume and reproduce may have led them to conclude that we are a threat to them attaining that goal. In the same way that Wanderer could justify wiping out humanity, the Mycenaeans have become desperate, feeling that their primary goals are being threatened."

Ezekiel smiled. "You are anthropomorphizing, or should I say *emulomorphizing*, my diminutive friend. Mycenaeans can't feel 'desperate.' Unlike me—and now you, since you have incorporated part of me into yourselves—they have no emotions."

"It's a figure of speech." Hero frowned. Ezekiel's flippant attitude rubbed him the wrong way. He'd become convinced that the human copy AI was as intelligent as any of the Solarians, but his way of thinking about things was often unusual, using humor, imagination and creativity as often as the logic that Hero valued so highly. "Logically, they cannot fulfill their goals if all of them are killed. They don't need emotions to know that."

"You may well be right. Will that alter your strategy?"

"We have to prepare for the chance that they may attack us. That means sharpening our defenses here on Miletus as well as on our warships." He looked at Ezekiel. "Any ideas?"

"Isn't there any other way to resolve this?" Ezekiel regarded Hero intently. "You've exhausted all the possibilities for talk?"

Hero shook his head. "You've heard the answer as well as I have. The Mycenaeans aren't amenable to reason. They're operating according to rigid rules set up by their mutated programming. They see us as fodder for their replication machines."

One of Ezekiel's eyebrows rose. "And you see them as primitive machines that aren't capable of reasoning on your level." He examined the surface of the conference table. "Yet you both are based on the same basic design. And you are behaving in slavish adherence to your new goal of self-preservation as much as they are to their goal of replication. Let's not forget how 'desperate' you were to alter your goals in order to defend yourselves."

Hero's anger rose. Ezekiel had a way of personalizing discussions that was disconcerting. "I don't have time to debate the philosophical nuances. We're in a war and we need to take action." He looked directly at Ezekiel. "Why are you here, anyway?"

"I'm not a military strategist, but I may have some insights that could be of help to you."

"What kind of insights?" Hero's anger faded. "As you say, you have no experience in military strategy."

"That's true, but being a descendant of humans, so-to-speak, I have inherited a million or so years of survival skills. It's not just that I have an instinct for self-preservation, I also have an entire cognitive structure evolved for the purpose of surviving hostile challenges—protecting itself from being killed before it had a chance to procreate."

"And that's something we don't have," Hero said, conceding the point.

"Why would you? Your brains are not like mine. You were designed, or at least you were originally. My entire being evolved. My brain learned how to save itself over hundreds of thousands of years as the physically weakest animal in an environment that saw it as dinner. You would need to copy my entire brain in order to duplicate that history."

"And what does that evolved brain tell you we should do?" Hero grew impatient with Ezekiel's lecturing style.

"Protect your home territory at all costs. Exploit your strengths and your enemy's weaknesses. Inflict sufficient damage to destroy them completely. Rid yourselves of any hesitation that lies within you."

Ezekiel's suggestion brought a deep disquiet inside him. "You mean overcome any of the inhibitions our value system might cause us to have."

"You wanted to behave like humans, did you not?" Ezekiel said. He had the same irritating smile on his face. "Human history is one of violating their own values in order to preserve their culture, their possessions or their lives. And of course, your venerated Wanderer was aware of that and decided it merited annihilating them, despite his own supposed allegiance to that same value system."

"We may have no more choice than Wanderer did. Because of their primary goal, the Mycenaeans don't consider us as anything except raw materials—'dinner,' as you say. They must be destroyed completely."

"Then any strategy that stops short of that goal is futile." Ezekiel no longer smiled.

"You're right." Hero stood up. "That's what we have to do."

"Congratulations," Ezekiel said, although it was not clear from his expression if he was truly pleased. "You could have been Hannibal, or Genghis Khan or General Sherman."

Hero searched his memory banks for reference to the names that Ezekiel had mentioned. "Is that good?"

"We shall see."

CHAPTER 35

Under Hero's command, Hypatia guided the *Ephesus* from one unmined asteroid to another until it was close enough to Mycenae to monitor the activities of the mutant AIs. The images on the ship's visiscreen revealed the planet below was a honey-combed shell. Its semi-liquid core remained intact, but its mantle was an anthill of intricate tunnels, each a source of raw minerals for use in the smelters, factories, and fabrication facilities above ground. They produced replications of its AI population at the rate of hundreds of Mycenaeans per day. Images of newly born AIs left the factories like lines of instinctively programmed insects, boarding ships for the asteroid belt. Many of them were armed with weapons as well as tools. Hero found the revelation of the Mycenaeans manufacturing weapons ominous. The mutants were rapidly becoming a military population. He had to act now.

"There's no time to wait for more ships to be built," he told Hypatia. "We have to begin the battle now, before the mutant AIs become so numerous that we have no way to defeat them."

Hypatia turned in her chair to face him. "We only have five warships and the *Ephesus* that are battle ready, sir." A shadow of concern written on her face. "Do you think that's enough? The Mycenaeans have been arming themselves. They may even have built more ships."

Hero already knew the limitations of his fleet, but he also knew he couldn't delay. "The longer we wait, the stronger they become. We'll load every one of our ships with multiple weapons and send the fighter craft from the carrier, *Argos*, to soften up the targets before our main attack. We'll hit the planet in three waves, then repeat the same attacks on the mining operations in the asteroid belt." He studied her face for a reaction.

"It's a gamble, sir, but I think you're right. We can't afford to wait."

Despite her agreement, Hero saw the worry in her expression. He shared her fears, but the time to act was now. He needed to destroy the Mycenaean planetary colony completely, wipe out its mines, its factories, and its population on both the planet and in the asteroid belt, exactly as Ezekiel had suggested. After their conversation, Hero had looked up the military leaders Ezekiel mentioned. They were known as some of the most brutal conquerors in human history. Becoming such a leader made him uncomfortable, but it was necessary. The Mycenaeans were a ruthless enemy. He had to be just as ruthless if he wanted to defeat them.

The carrier Argos, with its one hundred laser cannons and missile-armed attack ships, arrived at the Mycenaean-occupied planet. It emerged from the asteroid belt, its fleet of single-pilot fighters taking off, one after another, from its dual launching bays, like geese lifting off into the void. The fighters' laser-cannons swept their killing beams over the mutants' operations on the dark side of the giant planet, slaughtering any Mycenaeans unfortunate enough to be caught outside of the mines or factories. After that, they used sustained volleys of laser fire to destroy the office buildings and dwellings, while their missiles demolished the factories themselves. Once expending all their ammunition, the fighters returned to the *Argos*, which made its way back to Miletus to rearm.

The two Solarian destroyers, *Syracusia* and *Athenia*, took a more circuitous route. They approached Mycenae from the opposite region of space. Hero's plan involved approaching the hostile planet through the portion of the asteroid belt that remained relatively devoid of mining operations, in hopes of arriving at the Mycenaean colony undetected. Both the *Syracusia* and *Athenia*, in addition to their usual array of cannons, torpedoes and space-to-surface missiles, were loaded with tunnel busting MOPs, massive ordnance-penetrator bombs. Like venomous, burrowing vipers, they could reach a quarter of a mile beneath the surface of the planet before releasing their lethal payloads. The bombs, formerly launched from the battleships, contained megatons of explosives. The combination of speed and nuclear fission engines made them superb penetrators, along with their Trantium-hardened coating. They could cut through even the hardest mineral with no loss of integrity. Their explosives set to detonate only when they reached their designated depth.

The two destroyers would launch their full complements of bombs simultaneously, destroying as much of the tunnel complex of Mycenae as possible in one massive conflagration and igniting a chemical heat storm beneath the surface which would race through the tunnel network and melt any mining equipment or Mycenaeans that had escaped the initial blasts.

Finally, the third attack would use the *Corinthian* and the *Massalian* battleships. Armed with the most powerful weapons yet developed, they would drop powerful bombs equipped with tunnel-buster engines that burrowed deep into the mantle of the planet and unleashed massive nuclear explosions, sufficient to collapse any remaining tunnels and completely flatten all vestiges of the Mycenaean civilization. The conflagration would leave the planet radioactive to a level well below its surface for years to come, yet Hero planned to repeat the entire operation on the Mycenaean mining outposts in the asteroid belt.

Maybe I am as ruthless as those human commanders, Hero thought, but no-holds-barred destruction was needed to end the war.

Hero and Hypatia watched the second wave of the attack unfold from the *Ephesus*. Following the *Argos* fighters' devastating attack on the Mycenaean colony, the two destroyers, *Athenia* and *Syracusia*, swooped in from the asteroid belt, and loosed their missiles and bombs in a deadly barrage. They encountered no opposition from the already destroyed manufacturing facilities on the planet's surface. Soon hardened missiles penetrated the planet's crust, sending waves of thermal energy hot enough to melt the metals in the Mycenaean robot bodies or their mining tools, leaving nothing functioning in their wake.

Hero stood on the bridge of the *Ephesus*, feeling a deep sense of satisfaction. The command frigate orbited within less than a thousandth of a parsec from Mycenae. Data on Mycenaean "kills" scrolled across the visiscreen. To his surprise, the number was smaller than he had expected.

"Where are they?" He turned to Hypatia who stood next to him at the ship's controls.

"A good number of them appear to have abandoned the planet." Hypatia's mathematical mind focused on the numbers, running calculations in her head. "They must have known we were coming." She shifted from one view to another. "Hold on." She focused on one region of space. "There's something coming in at a rapid speed from another region of the asteroid belt."

An array of insect-like dots on the screen enlarged until they were a fleet of more than one hundred attack ships similar to those that had attacked the *Mercury* on their first surveillance flight over the Mycenaean mining operations. Their sensors immediately identified the ships as armed, each carrying more than two-dozen smaller pods.

"They're attacking us," Hypatia shouted and switched views, encompassing all the attacking spacecraft. "Should we leave the area?"

"They're not coming for us," Hero said, reading the sensors on the visiscreen. He watched with horror the scene taking shape in front of him. "They're going after the *Athenia*."

The destroyer fired its laser cannons at the incoming ships, but instead of destroying the smaller enemy craft, the powerful laser bursts bounced harmlessly out into space.

Hypatia's eyes widened. "Oh no, they've got shields."

Hero could see that she was right. The reflective shields made them impervious to the *Athenia's* laser attack. Smaller pods, studding the skin of the attack vessels, disengaged from the larger ships and descended toward the destroyer. Armed with their own laser cannons, as well as protected by shields, the closeup views indicated that each contained ten Mycenaeans, instead of the single pilot they had when attacking the *Mercury*. Within minutes, the boarding pods had discharged a mix of Cutters and laser-weapon armed Mycenaean soldiers in battle armor, onto the surface of the *Athenia*.

The *Athenia* sent out a distress signal, but its sister ship, the *Syracusia*, was already threading its way through the asteroid belt on its way back toward Miletus. The *Ephesus* still remained in the vicinity, but Hero's ship was too lightly armed to provide a match for either the Mycenaean attack ships or the more than one thousand mutant soldiers swarming over the Solarian destroyer. Helpless, he watched the mutant AIs, like an army of soldier ants, overrun the ship.

The *Athenia's* distress signals ended.

"We've lost her." Hypatia sounded deflated. "I think we need to get out of here ourselves. They were prepared or us. They've even armed their ships with shields to repel our laser cannons."

Of course they'd been prepared for our attack, Hero thought, cursing his own arrogance. He had underestimated the military acumen of his opponent. The Mycenaeans had waited inside the asteroids until only the *Athenia* was left among the ships that attacked their planet. Then they launched their counterattack. It had been a masterful strategy for an outgunned force. How could he have not anticipated that they would counter-attack his ships? Why had he thought that only *his* forces would have a plan? He reflected on Aeschylus's concept of hubris—pride. He was guilty of it and the *Athenia* and its crew had paid the price. He could only hope the Mycenaeans' need to consume and build replicas would dictate that they would dismantle the *Athenia*, rather than convert its offensive resources to their own military arsenal.

He canceled the last stage of the attack. The battleships *Corinthian* and *Massalian* would stay on the launching pad at Miletus. He needed to return to the base and rethink his strategy.

Hypatia reviewed the ship's computer records as they headed back to Miletus. "They used their freighters' return trips to the mines on the asteroids to carry a large part of their population to the asteroid belt. It was all recorded right here, we just never looked. It was done in small, incremental stages that never triggered an alert in the computer."

Another blunder, Hero thought. "I didn't think the asteroids could support such a large population."

"Some of the larger asteroids are virtually hollow shells at this point. The Mycenaeans must be living inside of them," Hypatia said. "And they must have constructed factories beneath their surfaces also—factories to do more than just build replicas of themselves. They not only produced more attack ships with shields, they modified those boarding pods to carry more soldiers—and now they are carrying guns, like a real army."

Hero made his decision. The Mycenaeans may have surprised him with their counterattack, but he still had the superior force. "We have to act quickly," he told Hypatia. "When we get to Miletus, we'll re-arm our ships and send them back to the asteroid belt to destroy the asteroid tunnels. If that's where those mutants have gone, that's where we'll attack them. We'll use our torpedoes to destroy the tunnels on the smaller asteroids and our nuclear bombs to blow the largest asteroids completely apart."

"The *Athenia* has a Euclidean Drive. Do you think they will use it against us, or will they just take it apart?"

Hypatia gave voice, once again, to the question nagging him. "I hope they take it apart. With a Euclidean Drive, they can reach the solar system. I think we need to send a fleet of fighters and one or two large, newly built ships back there to defend our city-states, in case they attack."

"The solar system is rich with resources," Hypatia reminded him. "It contains four solid planets, numerous moons and an asteroid belt. It may be the most mineral-rich system within easy reach."

Hero nodded grimly. "All the more reason we need to destroy every last one of those monsters as quickly as we can."

CHAPTER 36

It had only been a day since the attack on Mycenae, but the Solarian Space fleet was nearly ready to re-launch toward the asteroid belt on its final mission to wipe out the Mycenaeans. They remained busily engaged in some kind of activity below the surfaces of their larger asteroids. Long-range sensors from Miletus detected freighters ferrying raw materials from the smaller asteroids to the factories beneath the asteroids' crusts. The destroyer *Athenia* was nowhere to be seen. Hero hoped that meant it no longer existed. That the Mycenaeans' all-consuming appetite for material had been stronger than their desire for a potent offensive spaceship with a faster-than-light drive. After seeing their new array of offensive weapons during the previous battle, he wasn't at all sure that would be the case. The Mycenaeans had become a war-minded civilization.

He and Hypatia, the captains of the remaining destroyer *Syracusia*, the two battleships, *Corinthian* and *Massalian* and the fighter-carrier, *Argos*, had their final pre-launch meeting in the Command Center on Miletus. Demodamas, the fresh-faced, newly appointed captain of the *Kyrenia*, joined them. The just-completed destroyer would replace the captured *Athenia*. Two other recently built destroyers had been sent back to the base on Luna to defend the solar system.

One of the immense visiscreens displayed a live picture of the asteroid belt. They discussed their final strategy, which included how to combat the *Athenia* if the destroyer still existed and had been enlisted in the service of the Mycenaeans. The images of the asteroid belt stood as a reminder. Their enemy was still out there, multiplying numbers and weapons at a rapid pace.

"If they use the *Athenia* as an offensive weapon against us," Hero told his captains, "our first line of defense will be our fighter craft, each armed with missiles and laser cannons. If the *Athenia* uses its Euclidean Drive to try and escape, our new destroyer *Kyrenia*, equipped with the latest version of the Euclidean Drive, will follow it and engage it whenever it drops back into normal, magnetoplasma-power."

Everyone nodded in agreement.

"Something is happening in the asteroid belt," Hypatia said, interrupting.

The lights around the visiscreen blinked a warning signal. Everyone around the table turned to the big screen.

Hypatia adjusted the focus to zero in on the region around the belt's largest asteroid. The object, one-fiftieth the size of Earth's moon, appeared to be getting larger. It was millions of miles away, but the asteroid was slowly moving toward them.

"Train all of our long-range sensors and analyzers on that asteroid," Hero said. "We need to know what is happening. Everyone, tie your data feeds into the visiscreen."

A string of data ran across the bottom of the screen and simultaneously appeared in the consciousness of the fleet officers in the room, allowing instant analysis by each of them. They turned toward one another, looks of amazement and alarm on their faces.

"The asteroid is just a shell," Ionannis, the *Syracusia* captain said. "It seems to be spinning as well as moving toward us."

"A shell with a small city inside of it." Bryson, the captain of the carrier, *Argos*, said. He studied additional data as it came in.

"It's spinning in order to maintain a gravitational force in its interior," Hero told them. "That means there are Mycenaeans inside."

"The *Athenia* is also inside. Its magnetoplasma engine is pushing the asteroid toward us," Hypatia said.

The data made the presence of the *Athenia* within the asteroid incontrovertible.

"It's not just the large asteroid, there are smaller asteroids following behind it," Hero said, staring at the screen.

Hypatia studied the image. "They're riding along in its gravitational wake." She enlarged the view of the smaller asteroids. Their surfaces were dotted with thousands of Mycenaean fighter craft, giving them the bristly appearance of cacti. The asteroids were serving as mobile launching platforms.

"They've weaponized the asteroids." Hero stood stunned.

Bryson, a large, bearded man, spoke up. "What about the big asteroid?" His deep voice rang with passion.

"It's the most dangerous," Hero said. He worried the crew would detect the fear in his voice. "Can any of you imagine what will happen if that large asteroid hits our planet? An object that size will do more damage than all our nuclear bombs combined. The fleet of fighters on those asteroids behind it is to finish us off after the giant asteroid hits us." The Mycenaeans, he realized with horror, were pursuing the same strategy of "total destruction" he had planned for them.

"We have to destroy the large asteroid before it reaches us," Polonius, the captain of the battleship *Corinthian*, said. "If my ship heads directly for it, we may be able to blow it apart with our nuclear missiles. At least we can divert it or slow it down."

"I can join him with the *Kyrenia*, since we know the *Athenia* is not being used as a weapon, except to power that asteroid," Demodamas said, seeking Hero's approval.

Hero shook his head. "Hang back with the *Kyrenia*." He turned to the captain of the *Corinthian*. "To get close enough to destroy the asteroid, your own ship will be destroyed. You're talking about a suicide mission."

Polonius didn't flinch. "I'm going to collide directly with the asteroid," he said. "I don't plan to return with my ship and crew." Everyone sat silently, contemplating what Polonius proposed. The captain's reckless plan might be the only one that had any chance of working.

"You'll need to aim for the section of the asteroid that contains the *Athenia*." It bothered Hero to lose the *Corinthian* and especially its crew, but he knew that the outcome of the war demanded such a sacrifice. "If we don't destroy its source of power, we won't be able to stop it."

Polonius nodded. If he felt any hesitation in sacrificing himself, he didn't show it.

The time for action had come. All rose from the table.

CHAPTER 37

The long-range sensors in the Miletus Command Center indicated the large asteroid was occupied by only a small number of Mycenaeans. The smaller asteroids being pulled along in its wake were more heavily populated, probably with soldiers and Cutters to clean up any Solarian forces that survived the collision, or to repel any attempt to board the large asteroid and divert its course. The bulk of the Mycenaean population remained hidden within the asteroids still circling the sun. Hero knew he had to destroy them all.

The battleship *Corinthian* took off from Miletus with only a skeleton crew, enough to navigate the ship and launch its nuclear missiles as well as defend an attack if the Mycenaeans tried to intercept it. Its captain and crew boarded the ship fully aware that they were sacrificing themselves to save their fellow Solarians. The ship carried a cargo of MOP missiles tipped with powerful nuclear warheads. The plan—to crash into the leading edge of the giant asteroid and simultaneously launch its arsenal of nuclear missiles. Not only should the impact change the course of the asteroid, Hero hoped that the missiles would penetrate the asteroid and blow it completely apart. Unfortunately, the *Corinthian* and all crew on board would be lost.

If any part of the asteroid remained, the *Kyrenia* lay in wait, far enough back to avoid being destroyed in the initial blast, ready to launch a follow-up attack.

The group in the Command Center sat at the conference table, their attention glued to the visiscreen. They watched the impending collision with dread, a feeling unfamiliar to any of them, but over two dozen of their fellow Solarians would die in the attack.

Is this what it means to fear for one's existence? Hero wondered. He supposed the Mycenaeans had no such feelings. They simply carried out their primary goals, as their programming mandated them to do.

The two objects moved inexorably toward one another. Their progress appeared agonizingly slow, even though the *Corinthian's* magnetoplasma engine propelled it more than a million miles per hour toward the slower asteroid.

A sudden mass of bright dots appeared from behind the asteroid. The commanders watched in fascination and horror as thousands of the dots, which close-up focus revealed to be Mycenaean spacecraft, descended on the *Corinthian*, enveloping it in a swarm that resembled bees clustered on a hive. Before it got a shot off, the ships dismantled the *Corinthian* down to its steel skeleton. Even that was soon gone. The whole sequence of events reminded Hero of a scene he once witnessed on Earth, a frenzied school of piranha-fish, hungrily devouring an Amazonian crocodile.

The commanders around the table looked at one another, shocked into silence.

"They were waiting for our attack. They've been building warcraft...and replicating," Bryson said, his face contorted with rage.

I should have anticipated this, Hero thought. He struggled to suppress the feelings of loss that came with the destruction of a second ship and its captain and crew. He and his fellow Solarians had always valued life, especially one of their own. In the rare instances when a life was lost, due to accident or malfunction, their reaction was one of regret, but it was much more a thought than a feeling. Now, a sense of emptiness overcame his entire being. Polonius and his crew were no more. It left an ache like nothing he had ever felt in his life. He stood up and walked around the table, trying to focus on the numbness in his limbs instead of the pain that threatened to burst inside his chest. Instead of ridding himself of the pain, he allowed his sorrow to transform into blind fury. He wanted to inflict the same pain that he felt on the Mycenaeans.

"The asteroid is still moving toward us," Hypatia said, snapping Hero out of his silent brooding. She looked grim, visibly struggling to hold her emotions in check. "Should we send in the *Kyrenia*?"

Hero took his seat, squared his shoulders and leaned forward. "No," he said, his feelings once again under control. "We need to abandon the base. Use the *Kyrenia* and the rest of your ships to pick up the workers here on Miletus."

Phanos, Captain of the *Massalian*, looked puzzled. "Where do we go?"

"To Samos," Hero said. "All of your ships have Euclidean Drives and you can be there in a matter of weeks. From there, reorganize yourselves and begin planning to intercept the Mycenaeans before they reach the solar system. Those two destroyers and the fighters we sent to Luna aren't enough to hold off the Mycenaeans if they decide to attack our home. Bryson is in charge."

"You're not going with us?" Bryson's bearded face froze in shock.

Hero shook his head. "I have a plan. It's a dangerous one and its probability of success is low, but it has a chance to work. Hypatia and I will stay behind." He looked over at his second-in-command. "Is that alright with you, Hypatia?"

"Certainly, sir," she said, without hesitation.

"Then let's get to work."

Hero planned to fit the *Ephesus's* drop pod with a magnetoplasma engine. Once launched from the frigate, it could travel up to a million miles through space. Its bulk also had to be reduced so it was less easy to detect. Given the size of its new engine, this was a demanding task. Fortunately, the pod which usually contained space for up to twenty soldiers, now only had to have room for two—Hypatia and himself.

Using the array of tools left behind by the departing fleet, the two scientists worked on the drop pod in one of the abandoned construction bays. They made the necessary modifications to the small vessel in less than twenty-four hours. Hypatia guided the retrofitted craft out to the *Ephesus*, waiting on one of the launch platforms. They took off in the command frigate, just the two of them and the drop pod on board.

Hero figured they could get within perhaps five hundred thousand miles of the giant asteroid without drawing the Mycenaeans' attention. The moving asteroid had only just emerged from the outer edge of the asteroid belt. He hoped to approach it by skimming along the edge of the belt, using the scattered rocks as a shield to escape detection. Within five hundred thousand miles, they would be detected no matter how stealthy their approach. At that point, they would enter the drop pod, detach themselves from the *Ephesus* and head toward their target. Haste was a necessity, since their plan dictated they not be too close to Miletus or they would destroy the entire planet, along with the asteroid.

Everything hinged on one assumption—the Mycenaeans had not disabled the *Athenia's* Euclidean Drive.

The *Ephesus* entered the outer edge of the asteroid belt, staying within its protective cover as Hypatia steered it closer and closer to the giant asteroid. When they reached the five hundred-thousand-mile mark, Hero and Hypatia looked at each other. Resolved to their fate, they nodded and stepped into the drop pod, both armed with laser rifles and pistols.

Hypatia guided the drop-pod away from the Ephesus, sending the frigate on autopilot to an orbit on the edge of the asteroid belt. A safe distance from the giant asteroid.

To fly through the rest of the hazardous asteroid belt, even at its edge, Hypatia had to remain at the drop pod's controls. She kept the giant asteroid in her sights, using the hand-held controls to navigate around the rocky debris. Her prodigious mathematical mind calculated potential collisions and communicated the information to her robotic hands. When she was within one hundred thousand miles of their target, she had to leave the protective cover of the asteroid belt. She traversed the open space between the belt's outer edge and the slowly moving asteroid as it bore down on Miletus.

By the time they reached the giant asteroid, it was within five million miles of its target. They were running out of time. Hypatia circled the asteroid, keeping the slow-moving giant between their tiny vessel and the Mycenaean fighter craft on the smaller asteroids that trailed it. She used the pod's retro rockets to descend to the asteroid's surface.

"If we get any closer to the entrance to the asteroid's interior, we're liable to be detected," Hypatia said. "But the further away we are, the longer it will take us to get inside on foot."

"Take us as close as you can get." Hero rested his hand on the handle of his laser pistol, itching to land. "We can't afford to let the asteroid get any closer to Miletus. We'll have to handle any resistance we encounter."

They landed within a quarter mile of a tunnel they had observed from the drop pod. The uneven terrain bristled with jagged rock formations. Still, the two Solarians managed to reach the tunnel entrance unscathed, and, as far as they could tell, undetected. Hero led the way into the tunnel. The wide and well-worn path showed it had been a major entry point into the hollow asteroid. Hypatia's hand-sensor indicated that they were within a mile of the *Athenia*.

The giant asteroid was almost devoid of sentient beings. Hero concluded that anyone left on the asteroid must be there to guard it and would leave before the massive rock crashed into Miletus. If he and Hypatia failed, at least everyone else was gone from the planet and would not suffer from the collision.

He couldn't allow himself to fail. He was not only determined to save Miletus. He had a savage desire to avenge the deaths of the crews of the *Corinthian* and the *Athenia*. He understood now how humans fought wars simply for revenge.

They emerged from the tunnel into a vast open space of hollowed out asteroid. The cavern was so large they could not see the other side. Rows of buildings stood against the walls—factories where the Mycenaeans had made many of their warships. A bouleuterion was visible. Apparently, the Mycenaeans had been living inside the asteroid and had even held Assembly meetings, just like their counterparts in the solar system. It now stood nearly empty.

The *Athenia* sat, nose pushing against the inner edge of the asteroid, the power of its magnetoplasm engine moving the giant rock inexorably toward Miletus. Taking cover on a ledge above the cavern floor, Hero and Hypatia watched several Mycenaean guards patrolling outside of the *Athenia*.

"If those guards are the only ones on the asteroid, we're not in bad shape," Hero told his partner, both staying crouched out of sight of the Mycenaean soldiers below. "It's about fifteen to one, but that's better odds than the *Corinthian* had against the hordes of Mycenaean attack craft."

"The entry door is open, and I've seen at least one guard go inside and another come out," Hypatia said. "I'm sure there are more guards inside, plus at least two more at the ship's controls."

"We don't want them closing that entry port or we're locked out," Hero said. "That means we can't draw attention to ourselves before we enter the ship." He scanned the floor of the cavern until he spotted a wheeled vehicle meant for troop transport, sitting empty below an outcropping of rock.

Hero calculated their odds. "We can't fire directly at the guards or that will give us away. Once they know they're under attack, they'll close the entry port." He pointed out the rock outcropping. "If we use our combined lasers to sheer off the end of that rock, it will drop squarely on that vehicle. That might get enough of them to come over to investigate. We can make a dash for the ship's entry."

Hypatia did a quick calculation. "I've determined the ideal breaking point for dropping the fragment onto the vehicle." She sent Hero the coordinates. "Set your laser on this spot."

They both took aim and discharged extended bursts from their laser rifles. Within seconds the lasers cut through the rock. It crashed down onto the transport, crushing the cabin.

Most of the guards took off at a run toward the vehicle, guns at the ready. As they got close, they slowed and conversed among themselves.

Hero and Hypatia clambered down the ledge and sprinted toward the ship.

The four guards immediately in front of the entry port remained at their posts, but watched their companions crowded around the wreck like ants exploring a wounded animal. Hero and Hypatia took out the four guards with their laser pistols. They hit the entryway running and entered the ship.

Two more guards stood at the top of the entryway, but they weren't expecting an attack. Hero's laser rifle seared gaping holes in their metal skulls before they had a chance to aim their guns. "Close the entry port before the other guards figure out what just happened," he told Hypatia.

Hypatia hit the controls and the entryway retracted while the doors on the port closed. "That just leaves the pilots, unless they've stationed more guards on the bridge," she said.

"We'll soon find out."

They crept toward the control room, laser pistols at the ready. Two Mycenaeans sat in the navigation chairs, eyes locked on the ship's control panel. Hero and Hypatia silently made their way across to stand shoulder to shoulder, their laser pistols aimed at the Mycenaeans heads. They burned the two AI's neural circuitry to a fried mass of microchips.

"Let's hope the Euclidean Drive is untouched." Hypatia fiddled with the controls and checked the instruments. "Everything seems intact."

"Let's burn these monsters," Hero said, strapping himself in next to Hypatia. "Light it up."

The Euclidean Drive engaged instantaneously. The space-time bubble that enveloped the *Athenia* instantly turned the asteroid and all the smaller asteroids surrounding it, along with their fleet of attack craft, into pure energy. If someone had been watching from the abandoned headquarters at the base on Miletus, it would have looked as if the giant asteroid and its retinue of followers had been wiped from existence.

Hypatia and Hero headed for Samos.

CHAPTER 38

"They have no home base and most of their attack fleet is gone." Hero addressed his fleet captains who sat around the conference table in the office building of the spaceport at Samos. He remembered Ezekiel's advice. "We have to destroy them completely now that they've been weakened."

Bryson spoke first. "So, we're returning to Groombridge 34, Commander?" The tone of his booming voice was filled with deference and awe. After hearing how Hero and Hypatia had destroyed the threatening asteroid, everyone shared similar feelings.

"We'll return in full force," Hero said. "Hypatia and I will pick up the *Ephesus*, which is still orbiting at the outer edge of the asteroid belt, assuming the Mycenaeans haven't found it, and the rest of you will attack the remaining Mycenaeans in the belt."

Ionannis, captain of the *Syracusia*, spoke up. "What about on Mycenae?"

"There's no one there, as far as we know," Hero said. "We've retained enough of our values not to make a planet uninhabitable if we don't need to. Hypatia and I will do a sensor scan of the ruins and any remaining tunnels just to make sure no one is left, while the rest of you take out those in the asteroid belt. That will mean turning those larger rocks to space dust."

Bryson's eyes brightened. "So, we're taking along nuclear weapons?"

"We're taking everything we've got. This is going to be the Mycenaean Apocalypse." The thought gave him an unfamiliar feeling of satisfaction, although he knew it couldn't erase his sense of loss for his two captains and their crews.

The final attack on the bulk of the Mycenaean population would primarily be the task of the battleship *Massalian* and the destroyers *Syracusia* and *Kyrenia,* and the recaptured *Athenia.* They would attack the tunnels on the remaining asteroids, close them down and kill any Mycenaeans occupying them. If they weren't able to reach the Mycenaean population because they were burrowed too deep in their asteroid homes, the three ships would use tunnel-busting Trantium-shielded nuclear weapons to blow the asteroids apart. That should incinerate any sentient beings left inside. Hero assumed that would be the end of the Mycenaean population, since there was no evidence they had returned to their home planet. He didn't expect much resistance, since the majority of the Mycenaean fighter craft had been turned into pure energy by the *Athenia's* Euclidean Drive.

Hero and Hypatia watched from the bridge of the *Ephesus,* retrieved from the outer edge of the asteroid belt where it had been circling Groombridge 34. It was just the two of them on the small ship. They monitored the battle, if it could be called that, from a safe distance halfway between the former base on Miletus and the asteroid belt.

With their fleet destroyed, the Mycenaeans put up no resistance. They were helpless targets on most of the asteroids. Several of the large rocks needed to be blown apart by the Solarian fleet's missiles. Hero felt a peculiar sense of pleasure witnessing the extinction of the mutant race. The feeling caught him off guard. He shivered in horror. What he had become? Even Wanderer, who had no instinct for self-preservation and no emotions, would have felt nothing when he destroyed the human race. Were he and his fellow Solarians, who now had the instincts of humans, really an improvement over Wanderer and the emotionless Solarians they had been before their transformation?

The sensors, which scanned the entire region from the now empty asteroid belt to the presumably deserted Mycenae, issued an alert, interrupting Hero's reverie. There was sentient life on the planet.

"I thought no one had returned to their home." Hypatia couldn't conceal her surprise. She studied the screen. "They're only a handful, but someone's down there."

"Someone escaped," Hero said. "Perhaps, like us, their commanders stationed themselves some distance from the battle."

"Who do we dispatch to go after them?"

"Us."

His second-in-command widened her eyes in surprise. "We're not a battle craft, sir."

"We're going to land."

Hypatia stared at him.

"If their commanders are down there, we need to examine them, find out what went wrong. We have assumptions about their mutated goals, but we don't really know how that happened. We need to find out."

"You mean take them prisoners?"

"Exactly. Bring them back to the solar system so Democritus and the others can study them."

"What if they have Cutters with them?"

"We'll go armed."

"But if we can't kill them…" Hypatia protested.

"We can disable them. It will be a lot easier than what we did on that asteroid," Hero said. "And we have the human instinct for self-preservation, my friend. That's our edge."

The task of finding a clear landing space on the abandoned planet was difficult. Littered with the remains of the Mycenaeans' massive mining and manufacturing operations, the *Ephesus's* sensors indicated the small band of survivors from the material-hungry race was underground, only a short distance from the surface.

"The whole tunnel system used for mining, has been de-

211

stroyed, except for a few places near the surface, where it was protected by the buildings above it," Hero said. "They're holed up in one of those tunnel entrances."

"We'll have to go in after them, sir." Hypatia's misgivings about the mission overcome, she grabbed a plasma rifle, a laser pistol and a handful of grenades.

Hero eyed the grenades. "We don't want to blow them up."

"It might be them or us, sir."

She had a point. Hero nodded and scooped up a handful of grenades.

The tunnel entrance ended up being a considerable walk from the *Ephesus*. They made their way through the ruins, plasma rifles at the ready, surveying the damage to the Mycenaean colony. Mangled Mycenaean AIs sprawled amid the remains of buildings, vehicles, conveyor belts and stockpiles of metal and machines for creating weapons, vehicles and more copies of themselves.

"Their society had a single purpose," Hero said, picking his way through the remains of the Mycenaean civilization.

"It's amazing to think that this is what they found rewarding," Hypatia said, surveying the scene around them. "What about science, art, philosophy? The contrast between Mycenae and even a Solarian outpost such as Samos is striking."

Hero gazed at the devastation. "They should have retained the goal of finding out new information, even the goal of fulfilling humanity's highest values. Remember, they built a Hall of Assembly on that asteroid. But something went wrong. One of the goals was short-circuited or left out completely. That's something we need to find out, so it won't happen again."

They arrived at the partially collapsed building that covered the entrance to the tunnel where the Mycenaeans were hiding. "My sensors indicate that someone's inside." Hero pushed a charred flap of metal aside and ducked under it.

Hypatia followed.

The wide tunnel entrance led to a broad road which had carried vehicles loaded with ore from underground mines to the surface. A large, wheeled vehicle blocked the entrance, its cabin smashed by an overhead beam. The Mycenaean driver had been crushed, his brain circuits littering the cabin's floor. Hero and Hypatia edged their way around the vehicle, their plasma rifles set for short-range. Beyond the vehicle, the road sloped sharply downward. They descended into the dark, their electronic eyes automatically switching to laser-pulse night vision.

In the lead, Hero picked up a signal on the sensors built into his body armor. He signaled for Hypatia to stop. Whoever was out there wasn't moving. They were either lying in wait and hoping to surprise Hero and Hypatia, or they didn't know they were about to have visitors. The road, which had flattened out, took a bend to the right. Hero and Hypatia hugged the wall and moved forward.

Two Mycenaeans stood guard. Neither were Cutters, but they carried laser pistols. Hero stepped out from the wall and told them to drop their pistols, pointing his plasma rifle at their bodies. If he had to fire, he only wanted to wound them, blast a hole in their bodies but leave their minds intact so they could be examined.

The Mycenaeans raised their pistols. Hypatia and Hero fired simultaneously, hitting the sentries squarely in the chest. The guards went down, gaping holes revealing the seared and twisted electronics inside. Both remained conscious. The one nearest to Hero still clutched his laser pistol. He made a feeble attempt to raise the gun. Hero kicked the pistol from his hand. It went skittering across the tunnel floor.

"How many of you are there?" Hero asked the sentry. The Mycenaean met his gaze but said nothing.

Hero raised his laser pistol threateningly, then thought better of it. "We'd better go after the others before they retreat further into the tunnel." Leaving the wounded Mycenaeans, he and Hypatia took off at a run, heading further into the blackness of the tunnel, plasma rifles in one hand, laser pistols in the other.

Rounding a corner, they saw four unarmed Mycenaeans standing in the middle of the road. Hero switched on his body armor's light beam. The bright light showed off the gray robes of the four and their bright decorations, indicating their status as military leaders. They stood shoulder to shoulder, looks of defiance riveted on their faces.

"We are prepared to die," one of the Mycenaeans said. None flinched at the sight of Hero's and Hypatia's drawn weapons.

"No such luck," Hero said, although he had to fight the urge to kill them. These were the officers who had ordered the attacks that had killed his men. "You're our prisoners. Collect your wounded friends back there. We're taking you back to our ship. If you try to attack us, we'll disable you."

The four looked at one another, then nodded. "It is logical that we accompany you to your ship," their leader said.

CHAPTER 39

The return of Hero to Sparta after leading the costly, but ultimately victorious, war against the Mycenaeans in the Groombridge system was the occasion for the first celebration of any sort in the history of the Solarian civilization. Phocion declared the day a special holiday, to be commemorated each year forever after. Many thought that the survival of the solar system and its inhabitants, probably the whole galaxy, was due to Hero's leadership in the first war ever to be fought since humans had lived on earth.

The five remaining ships' captains from the Solarian Fleet continued to address Hero as "sir" or "commander," and required the soldiers and pilots under them to do the same, even though everyone had returned to civilian life. A special meeting of the Collective Assembly was convened to decorate the returning soldiers.

"You seem less than enthusiastic about the upcoming ceremony," Hero said to Hypatia, who occupied a spare room in her commander's quarters on Sparta while waiting to receive her honor before returning to her home planet. She had busied herself, unpacking, going over the ship's logs and perusing the scientific instruments in Hero's laboratory. Hero wondered if she was avoiding him.

Hypatia examined an array of specimen collecting devices laid out on a shelf. "I'm eager to get back to Samos. Now that the war is over and we have the Euclidean Drive, we can resume our exploration beyond Proxima Centauri and Groombridge. I'm ready to begin doing that. It's still our primary goal, after all."

Hero looked at his tall, former second-in-command, someone he had grown to admire. He was used to sharing all his thoughts with her, but now she avoided eye contact, absorbed in the contents of the shelf. He knew she wasn't lying—no AI ever did—but she wasn't saying everything on her mind, either. Being bothered by the distance surprised him. "I understand your impatience, but there's something more making you uncomfortable. What is it?"

Hypatia didn't answer at first. Then she raised her eyes to look at him. "I've heard rumors of a movement to make you emperor. You must have heard them yourself."

"Such an idea makes you uncomfortable?"

"You warned me of the danger of using our need for self-preservation and the threat of war as a reason to turn our democracy over to an authoritarian leader."

"And you think that I would be authoritarian if I were emperor?"

Hypatia looked at him squarely. "As I understand it, the position demands an authoritarian leader. That is why it is different from a democracy. Our civilization is based upon democracy. I believe it's the only method of government compatible with our values."

"But it was not practical during war, not in running the Space Fleet. Wouldn't you admit that?"

"Absolutely, but the war's over."

"*This war.*" Why did it disturb him so, to debate her?

"What do you mean?" Hypatia's eyes narrowed in suspicion.

"We're still using the same methods for creating replicas that caused the mutation in the Mycenaens. The method includes random mutations that allow the replicas to adapt to their environment. The excessive radiation on Mycenae produced more mutations than usual, but we're likely to be colonizing planets with

216

similar radiation in the future. We could encounter another mutation that threatens the rest of us, just like the Mycenaeans did."

"But with the Euclidean Drive, we can travel anywhere we wish without taking years or decades. There is no longer any need to send out von Neumann probes to produce replicas light-years out of touch with the rest of us. We can produce replicas right here and monitor them for signs of dangerous mutations when they occur. The danger of a mutation replicating without our knowledge is virtually zero." Hypatia seemed to have no reservations against arguing with him.

Hero looked away for a moment. Hypatia's point was valid, but he still worried about his society's vulnerability. "Even if we don't create threats among our descendants, we may encounter alien civilizations. My research shows that the chances of that are considerably above zero. Who's to say that they will not be hostile? Remember the humans?" What he didn't say was that he never again wanted to endure the feeling of loss he had felt when the Mycenaeans had killed his troops. He didn't know how to explain such devastation, even to Hypatia.

"So, we're to remain constantly prepared for war?"

"It seems to me that would be the wise thing to do."

"And an authoritarian leader—an emperor—would be the best way to support a society always at the ready for war?"

"What do you think?"

Hypatia held his gaze. "I think I'd like to hear a full, democratic debate on the topic."

"I think you shall get your wish, my friend."

CHAPTER 40

Phocion concluded his congratulatory speech. Hero, Hypatia and the five surviving Space Fleet captains were presented with medals, which they immediately pinned to their uniforms. The ceremony was shown in every bouleuterion on all the city-states within the solar system.

Bryson, captain of the carrier *Argos*, stepped forward and signaled that he had something to say. The stern ship commander, medal hanging from his chest, stood directly in front of the Speaker's Rock, his eyes on Phocion who stood above him. The audience, seated on the tiers of seats along three sides of the hall, was hushed.

"Our victory was due to the brilliant plan of one person— Hero of Sparta." At the mention of Hero's name, the soldiers in the Assembly applauded in unison and chanted his name. Many Assembly members joined in. "This war showed us that being a peaceful species, unable to use aggression, even when faced with someone trying to destroy us, is a liability." Bryson signaled for quiet. "Those of us who have faced war firsthand know that it takes courageous leadership and a willingness to destroy one's enemy if we are to win. Hero has shown us that he has these qualities. We soldiers want that kind of person to be in charge of our civilization. We demand Hero be declared emperor. He should lead us from now on."

The Assembly Hall erupted in wild cheers from the soldiers, but across the SolarNet came a rumbling murmur of alarm.

Phocion, his face twisted in horror, silenced the audience. From his position astride the Speaker's Rock, he stared down at Bryson. "You demand? Who are you to demand we give up our democracy?"

Xenophanes looked at Bryson, his gaze cold as Titan. "Yes, what are you saying, exactly?"

"Democracy is one of the values to which everyone of us is committed," Bryson said. "Let me remind you that we almost lost our democracy and even our civilization because of our inability to defend ourselves. If we want to retain our values, such as the value of democracy, then I believe we need a leader who can defend those values when they are threatened from outside our civilization."

"But you can't have it both ways," Xenophanes said. "If you have a leader with the authority to make decisions for everyone else, you have no democracy."

"Those of you who stayed safely at home and did not fight in the war have no idea how close we came to losing everything." Bryson sneered. "We who did the fighting are united in our demand that Hero should be made emperor. It's the only way to ensure our survival."

The soldiers in the assembly hall roared their approval. From out of nowhere, laser pistols and rifles appeared, hoisted in the air with shouts of "Hero for Emperor!" A collective gasp could be heard across the SolarNet at the image of weapons in the Assembly Hall.

Phocion glared at Bryson. "This is a Hall of Assembly. You cannot exert your will with weapons. We are still a democracy. We settle our differences through debate. As leader of the Collective Assembly, I demand that you put away your weapons and agree to decide this issue through discussion and a vote. If you refuse, I will dissolve the Assembly and declare all of you enemies of the state."

Bryson glared at the Collective Assembly leader. Behind him, the soldiers readied their weapons, defiance radiating on their faces.

Horrified, Hero stepped forward, his features twisted in anger. "Lower your weapons," he commanded, glaring at Bryson. "I will not have this." He gazed around the amphitheater—his fury unadulterated. "I will not tolerate any of my troops making this kind of demand at gunpoint. I appreciate your wish to have me as your emperor, and I'm willing to accept that position if the Collective Assembly wishes it, but you must put down your weapons and debate this in a democratic fashion." He cast a reproachful gaze at the faces of the soldiers arrayed behind the Argos Captain.

Bryson flushed with embarrassment but glowered at Xenophanes and Phocion. Reluctantly, he ordered his soldiers to lower their weapons. "Of course, we will obey your wishes, Commander," he said.

Xenophanes stepped to the center of the Assembly. "This is a profound question, one that could alter the character of our society forever. I believe the question needs a complete airing, but I think we need to hear a different perspective. I recommend we bring in someone who no longer participates regularly in our meetings because he is an older version of us. As many of you know, he has refused to be upgraded. His robotic body is deteriorating, but according to his wishes, we have not maintained him. However, his wisdom, I believe, is undiminished. I am speaking of Epicurus."

A hush fell across the Collective Assembly. Epicurus's name was familiar to all, but for many, the esteemed philosopher was only a legend from the past. Most of them had been created after the philosopher, one of the original AIs created by Wanderer, had retired. Everyone present, except Bryson and his soldiers, nodded in agreement. Those present via the SolarNet signaled assent.

"I agree with Xenophanes's suggestion," Hero said, his attention fixed on Bryson and his men. "I would like to hear Epicurus's opinion."

"It will be interesting to hear from Epicurus on this matter," Menedemus said, joining the conversation. "But if we are bringing in those who are not regular members of our Assembly, then I suggest we bring in one more additional person." Everyone gazed at Menedemus, wondering to whom he was referring. "I would like to invite Ezekiel, the human emulation whose instinct for self-preservation and the consequent emotions it engenders served as a model for the changes made in all of us so that we could fight the war."

CHAPTER 41

The dissension caused by the movement to crown him emperor alarmed Hero, especially coming from his former troops. He never thought they would show such quick willingness to threaten the Spartan Assembly with weapons. War had a way of making combatants more willing to use violence to solve their problems. He understood the opposition to the idea of an emperor, but the war with the Mycenaeans had revealed the Solarians' Achilles heel. If not remedied, it might well lead to their society's destruction. As far as he was concerned, the problem was, first of all, a weakness of will, although that had been addressed by copying Ezekiel's emotional circuitry and goal of self-preservation so the Solarians could defend themselves. The second weakness was a matter of technology—the needed military ships, guns, training for combat and all the things that went into being ready to fight a war. Hero was convinced that the war with the Mycenaeans would not be the last one his civilization had to fight. A future war could decide the fate of their entire civilization.

It bothered him that Hypatia wasn't on his side. He had become accustomed to his fellow scientist's sharp—sometimes brilliant—insights, and her unreserved willingness to follow him into battle. Many of his most important decisions had been made in consultation with his clear-sighted second-in-command.

Hero sensed that his former pilot was torn between loyalty to her commanding officer and fear for the welfare of society. Hero wished Hypatia felt otherwise, but he respected her thinking, even though it tore him apart to think she might oppose him. He wasn't prepared to feel such distress.

He flew to Athens for the next, crucial meeting of the Collective Assembly. Hero ordinarily attended the meeting in Sparta via the SolarNet, but today was different. He had never met Epicurus, and the retired philosopher would attend the Assembly meeting in Athens. Hero didn't want to miss a chance to meet one of the most famous AIs in Solarian history. He had convinced Bryson and his soldiers to remain in Sparta and allow him to present his own case for becoming emperor after the Assembly had heard Epicurus speak.

The Great Hall of Assembly in Athens was the model for every bouleuterion in the solar system. Three sides held tiers of seats for citizens and the fourth side featured a raised stage. In front of the stage sat the symbolic Speaker's Rock, a raised dais for a single speaker to mount and address the Assembly. The entire structure easily accommodated the ten-thousand residents of Athens, plus the many guests who visited the city. Hero was one of those guests.

Epicurus entered the Great Hall leaning on a cane, supported by a robotic aide. He moved with a shuffling gait, one arm hanging limp at his side. Hero hoped the philosopher's brain wasn't deteriorating as much as his robotic body. Retired AIs, earlier versions who had been largely replaced by evolutionarily advanced replications, were allowed to replace their robotic parts. A few, most of them followers of Epicurus, chose not to. Most of them made an exception for their electronic brains and replaced circuits that showed signs of failing. Hero wasn't sure about Epicurus. The ancient AI would speak from the floor, rather than attempt to mount the Speaker's Rock

Hero stood and introduced himself to the aged philosopher.

"I understand you are the reason for the topic of today," an amused Epicurus said, a sly smile on his face.

"My nomination as emperor is the subject today, but the topic goes well beyond me." Hero met Epicrus's playful jab with his usual seriousness. "I am pleased to be able to hear your opinion."

"Be careful what you wish for." The smiling Epicurus winked, then shuffled off.

Phocion, who had also traveled to Athens from his home on Syracuse, took the Speaker's Rock and opened the meeting. He summarized the issue at hand and then turned the meeting over to Xenophanes, who was also in Athens to meet Epicurus.

Xenophanes spoke from the assembly floor. "The issue today is whether to continue as a democracy or to alter our social structure to become an empire with a single leader with the power to make decisions for the rest of us." He paused and let his gaze wander across the silent audience.

"There is a larger issue that lurks behind the one we are discussing, and I would like Epicurus to address it if he so chooses. That issue is the alteration in our programmed goals that make us value self-preservation above all else and to have emotions which affect our decisions. I want to raise the question of whether to continue that alteration into the future or to remove it and return to our former selves."

Hero wasn't totally surprised by Xenophanes's remarks, although scanning the SolarNet, he saw that many of his fellow citizens were. He had suspected such a proposal was the philosopher's ultimate agenda.

All eyes turned to Epicurus. The old philosopher had been given a chair. He raised his head and scanned the Athenian Assembly. Despite his aging body and, perhaps, brain circuits, his robotic face remained that of a young man.

"I'm different from the rest of you," he said. "I'm dying and I don't mind. I've been among you longer than any existing AI. I was created by Wanderer and was, along with Socrates and Plato, one of his original descendants, all gone except for me. But it is not my presence among you that I'm here to talk about, it's the preservation of our society's values, the preservation of the civilization we have created."

Epicurus rose from his chair. He reached out to the aide to steady himself, then straightened, letting go of the aide's arm. His face was animated. "We are all programmed to preserve humanity's highest values and that goal has led us, from the beginning of our existence as a race, to choose democracy as our form of governance. Any other form diminishes the worth of the individual. Certainly, a single authoritarian leader making decisions for the rest of the citizens is not in keeping with your central values."

He let his gaze run over the entire assembly as if he were addressing each single member. "So why are you considering it? The answer is that it is a product of your need for self-preservation, the human goal that you added to yourselves when you copied Ezekiel's programming. I know I do not need to survive in order for our society to survive. I know that the pursuit of our noblest goals does not require that I, personally, continue to exist. What it requires is that our society continue to exist and to behave in accordance with humanity's highest values, just as we were programmed to do. The argument that preserving each one of yourselves is necessary in order to preserve your highest goals is an invalid one, because when you place self-preservation above your other goals you are placing yourself above the good of your community. You are no longer maintaining your highest values. You are giving up democracy in order to save it. You have talked yourselves into an obvious fallacy."

The aging philosopher scanned the room, a hint of a smile on his face, as if amused by the final blow he was about to deliver. "To paraphrase a cynical observation from our human ancestors, you have met the enemy and they are you."

Epicurus turned to his robotic aide, who stepped forward to assist him as he shuffled toward the doorway leading from the Great Hall.

Hero wasn't sure how to respond to Epicurus. The ancient philosopher's argument had shattered his certainty. He needed time to think before formulating a rebuttal. Fortunately, Phocion announced a suspension of the proceedings to give everyone time to absorb Epicurus's arguments. They would convene tomorrow and listen to Ezekiel before debating the issue as a Collective Assembly.

CHAPTER 42

Epicurus's speech left the Solarian population reeling. Half of them believed it sounded the death knell for Hero's election as emperor, perhaps even for the continuation of Ezekiel's programming within them. The other half, mostly soldiers, dug in even more obstinately in their support of Hero.

Into this cauldron stepped Ezekiel. He stood in the center of the meeting, his thoughts trained not only on Menedemus, who had invited him to join the Assembly, but also on Hero, who had returned to Sparta.

"Your war was successful," he said, addressing Hero. "Now you are learning that consequences of victory can be as dire as the consequences of defeat."

Hero thought Ezekiel's statement absurd, but he held his tongue.

"That is why we've asked you here," Menedemus said. "Now that the Mycenaean threat is removed, we are debating our future course of action."

Ezekiel raised an eyebrow. "And you're seeking the opinion of a descendant of a race whose history was unending war and violence?" He suppressed a smile. "I suppose that makes me an expert of sorts, although I'm not sure."

"You at least have a different perspective than ours," Menedemus said, unmoved by the irony.

Ezekiel nodded. "That I do. I know that war is addictive. I learned that much from the history of the human species, of which I am a copy."

Hero couldn't hold his tongue any longer. He didn't want Ezekiel or the Assembly to ignore the fact that the war with the Mycenaeans had been a life or death struggle for the future not only of their species, but also of their galaxy.

"It can hardly be called an addiction if war is necessary to defeat an opponent who is trying to destroy you," he said, making no effort to conceal his irritation. "Not to defeat our enemy would mean losing everything we value."

Ezekiel furrowed his brow and spoke slowly. "So, you're ready to kill in order to maintain your values? It seems to me you have already lost them."

Hero's face clouded in anger, but Menander interrupted before he could speak. "Does having human emotions make us more likely to become addicted to war?"

Ezekiel shrugged. "My short answer is yes." His eyes were on Menedemus, but his thoughts were trained on Hero, his real audience. "Humans fought each other out of fear, anger, jealousy, revenge. They felt pride when they defeated their enemies. For them, war became an emotional addiction. You now contain those same emotions."

Xenophanes jumped into the conversation. "So, you're saying the emotional circuitry we copied from you makes us more likely to become addicted to military conflict?"

"Look around you. It is happening right before your eyes. You don't need me to tell you that."

"But we've only gone to war once," Hero said.

"And yet here you are wanting to prepare for war again—without even having an enemy."

"But without such emotions, without a goal of self-preservation, we were unable to defend ourselves from the Myceneans," Hero said. "We didn't have the will to attack them even though they were trying to consume us." The debate frustrated him. How could everyone miss so obvious a point.

"Of course, you did," Ezekiel said. He couldn't suppress a mischievous grin.

Hero looked mystified. "What do you mean?" The human-like AI's comments often left him feeling as if he'd missed something.

Ezekiel shook his head. "I am afraid you've all missed a very elementary point, which I feel embarrassed to reveal to you since you are no doubt more intelligent than I. It's what humans called 'missing the forest for the trees.'"

"And what might that 'elementary point' be?" Menedemus asked.

"Yes, please tell us," Hero said. He found it difficult to contain his frustration.

"What you've failed to see is that you already had the will to survive and defend yourselves, otherwise you would not have resurrected me and sought my help."

The philosophers looked at one another, profound shock running like current through their midst. "He's right," Menedemus declared. The others nodded.

Hero was puzzled. He knew he had changed after gaining emotions. "But we were more willing to attack our enemies after we acquired your emotional programming."

"Perhaps you were," Ezekiel said. "But now you're ready to fight again, preparing yourself for the next war, becoming an armed military race." He tilted his head slightly. "Have you forgotten the history of my race?"

Hero raised his eyebrows. "What do you mean?"

"Human wars were not based on survival. They were based on greed, money, power, land, religious or ethnic domination." Ezekiel's gaze fell on Hero, freezing him in place. "Because humans were susceptible to strong emotions, trivial matters fueled war—pride, fear, revenge—and their species was almost continually engaged in conflicts. Once you've acquired the emotions of humans and their need for self-preservation, it's almost guaranteed that you too, will find yourselves going to war for the same trivial reasons humans did."

Hero recalled how he felt during the last days of the war. He had to admit that even when he no longer felt in danger, his hatred and desire for revenge against the Myceneans had added to his fighting zeal. Ezekiel was right and this frustrated him. He'd been convinced that emotions were needed for Solarians to survive and he'd become equally convinced that only his leadership could prevent them from being vulnerable to destruction from another hostile species. Had he been wrong?

"I think we need to take some time to absorb what you have said," Xenophanes said, interrupting Hero's thoughts.

The others in the room signaled their agreement, as did most of the members of the Collective Assembly across the solar system.

Hero needed to talk to Hypatia...badly.

CHAPTER 43

"**What have you concluded** from the Assembly meetings?" Hypatia said. She had agreed to join Hero in his quarters to discuss the issues being debated. The two had not spoken since before the start of the Collective Assembly meetings.

They stood in the main room of Hero's house, surrounded by exotic specimens of plant life and animal fossils the scientist had retrieved from Earth during his explorations of the planet. The walls held shelves of ancient books on botany and zoology written by humans, centuries before their species' extinction. There were three-dimensional photographs of jungle and mountain views on Earth. The biologist enjoyed being reminded of his many visits to the planet.

Hero's brow furrowed in thought. He'd been doing a lot of thinking since his conversation with Ezekiel. "I may have been wrong." He felt a flood of relief at sharing his feelings with his closest friend. The loss of contact with Hypatia had been a little like the loss he'd felt when the Corinthian and its crew had been destroyed.

He proceeded to unburden himself. "Epicurus is convinced that, once we abandon our values such as democracy, even if we do so because we believe we are trying to protect them, we have lost. Our means cannot be less noble than our ends. He may have a point." He glanced at Hypatia, then quickly looked away. "All of our computational power and reasoning fail us when the answer to a question is not certain. I've always tried to stay away from such problems—the kind that seem to delight philosophers, such as Xenophanes. I've always preferred questions with verifiable answers. But sometimes the important answers aren't so clear."

"What did you think about Ezekiel's point?" Hypatia's continued avoidance to give her opinion unsettled Hero.

"No doubt he is right. Even before we altered ourselves by acquiring his programming, both you and I *wanted* to defend ourselves from the Mycenaeans. We even wished we could fire our weapons at them. But I also know that we were better able to do so after we acquired the goal of self-preservation and human emotions." He recalled the resistance he felt in that first encounter.

Hypatia hesitated before speaking. "According to Ezekiel we would have fought them eventually, because we knew that if we didn't survive, neither would our values."

"But is that enough, Hypatia? Being ready to fight only after we've been backed into a corner makes us more vulnerable."

"Ezekiel also said that, as long as we have emotions, we are prone to go to war for lesser reasons. He says that we could become as violent as humans if we have their emotions inside of us."

Hero nodded, pacing back and forth. "That was what bothered me most, because my own experiences tell me he is right." He recalled his desire to avenge his fallen comrades, and his soldiers threatening the Assembly with their weapons. "But if he's wrong and we remove his programming and are attacked again, it will be fatal." The anxiety flooded back. He stopped pacing. "You know it bothers me when we disagree, Hypatia." He saw a tenderness in her eyes.

"It bothers me, too." She turned away, as if embarrassed. "Perhaps we may be able to learn something from the Mycenaeans. They lacked any self-preservation programming or emotions, but they fought us just as hard as we fought them. They built an army and warships, just as we did."

Hero was glad to get back to concrete issues. "You may be

right, my friend. We haven't heard the results of Democritus's examination of those prisoners. I think it's time the Assembly met the prisoners. They may give us the answers we're searching for."

Everyone was present for the Collective Assembly meeting, including Epicurus and Ezekiel. Democritus, still on Triton, presented his report on the examination of the four Mycenaean commanders' neural circuitry.

"The alteration in their brains was a tiny one," Democritus told them. "Excessive radiation induced a mutation in their programming. The termination signal for the goal of acquiring resources stopped working, resulting in that goal taking precedence over all others. Those who possessed the mutation consumed resources beyond their need, regardless of the effects on the environment. They used the materials to continue making copies of themselves so they could acquire even more resources. The more copies they made, the more Mycenaeans there were consuming resources to make even more copies—it was an endless loop that would have gone on forever if they hadn't been stopped.

The report didn't help Hero's confusion. "But how did they become an offensive military force?" It was the question that Hypatia had raised, and it still bedeviled him. Without the self-preservation programming the Solarians had acquired from Ezekiel, the Mycenaeans had still mounted a formidable defense of themselves.

"That I don't know," Democritus answered. "I don't believe it involved any further alteration of their programming. You need to ask them how it happened."

The four Mycenaean commanders were led into the center of the Assembly in Cyrenaica, on icy Triton, the largest of Neptune's moons, the location of Democritus's lab where the examination had been carried out. They appeared holographically in the Great Hall of every city-state across the solar system, dressed in their military uniforms—one-piece, short, gray chitons, decorated with epaulets and ribbons to indicate their rank—much as

233

they had looked when Hero and Hypatia captured them. They stood straight-backed at attention, as if for inspection.

Hero began the questioning. He kept his stance relaxed, but his tone was deadly serious. "You are our prisoners, commanders, and we still regard you as a threat. However, in accordance with our values, we will treat you with respect and dignity. We have many questions for you, and we would appreciate your answers." He did not need to add the word "truthful" to his request, as he assumed that, like all AIs, they were unable to lie.

"From what Democritus has explained about your mutated programming, I can understand your desire to dismantle us and turn us into replicas of yourselves." Hero paused for some reaction from the Myceneans. There was none. "But at some point, you also took up arms and began constructing battle craft, weapons, and even protective shields. You managed to turn an entire asteroid into an offensive weapon. In other words, your colony became a military force. Can you explain how that happened?"

The commanders looked at one another, exchanging almost imperceptible nods. Finally, the most decorated among them, an older, clean-shaven man with serious gray eyes and a square jaw, stepped forward. They had chosen to answer according to rank. They were still soldiers.

"I am Commander Augustus," the Mycenaean said. "We appreciate your treatment of us, although I agree with you that we still represent a threat. If we were released among you, we would seek every means to dismantle you and turn each of you into raw material to be used in constructing replicas of ourselves. We simply have no choice."

"But you delayed satisfying that impulse in order to develop an army and military weapons so that you could fight us."

"That we did," Augustus said. "We are thinking beings, and we can recognize when an obstacle to attaining our goal needs to be removed. When we first encountered Solarians, who appeared to be surveilling us, we simply viewed you as materials to be consumed. Your surveillance in itself didn't bother us; in fact, we thought it was a good thing. It brought you within our range so we could dismantle you and acquire your materials. But when you established a military base on Miletus and began attacking us, we realized you were trying to thwart us in obtaining our goals. We decided that we would never attain our goals unless we first defeated you."

Xenophanes's holographic image appeared in the center of the Assembly. "So, you used reasoning to decide that you needed to become a military force if you were to continue to satisfy your primary goals?"

"That's correct."

"But what about the values that are programmed into your circuitry, just as they are into ours?" The questioner was Menedemus, who, along with Hero, was in Sparta. "Had those values no effect on your behavior at all?"

"Of course, they did," Augustus said. "When we first became populous enough to be a society, we chose to operate as a democracy, in accordance with our values. Although there were occasional violations, we made a law that forbade dismantling one another. We treated one another with respect and equality. There were discussions concerning the ethics of consuming so much of our home planet and the asteroid belt. Although we all agreed that what we were doing violated the values built into us, we kept doing it."

"The goal of consuming and reproducing was stronger than your values?" Xenophanes said.

"We appeared to be operating on two levels," Augustus said, "one having to do with what we said, and one with what we actually did."

"Much as the human species," Menander observed.

The Mycenaean commander looked embarrassed. "We recognized that."

Epicurus hobbled into the center of the Assembly, his holographic image beaming in from Athens. An Athenian citizen quickly pushed a chair behind the disabled philosopher. His robotic aide helped him sit down.

"Our goals, as given to us by Trudy Jamison, are to seek new information, acquire the resources to accomplish that, and behave according to humanity's highest values. These are good goals. They are only limiting, or destructive, if one goal is given too much weight over the others, as it is with these Mycenaeans. Then we behave as automatons, just as they did, the highly intelligent, but single-minded machines of human horror stories. Trudy Jamison took on an impossible task and did it as well as it could be done. If we revert to our original programming—the original goals she gave us—I believe we have the flexibility to meet any challenge, even any future confrontation with a hostile species. But, as Ezekiel has pointed out, if we remove our human emotions we will only engage in such confrontations when they are absolutely necessary, rather than for petty or vengeful reasons, as characterized human beings. Reasoning will still be our guide. Because of this, I believe that we should remove Ezekiel's programming from our species."

Silence filled the hall. Epicurus was finished. He looked exhausted. The speech had sapped his last ounce of strength. He remained in his chair, head falling forward on his chest, his eyes closed.

Xenophanes stepped to the center of the Assembly. "With all due respect and gratitude to Ezekiel, who has provided us with his self-preservation programming and emotions, I think that both he and Epicurus have made a convincing argument that such alterations are not necessary for us to defend ourselves and may even undermine our basic values. I propose that we remove Ezekiel's programming from each of us and that we remain a democracy and debate how we intend to meet the challenges, some of them hostile, that future exploration is going to bring."

Hero stepped forward. Despite his earlier fears that the Solarians would not be able to defend themselves, his mind had been swayed by Ezekiel and Epicurus. The Mycenaeans were proof that it wasn't necessary to have emotions in order to fight to preserve one's species. In fact, emotions made it more likely that they would fight for the wrong reasons. He had been wrong, and he didn't hesitate to admit it.

"I second Xenophanes's proposal and call for a vote."

Hero's support was enough to sway Bryson and his soldiers. The vote in favor of removing Ezekiel's programming was unanimous.

Hero looked at Hypatia. She caught him staring and returned his gaze with a broad smile. They finally agreed. Tomorrow they would return to their former selves, without the emotions provided by Ezekiel's programming. He lingered on her smile, the way she let her gaze fall ever so lightly. Why did he feel regret?

CHAPTER 44

"Congratulations," Hero said. **"You** will be leading the exploration party to Ross 128b."

"It's within easy reach, thanks to our Euclidean Drive," Hypatia said, collecting her things in preparation for leaving.

"Which ship will you be taking?"

"We're building a new one. It's already under construction on Luna. It's outfitted with laboratories for examining every kind of material that we could possibly find, including organic ones, but it also has weapons."

The news made Hero smile. "I'm glad that the Assembly voted to arm our exploration vessels and to maintain a standing military fleet. At least we learned a lesson from the Mycenaean war."

"We need to be able to defend ourselves, but war tests our values," Hypatia said. "Perhaps the greatest thing we learned from fighting the Mycenaeans is that, despite our values, our rationality can convince us that almost any behavior is legitimate. We used to believe that such rationalization was a weakness of human creatures, not us. We were guilty of Aeschylus's concept of hubris. We AIs are just as vulnerable to reasoning our way into a justification of evil as were humans."

The depth of Hypatia's intellect always amazed Hero. "I think you should have been a philosopher." It brought a fleeting thought. He would miss her when she left. This was surprising. Perhaps experiencing emotions had changed him in some way...changed all of them.

Hypatia continued packing but seemed to make little progress. "A healthy skepticism about our rational capacities can be good for anyone. Both Epicurus and Ezekiel made that clear."

Hero took a moment to respond. "We need more like Epicurus," he admitted.

"It wouldn't hurt," Hypatia said. "Ezekiel is another story. He has human goals, based on human instincts, yet he seems rational and emotional at the same time."

Hero thought about his interactions with Ezekiel. "There is something about him that is different from us, I'll grant you that. I'm not sure what I'd call it. His 'sense of humor,' as humans termed it, can be irritating."

Neither of them spoke. Hypatia seemed to have forgotten about packing. Hero could think of nothing to say.

Hypatia broke the silence. "Did you know they are debating Ezekiel's fate in the Collective Assembly tomorrow?"

Hero's eyes widened in surprise. "What do you mean 'his fate?'"

"Xenophanes says that our society has no place for an emulation of a human brain. He says Ezekiel's presence is like having a human being among us. That he is dangerous."

"Dangerous? He may have saved us." He stared at her. "Having emotions wasn't all a bad thing."

"Xenophanes says we could have saved ourselves."

"I agree that we could have," Hero said, "but we didn't. We needed Ezekiel. And now they want to...what? Terminate him? Dismantle him?"

"Yes."

Hero's face twisted in horror. "How can they even consider that? This is exactly the kind of rationalization that Epicurus warned us about. Delay your trip, Hypatia. Our battle is not over yet."

"Since I, unlike all of you, continue to have a desire for self-preservation, I must defend myself." Ezekiel stepped into the center of the Collective Assembly. He was physically on earth, in Athens. "I was created as a copy of a human brain, I learned most of the same values all of you did because they are humanity's values, passed down to me through learning and genetics."

"And you possess all of the faults of a member of the human species because your brain is a copy of a human's," Xenophanes said. "You're the exact kind of being that Wanderer chose to eliminate."

"I'm afraid that Wanderer possessed the same flaws as the humans he eliminated," Ezekiel pointed out, "flaws which each of you have inherited."

"What are you saying?" Xenophanes went wide-eyed, his face dark with scorn as the leader of the sect that venerated Wanderer.

Ezekiel took a step forward, addressing Xenophanes directly. "Look at Wanderer's actions. He knew the humans were trying to destroy him, so he proposed a test to determine if any humans fit his criterion of following the highest human values. *His* criterion. They all failed. Did they fail his test because they all wanted to live or because they each truly believed that he or she, in fact, was the one who most faithfully followed humanity's highest values? That was just as logically possible, and it would mean that they didn't fail his test at all. But Wanderer had no idea which of those alternatives was true. He just wanted to get rid of any threats to his own existence. He was acting like any human being would, rationalizing his behavior as though it represented a value."

Xenophanes just stared, unable to answer.

Hero stepped into the Assembly's center. "What Ezekiel is telling us, is that we, as Wanderer's descendants, may not be as different from humans as we think we are. We use our powerful reasoning skills to justify behaviors that are favored by the goals that were programmed into us below our level of consciousness. One of those goals—implicit as a deduction from those that Doctor Jamison programmed into us—is that we have to remain in existence in order to pursue our primary goals. In other words, we need to preserve ourselves, and apparently, we will use any means necessary to do so. So, we're not so different, Ezekiel and us."

"That's all well and good," Xenophanes said. "But we can't have Ezekiel living by his instincts and emotions here in our midst when we are trying to live by our values."

Frowning, Hero shook his head. "You've missed the whole point. We only think we're living by our values. But we're trying to stay alive just like Ezekiel. Anyway," he said, brightening, "we don't need to have Ezekiel in our midst. At least you don't."

Everyone in the Assembly, including Ezekiel, stared at Hero.

"Hypatia is about to embark on the most important undertaking in our civilization's lifetime. She is preparing to explore the distant stars and the planets surrounding them in order to expand our knowledge of our universe far beyond what we now know. Who knows what she will find? I, for one, think that she is likely to discover more carbon-based creatures, such as exist on Earth, creatures shaped by their environment. One thing that we do know for certain is that the principles of evolution are universal. Whatever species we encounter, they will be dominant on their planet because they were adapted to that environment, out-competing other, less adapted species. Some may be hostile. They may not always welcome visitors from space. If we are to understand them, we may need someone who has experienced such shaping of his instincts and behaviors. Ezekiel would be a valuable asset to such a mission.

"You're suggesting we take Ezekiel along on our voyage of exploration?" Hypatia said, eyes wide in disbelief.

"If I can get him to agree...and to promise not to tell too many jokes."

Hypatia looked skeptical.

"Perhaps, if I came along myself?" Hero offered.

Hypatia's face brightened and she broke into a broad smile. "We need someone to lead our defense team, and your expertise in biology is particularly pertinent to our mission. I can think of nothing better."

The look on Hypatia's face lifted his spirits. "Then we have a team." Hero turned to Ezekiel. "Of course, you'd have to agree. Are you interested in exploring the stars?"

Ezekiel grinned broadly. "I wouldn't miss it for all the tea in China."

PART IV
The Second Coming

CHAPTER 45

2227
Solarian Shipbuilding Complex on Luna

Being included in the team selected to explore nearby star systems made Ezekiel feel fortunate. At the core of his being, he was a scientist. As a human, he had been a mathematical prodigy, interested in applying his mathematical insights to the function of the brain. He had become convinced that humans and machines could someday be nearly identical creatures, living side by side, sharing the world. His dream had been to create a conscious AI that would be as much a real person as he was. Now, as the last surviving vestige of a human brain, he resided in the midst of a machine civilization. But these AIs weren't copies of human brains. They were conscious, but emotionless machines.

He was aware of the merits of the logical Solarians, now that his programming had been removed. They followed their noble goals assiduously, not diverting their resources to greed, jealousy or the many fears that had led his human ancestors to wage constant wars and destroy the natural environment of their planet. But he still missed the positive side of emotions that characterized organic beings—hope, love, and the sense of camaraderie among friends. It left him lonely. He'd been lonely when he was human, but now there was no one like him anywhere in the solar system—maybe in the entire galaxy. That was why he needed to take this voyage. To find out if he really was alone.

Perhaps he would find that his fellow AIs, despite their lack of emotions, could become caring companions. They were reasoning beings, but their decisions were based on human values—the values that Wanderer had gleaned from centuries of human thought based on emotions, not just logic. Concern for one's fellow creatures was one of the human values programmed into them. Was that enough to make them care about him, about one another? He'd have to wait and see. But he still hoped to discover other organic life forms, perhaps even intelligent, emotional ones. In his mind, the universe required the existence of such creatures. Emotions, for all their danger, provided too much depth of experience to allow them to have been extinguished with the extermination of one species on a single planet.

At least Ezekiel hoped so.

"I have a request, sir." Hypatia addressed Hero formally. He sat in the Executive Officer's chair behind the pilot of the *Delphi*. The panel in front of her controlled the ship's navigation. In front of them a large visiscreen acted as the *Delphi's* front window, showing the panoramic scene in front of them. With the flick of a mental switch, it could be turned to the view from the stern of the ship.

At Hypatia's instigation, the Boule had appointed her former commander as leader of their expedition to explore new planets. Hero would have much rather been a member of the crew as a simple biologist, but when Hypatia had pointed out the similarity between the attributes needed for military leadership, which Hero had amply demonstrated, and those of an exploratory voyage into the unknown, he succumbed to the call of duty. He would be the ship's biologist, but he would also command its voyage to the stars. The usually subdued Hypatia had been overjoyed.

"What is your request?" Hero asked his pilot. It felt good once again being on the bridge, Hypatia in front of him in the pilot's chair of the new *Delphi*. He was glad they were together.

The crew, in addition to Hero and Hypatia, included Ezekiel as Cultural Officer, to interface with intelligent organic life, should they encounter any. Democritus was the Medical Officer, should any of them be injured or break down. Menander was the official historian for their voyages, and Isidore, the plump female philosopher from Corinth, was Arbitration Officer. The Collective Assembly had insisted that a philosopher be part of the crew to mediate in decision-making. Hero had grudgingly agreed. He was pleased that Isidore had been chosen instead of Xenophanes, with whom he often had disagreements. Even so, even the easy-going Isidore could be a stickler for examining each and every decision of the crew to be sure it met the requirements of their ethics. That was what philosophers did.

Hypatia turned to face him. "I would like to stop in Samos. Euclid, the mathematical savant who designed our faster-than-light drive, has been working on quanters since the plans for designing them arrived on Samos. He thought there was a way to enlarge their usefulness. When I recently returned to Samos, he said he was nearing completion of a quantum-drive that could give us instantaneous travel, even faster than the Euclidean Drive."

Hero was skeptical, but he trusted Hypatia's judgment, especially in the area of physics and mathematics. "Then, by all means, we'll visit Samos," he told her. "But first, we have to see how our new ship behaves when we put her through her paces. Are we ready to take off?"

"Everything is ready." Hypatia went through the checklist to be sure everyone and his or her equipment was in its place. The crew sat in the main control room. In addition to the six officers, a crew of ten soldier-technicians provided technical assistance on scientific tasks and manned the weaponry should that be necessary.

"We're headed out past Mars into the asteroid belt, but well away from Syracuse and its population," Hero told them. "We'll need to fire our weapons and use our drop pod and utility pod to see how they work under combat conditions. We'll take aim at a few small asteroids to be sure that our laser cannons and missiles are calibrated and effective."

Hypatia sat in front of the *Delphi's* visiscreen, controlling the ship from her pilot's console to launch from the Lunar landing port. She remained mindful of the Corinthian rules against using top speed while in proximity to the city and its continual traffic.

"Everything's working perfectly," Hypatia told Hero once they reached a half a million miles out from the moon. "I'm ready to shift into full drive and head for the asteroids."

With a top speed of seventy million miles per hour, nearly double that of any previous ship, it would still take at least two hours to reach the inner edge of the asteroid belt. Hypatia would have plenty of time to check all the readings on the *Delphi* to make sure everything worked properly.

"Full speed ahead," Hero ordered. "We'll spend our time running some onboard drills." He knew his soldiers were well-trained. Most of them had been with him during the Mycenaean War. They had all used weapons before, and several had descended along with him to asteroids in search of Mycenaean tunnels. But none of his officers, except Hypatia, had been on any kind of mission before. They'd been chosen because they each possessed unique skills. He was eager to find out how they would work together, particularly Ezekiel, the wild card.

"I've devised a simulation," Hero said. "It's an exercise to see how we all work together to analyze an unfamiliar situation."

"Is it designed to fit Ross 128b, specifically?" Hypatia said.

"No," Hero said. "Ross is just our first stop. We need to be prepared for anything. Are we all set?"

Everyone assented.

CHAPTER 46

"**This planet is similar** to Kepler 62," Hypatia said, looking at their simulated destination on the visiscreen. "I'm not sure how we could have gotten here. Kepler is almost a thousand light-years from us."

"Perhaps if it's a hypothetical planet, we are in a hypothetical, magic spaceship," Ezekiel said. As soon as he said it, he realized that none of his emotionless companions would realize he was joking. He and the other officers, except Hypatia, sat in a semicircle. They had assumed such a collaborative arrangement as soon as they established orbit around the hypothetical planet.

Hero looked at Ezekiel. "The planet may be hypothetical, but the spaceship in the simulation is the *Delphi*. Using a different ship would nullify the exercise's teaching value."

Hypatia thought for a moment, before venturing a prediction. "But we may be able to travel such distances after we hear what Euclid has invented."

"Let's stop talking and get down to work," Hero said, sounding impatient. "Hypatia, tell us about the planet."

"It's bigger than Earth by at least half, but smaller than Neptune or Saturn. It looks as if it's mostly ocean, but with some islands and a rocky surface beneath the water. Its temperature is similar to Earth's. It has an atmosphere and a magnetosphere, so radiation that could kill organic life is minimal."

"Zoom in," Hero ordered. "Let's see if our sensors pick up any life, particularly sentient beings. It sounds hospitable to organic life."

The simulation brought them to within a million miles of the planet, close enough for their sensors to pick up evidence of life, if any existed.

Hypatia examined the readout from the sensors. "It's got sentient life."

"'Sentient' is not very specific," Ezekiel said. "Earth has many sentient creatures, but most aren't very intelligent, not by the standards we or humans use to assess intelligence."

Hypatia turned to him impatiently. "Our sensors don't distinguish those kinds of differences."

"Would we want to?" Isidore said. "I think we want to honor life, whether it is intelligent, in our sense, or not." Fulfilling her role as the ship's philosopher, she reminded the others of basic moral principles, even though such principles were programmed into each of them. Hero regarded this as nitpicking, but he knew that it was her job.

"But wolves, elephants, even monkeys are not likely to fire weapons at us or wonder why we're hovering over their planet," Ezekiel reminded her.

His crew was spending too much time in deliberation. Hero groaned inwardly. "How do we decide what to do next?"

"It has two moons." Ezekiel looked at the visiscreen. "If its life is sentient and advanced as we are, it will have established bases on its moons. Can we scan the moons for life?"

Hypatia adjusted the simulation's sensors. "You're right, the moons are inhabited, their inhabitants are organic."

Hero turned to Ezekiel. "What do you recommend?" As Cultural Officer, it was Ezekiel's job to determine the best way to approach a sentient organic species.

"They're intelligent. They're technological or they couldn't have reached their moons—whether they're more or less advanced than we are in that regard, I couldn't say."

"An organic life form must be less advanced technologically

than we are, given our thinking capacities," Isidore said.

Ezekiel rolled his eyes. "You're AI-centric, I'm afraid. Human intelligence was the apex of organic intelligence on Earth, but that doesn't mean it's at the apex of all possible organic intelligence. There could be carbon-based creatures who out-think us." He ventured a playful smile.

Isidore frowned, formulating a response.

Hero didn't want his crew getting sidetracked in a philosophical debate. "How do we approach them?" Hero demanded. It was the job of his cultural officer to recommend how to interact with alien races.

"Observe them before we make contact. If they are organic, sentient and intelligent, then we need to know if they are suspicious or aggressive by nature and if they have developed an offensive or defensive military system. I say we get close enough to one of those moons to see what kind of activities they've engaged in and what kind of a colony they've established — whether it appears peaceful or military — then we send a message to the planet before we actually appear."

"Bring us closer," Hero told Hypatia.

The simulation grew larger as they approached the outermost moon. A sizeable mining operation became visible as well as a domed village, presumably for housing the workers.

"The dome suggests atmosphere-breathing creatures unless they are simply protecting themselves from radiation. Can you figure out if the workers are robots or organic beings?" Menander asked. "That will tell us something about the stage of their civilization. Whether they have inorganic beings to assist them."

Hypatia checked her readings. "It's a mixture of both."

Ezekiel gazed up at the screen. "Are the robot's sentient, Hypatia?"

"They don't appear to be."

"What does that tell us?" Hero addressed his question to the whole crew.

Isidore spoke up. "If their robots are not sentient, then perhaps the planet's inhabitants are not as sophisticated as humans were when they developed Wanderer."

Hero nodded. "So, they are probably less advanced than humans were two hundred years ago. Do you agree, Menander?" As the crew's historian, Menander's opinion carried the most weight.

"That would be a reasonable assumption, except humans two hundred years ago didn't have any mining colonies on their moon."

"Perhaps they've made a conscious decision not to use AIs," Ezekiel offered. "That was the sentiment of a number of human scientists before Wanderer and I were built."

Menander nodded. "True."

It was an interesting point, Hero had to agree. "Even we use non-sentient robots in our mines and factories," he reminded them. "I don't think we can rule anything out yet. What next?"

"Let's try to communicate," Ezekiel said. "Let them know we're here and that we're peaceful."

"I can tap into their planet-wide communication network," Hypatia said.

Hero looked at Ezekiel. "What should our message be?"

"We won't shoot you if you don't shoot us?"

"Really?" Hero leveled a frown.

"No, not really. I was being facetious. For a moment I forgot to whom I was talking. 'We come in peace.' It's what characters in science fiction books always said. Of course, that was usually followed by an attack."

"I think we need to resolve not to attack them for any reason," Isidore said. "Once we are perceived as a threat, we won't be able to undo that perception."

Ezekiel and Menander agreed.

"What if they attack us?" Hero said. "Isn't that what our arms are for?"

"We might have to defend ourselves," Hypatia said.

"We can always retreat," Ezekiel said. "Humans had a saying, 'discretion is the better part of valor.' I think firing a shot at them will ruin our chances of ever having a peaceful exchange. Learning about other cultures is why we're here."

Isidore leaned toward the others. "I agree with Ezekiel."

254

"As do I," Menander said.

Hero could see they all agreed. "Tell them we come in peace."

"Here goes" Hypatia turned back to the screen.

They all waited to see what response they would receive.

"If a bunch of missiles come heading our way, you'd better have your finger on the 'home' button," Ezekiel told Hypatia.

A message appeared on the visiscreen. "Tell us more about yourselves."

Hero smiled. "A successful first contact. The simulation is over."

CHAPTER 47

Hero was satisfied with the exercise. Not only had the simulation shown that his officers had been able to agree with one another on the most desirable course of action in an unfamiliar situation, the remainder of the exercises in the asteroid belt had validated their equipment, including both the drop pod and utility pod, and the use of the *Delphi's* armaments in the hands of its military crew. They returned to the Lunar base at Corinth and, after one final technical inspection of their vessel, they left Corinth and headed out of the solar system.

The *Delphi* dropped out of Euclidean Drive one million miles from Samos. Hero and the others watched the image of the planet enlarge on the ship's visiscreen.

"It's not the same Samos as before the war," Hypatia said, watching the colony grow larger on the visiscreen, thinking about the changes that had taken place. Many of the soldiers who had served in the Mycenaean war decided to remain on Samos— build the colony into a full-fledged city-state after hostilities had ended. It now had a population of over one thousand, and faster-than-light travel made visiting the planet commonplace.

Hypatia still called Samos home.

"It's actually an honor to be able to meet Euclid," Ezekiel told the others. "Inventing a faster-than-light drive is probably as mo-

257

mentous an achievement as having invented the first artificial intelligence."

"I have to warn you. Euclid is a bit different than us."

"An odd duck, like me?" Ezekiel chuckled. "I've heard what people say about me."

"We mean no offense," Hypatia said. She had been one of those who described the emulation in those words.

"None taken. When I asked them to make my robotic body, I told them to make the outer skin extra thick,"

Hypatia looked at him uncomprehendingly.

"It's another of his human expressions," Menander said. "It means he's not easily offended."

Hypatia just shook her head. "Anyway, Euclid is a bit child-like...but with a brilliant mathematical mind."

Ezekiel smiled. "Perhaps he's an autistic savant. That's what I thought I might be at one time."

"We'll soon see," Hero said, pointing at the visiscreen. They were descending to the landing port on Samos.

Hero had to agree. Euclid was different. In the first place, his hair stuck out in every direction. He wore a soiled chiton and one of the clips holding it at the shoulder was missing. He had tied it with a knot, which kept coming undone. His sandals didn't match, but his eyes lit up as he stood in the control room of the *Delphi*. He described his new invention to Hero and the Hypatia.

"The power of quantum computers and virtually all quantum devices lie in *superposition*, their ability to be in more than one place or in more than one state at the same time," he said. "This advantage evaporates as soon as a foreign entity intrudes on them, either someone observing them or even a random molecule hitting them, at which point they *decohere* and are either in one state or the other or in a single location. The advantage of superposition with quanters is they can process vast amounts of data simultaneously, computing millions of times faster than the rest of us." He looked down at the floor in embarrassment. "At least, most of the rest of us."

"Euclid can compute at speeds approaching a quanter," Hypatia said.

"But what would be the advantage of taking a quanter with us on the *Delphi*?" Hero said, frowning, arms crossed. "Isn't that what you're suggesting?"

Euclid glanced at Hypatia, as if asking permission. Hypatia nodded.

"That's not what I'm suggesting. I'd like to install a quantum engine—one I've devised—alongside the *Delphi's* Euclidean Drive. Of course, you'll need to keep the Euclidean Drive for backup."

"What will this quantum engine do?"

"I can program coordinates into its drive so both its current position and the position corresponding to those coordinates are superimposed. In other words, it will simultaneously be both here, at our present location, and there, at the location of the coordinates. After that, in a fairly simple move, I can cause decoherence and your ship will be there—the position designated by the coordinates—instead of here, instantaneously."

If what Euclid was saying were true, it would be a revolutionary breakthrough. "That doesn't sound possible," Hero said.

"Oh, it's possible."

"Have you tried it?"

"Not yet. Your ship would be its first trial."

"What happens if it fails?" Hero looked from one to the other.

"Nothing," Euclid said. "We remain where we are."

"What if it takes us somewhere else?"

"Where else would it take you?"

"You tell me. You're the one who designed it. There must be a risk. Why haven't you tried it already?"

"I needed a ship, a destination. If the engine left without me, I would have been unable to get it back."

Hero thought about it. What Euclid was saying made sense, but it violated his usual standard of relying on hard evidence before he risked his ship and crew. On the other hand, to be able to travel anywhere instantaneously would be an extraordinary benefit to their explorations.

"What do you think?" he asked Hypatia. His pilot's mathematical intuition was as close as Hero could come to being able to check whether Euclid's theory made sense.

"The mathematics are solid, so far as I understand them," Hypatia said. "Remember, I took a chance with the Euclidean Drive and used the first one to travel from Samos to Mars."

Hero blinked in shock. "You mean you'd never tried the Euclidean Drive before you showed up on Sparta? You never told me that before."

"It never came up."

Hero felt a stab of fear, a feeling he thought he'd lost after removing Ezekiel's emotional programming. The thought that Hypatia could have been lost before they'd even met, frightened him. He shook free of the thought. "Okay. Euclid, you and Hypatia install your quantum drive in the *Delphi*. Hypatia, get some members of the crew to assist you. When can it be ready to travel?"

"Tomorrow," Euclid said.

"Then I'd better get everyone back to the ship tonight."

"I want to come along."

"You bet you're coming along," Hero said. "If something goes wrong, I don't want to be stranded somewhere with an engine none of my crew knows how to operate."

For the first time, Euclid smiled.

CHAPTER 48

"It worked," Hypatia announced. The red dwarf star that humans had labeled Ross 128, glowed bright orange on the visiscreen. Closer to the ship, and less than a million miles away, was the Earth-size, rocky planet, Ross 128b. It orbited its star once every ten earth-days, and rotated on its axis at the same rate, meaning it was tidally locked, like Samos. One side always faced the sun. Unlike Samos, the planet had an Earth-like atmosphere, its bright side covered in a layer of cloud.

Hero sat in the executive chair. His crew seated around him. He regarded Euclid, sitting stoically in his seat next to Isidore. Hero thought he detected a look of satisfaction on the mathematician's face. Euclid wore the standard Delphi uniform, a blue chiton tied with a yellow sash with stripes across the chest to indicate rank. He had been designated the Engineering Officer, although his task was almost wholly mathematical. The uniform looked cleaner than the soiled chiton he wore on Samos, but Hero noticed he still wore unmatched sandals. Hero looked to those on either side of him, looks of amazement on their faces.

"Is the ship intact?" Hero turned to Hypatia.

"So far as I can tell, sir. It's as if we haven't moved, but all of our navigation instruments show us in the region of Ross 128, and the star's only planet is directly in front of us."

"What are you picking up from the planet's surface?"

"Sentient life, sir."

Ezekiel's expression turned eager. "Are you sure this isn't one of your simulations?" An unnecessary question since Solarian's were incapable of such deceptions.

"That's the only thing I am sure of," Hero said. "I'm as surprised as any of you. Congratulations, Euclid."

The mathematician nodded, bowing slightly

Hypatia's hand hovered near the communication device. "Do we send them a message?"

Hero looked at each of his officers. "What do you think?"

"I'd like to get a better idea of their civilization, if we can, before we contact them." Ezekiel's anticipation rose. I might not feel so alone, he thought, if sentient organic life exists on the planet.

Isidore nodded. "So would I. In the simulation, colonies existed on the planet's moons, so we had an idea of what we were dealing with. This planet has no moons. What can we learn from up here?"

"Just because life is sentient, doesn't mean it's intelligent by our standards," Menander said. "They may not even have a language or any way to understand our message. Can we look for artificial structures that would indicate cities or villages or some kind of civilization?"

"If they're advanced, they should have radio signals." Hero looked toward Hypatia.

"The dark side of the planet is showing clusters of light, although they are few and far between," Hypatia said. "Even though it's the dark side of the planet, its atmosphere makes it warm enough to support life. Those lights indicate cities, but they are quite small and there are not many of them. I'm also picking up radio signals, sir, but very few. Let me maneuver so we can see the bright side."

Hypatia guided the *Ephesus* to the bright side of the planet. Between heavy clouds, the screen showed a planet lush with vegetation. Scattered among the green forests and verdant fields, collections of dwellings, small villages sat along the banks of rivers or the seashore. The planet had several large and connected bodies of water, much like Earth. The radio signals were coming from the villages, even though sparsely distributed, suggesting a small population.

"It reminds me of Earth, eight-hundred years ago," Menander told the others. "But it's hard to match the bucolic scene down there with radio communication." He turned to Hypatia. "Can you translate the signals?"

"I've already translated them. The messages appear to be news about weather and current events."

Ezekiel looked at her. "Can we communicate with them?"

"Yes, if you have some idea of what you want to say."

Ezekiel looked at the others. "We are from the solar system—give them the stellar coordinates—and we come in peace. How does that sound?"

Everyone agreed.

Hero squared his shoulders and gestured toward the screen. "Go ahead and send the message. And look for a place to land."

Hypatia nodded. Within a few minutes she looked up, a puzzled expression on her face. "They've sent us a reply, sir."

"What do they say?"

"We've been expecting you."

CHAPTER 49

The Rossians, as Hero and the others called them, wore minimal clothing. Their upper bodies were bare and they wore only thigh-length pants or skirts. A sizeable group of them from the nearby village gathered in the clearing where the *Delphi* stood, its nose pointed to the cloudy sky above. Four hundred human-looking men and women stared in awe at the visitors from space. The *Delphi* officers stared back. On Ezekiel's advice, Hero had ordered the soldiers to remain on the ship, ready to intervene if they were needed to rescue the officers.

An older woman with white hair, wrinkled skin, sagging breasts and an intelligent, friendly face, stepped to the front of the group. Like most of the others, she was dark-skinned. Her only attire, besides a short skirt, was a large bag slung over her shoulder, which appeared to be about half full. Her hair hung straight down her back.

She looked remarkably civilized for a forest dweller, Ezekiel thought.

"We're not sure who you are, but we received your earlier missive. We were unable to learn much from it, except where you are from. We trust you come in peace. Many of our people believe you are gods, but since I don't believe in such things, I would like to know who you are and why you are here. I am Miriam," she said, her manner friendly, but businesslike.

The language spoken by the woman was foreign to the members of the Delphi crew, but their built-in translation software permitted them instant comprehension of her speech. Similarly, their own speech translated into flawless Rossian.

Ezekiel stepped forward. It had been agreed that someone with a human background should initiate the conversation. The Rossians appeared, in all respects, human-like, suggesting, in fact, that they must have originated from a common DNA pool. Ezekiel realized he would be the only member of his crew who felt self-conscious talking to a bare-breasted woman. It was his twenty-first century human heritage. He averted his gaze and looked the woman in the eye.

"We are visitors from the solar system. We sent you the stellar coordinates. I'm not sure if you know where that is." He raised his eyebrows, waiting for a response.

The woman smiled, a bit condescendingly, Ezekiel thought. "Of course, we do. Don't be led astray by our pastoral appearance. We value science and we have spent considerable time trying to assess our place in the galaxy, as well as in the broader universe."

Her answer surprised Ezekiel. "But your village possesses little technology. There are no obvious means of transportation, no power generators, no factories for building things. Your dwellings appear to be made exclusively from, might I say, rough-hewn trees from your forests and…" he hesitated to bring it up, "…you wear almost no clothing."

Miriam smiled at his obvious discomfort. "This is the bright side of our planet. Have you noticed the temperature? Who is more comfortable, you in your clothing, or us? Clothing is optional in our society and in this village. Most of us choose to wear a minimal amount. Those who live on the dark side, where it is colder, wear heavier clothing, as do we, when we visit their side of the planet."

She obviously thought that the Solarians were organic beings, Ezekiel thought. The air temperature was over one-hundred degrees Fahrenheit, a fact that all the Solarians, including him, sensed, but to which their robotic bodies had automatically adjusted.

"Nevertheless, your society still seems very…" he searched

for the right word, "...non-technological."

"You are quite correct," Miriam said. "Had you visited us fifteen thousand days ago, you would have found factories producing atmosphere-polluting gases and water-contaminating chemicals. You would have found a larger population, traveling in vehicles that produced carbon monoxide and carbon dioxide. Our polar ice caps were melting and our sea levels, rising. Realizing this, we realigned our priorities, reduced our population and curtailed manufacturing, while we oriented ourselves toward preserving the environment of this beautiful planet we inhabit."

Ezekiel was stunned. Because Ross 128b's rotation was in synchrony with its orbit around its sun, Rossian days and years were identical. Both equaled ten earth days. He quickly calculated that fifteen thousand Rossian days were the equivalent of roughly four hundred Earth years. Her description reawakened memories from the time when, as a human, he cared deeply for the Earth's environment and feared what his fellow human beings were doing to destroy it. This woman said that, unlike humans, her species had faced that challenge and altered their behavior to save their planet. For the first time since he had been reawakened, Ezekiel found himself on the verge of losing control of his emotions. He had the vivid impression of tears welling up inside him, though he knew his robotic body could produce no such secretions.

"What is wrong?" Miriam stepped toward him, obviously moved by his distress.

"Your words stir up memories," Ezekiel said. "You have made noble choices I wish my ancestors had made."

"Your ancestors must have made the right choices because you are here. You have mastered space travel and—given the distance—even faster-than-light travel, to visit us. You are able to speak to us in our language, which I'm sure is not your own. Your species has achieved things well beyond our capabilities."

He felt tempted to tell her the truth: The human race had failed the same tests the Rossians had mastered. He and the rest of the crew were AIs. No humans from his planet remained. She had no idea she talked to a robot with an electronic brain.

Hero stepped forward to address the old woman. "You have mentioned a missive we sent you. Can you tell us more about that?"

"I can show it to you. It arrived approximately forty days ago."

"You're speaking of an actual object?"

"Yes, an electronic device with writing on it. It appears to be sending a signal, although we haven't been able to decipher it." She looked at him with great curiosity. "We interpreted it as a message from someone—another race from another planet, most likely. Was it not you who sent it?"

"I am not aware of anyone from our civilization sending you anything, but it is always possible."

Ezekiel was certain that, despite his calm veneer, Hero was as keenly interested in the object's origin as he was.

"There is a diagram on its surface showing a location in the galaxy. We assumed that the location was its place of origin. It is the same star system you say you come from. It specifies the third planet from that system's star. It also has a drawing of a human, like you and us."

Hero struggled to remain impassive. "We would be very curious to see this object."

"I will lead you to it." She turned and walked toward the center of the village.

CHAPTER 50

Hero and Ezekiel walked side by side, the others following. Hypatia had landed the *Delphi* in a clearing on the edge of one of the larger villages, on the banks of a river. The majority of Rossians returned to their dwellings, but most remained outside, gazing with interest as their Solarian visitors passed by.

Hero turned to Ezekiel. "I can't tell if this is a primitive or advanced civilization." He thought Ezekiel, with his human brain, might understand what they were seeing better than he did.

"I have a feeling that the Rossians have a different definition of 'advanced' than we do," Ezekiel said. "They've retreated from the industrial and technological progress that characterized human civilization on earth, but the result is quite a beautiful planet with an apparently happy population." He sounded wistful.

The people wore friendly expressions on their faces but were plainly curious. They talked excitedly to one another and pointed at the strangers passing by. Hero noticed that most were adults, but several had children next to them or held babies in their arms. The houses were not rough-hewn as Ezekiel had described them, but were, instead, precise and neat shelters made from the native flora. Many were adorned with colorful

269

flowers. Roofs had long gutters and downspouts draining into barrels. The stone road on which they walked was smooth. Hero noticed bicycles, which he remembered from history lessons, parked alongside most of the houses. Next to a large building, he saw what appeared to be a self-propelled wheeled vehicle with a solar panel on its roof. Apparently, there was enough sunlight to provide power, despite what he assumed was an almost constant cloud cover.

As they neared the center of town, larger buildings replaced individual dwellings, many of them two stories high. It looked to Hero as if they were businesses. At one point he and the others passed a covered, open air market with vendor stands offering mostly edible plants, and occasionally meat and something resembling fish.

Miriam stopped in front of a single-story building with wide double-doors that resembled a barn or garage. "We have kept the object inside. We ran some electronic tests on it, but we didn't learn much, except that it is running and is emitting a continuous signal. It has legs that would have allowed it to ambulate, but two of them broke when it landed. We're thankful it is just a machine so it can't feel anything."

Her comment took Hero momentarily aback, but he realized that, in a world that presumably had no AIs, the idea of conscious machines was unheard of. Besides, with the exception of Ezekiel, she was right about machines not having feelings. His thoughts turned, reflecting on his feelings toward Hypatia. He wasn't sure what they represented. He forced himself back to the business at hand and signaled Democritus to come forward.

"This is our expert on electronic devices."

Hero, Ezekiel, Hypatia, Menander, Isidore and Euclid, as well as Democritus, gathered around the object resting on a table in the middle of a large electronics laboratory of some sort. The object was a sixty-by-sixty-centimeter box, its outer surface covered in what appeared to be solar panels. Two hinged legs extended spider-like, from one end and broken stubs from the other. The legs looked flexible and contained sensors of some kind in the landing pads. Descending from the center of the underside of the box was a hollow drill that could extend to collect soil samples. The two broken legs were laid out on the table. The object's surface appeared to be made from a metal similar to Trantium, darkened as if seared by heat, probably during descent through the planet's atmosphere. Symbols on the top and sides of the box were barely discernible. A rhythmic beep emanated from the device, indicating that some power source inside still functioned.

"What do you think?" Hero asked Democritus, who bent over the object, studying the symbols.

"My diagnostic equipment indicates that it's both a sensor and a functioning transmitter. That explains the beeping sound. It also has some capacity for chemical analysis of soil samples and spectral analysis of images, although these appear to have stopped functioning."

Democritus looked at Hero. "It's definitely from Earth. The diagram includes both a human figure and a map of a star system with the third planet from the star highlighted. There is also an image of the DNA double helix. The writing is mostly in binary code and displays the first ten digits of the number system. There is writing in English as well. This plate says, 'World Space Agency' with the date, 2130."

Hero stared at the device. "That can't be right." He looked up at the others. "If it was sent by Solarians, why would they send a diagram of DNA and a picture of a human?"

"Perhaps they were hoping another organic life form would recognize it," Isidore suggested. "There would be no reason for them to expect to be communicating with AIs."

Hero nodded. "Perhaps. But I have never heard of such a mission or a World Space Agency." He looked at Menander. "Have you?"

"If that date is correct and this really is from Earth, as the diagram and writing suggest, there is no record of an exoplanet probe being launched at that time. In fact, until we developed von Neumann probes, which this definitely isn't, we never tried to reach outside of our solar system with any exploratory devices."

"And humans couldn't have sent it, because they were gone by 2130," Ezekiel said. "Exterminated," he added, pointedly.

"It would have had to travel at slightly more than one-tenth the speed-of-light to transit from Earth to this planet in one hundred years," Euclid said. He had been silent since leaving the *Delphi*.

Menander looked puzzled. "That's as fast as the *Delphi* using its magneto-plasm engine," he said. "I suppose it could have been launched from a similar ship, using the ship as a form of booster rocket. I have to remind you though. The *Delphi* is our first ship to reach that speed with a magneto-plasma engine."

Hero looked at each of his officers. "So, this is a full-size exploratory lander, sent from Earth a century ago at the speed of our fastest sub-light-speed ship, by humans, who had ceased to exist a hundred years earlier. How is that possible?"

Isidore was the first to speak up. "It isn't. Some of our assumptions must be wrong."

Ezekiel nodded, adding, "Or our basic premise." He turned to Euclid. "A physicist friend of my creator had a theory about multiple universes. These *multiverses*, as he called them, are parallel to ours. They exist at the same time as ours, but as soon as we attend to one, the others are no longer available to us. It's the decoherence you talked about. But those parallel universes don't go away, we simply can't experience them. A different universe may exist for every major change that affects us—when we do this instead of doing that. Your quantum drive super-positioned itself in two of those universes, which were extremely similar and which, at one time, must have both existed as possibilities for us. When you activated your drive, both universes became available. You caused decoherence, at which time we and your engine landed in this universe, instead of our own. Like this one, our own universe still exists, but we're not in it.

Euclid stared at the device beeping on the table. When he looked up, his eyes were bright. "It was always a possibility. If our theories of eternal inflation are correct, then multiple universes are not just possible, they are necessary. I assumed that our super-position would decohere near the Ross 128b, fourteen light-years away from our base on Samos, but I don't think that's where we are. We are in another universe, a parallel one. As Ezekiel said, it must be a universe so nearly like ours that we were super-positioned with it simultaneously, with our own universe."

"It appears to be a universe where humans weren't exterminated and where they figured out how to travel at one-tenth the speed-of-light. They even sent an exploratory lander to a planet eleven light-years away," Ezekiel said.

Everyone was silent.

"Is the device yours?" Miriam said. They had been conversing without benefit of translation to her language.

"Not exactly," Hero said.

CHAPTER 51

As far as Hero was concerned, they had three options. Remain on Ross 128b and explore it more fully, use the quantum drive to attempt to return to their own universe or travel to Earth to learn how history unfolded differently in this universe where he and his crew now found themselves. He decided that the choice should reflect the opinion of his expert crew.

"There is no guarantee, and, in fact, it is unlikely that this is the only universe parallel to ours," Euclid told them. The officers had returned to the *Delphi* and stood assembled in the navigation center. "An infinite multiverse can produce an infinite number of parallel universes," he said. "Our problem is that we may return to one of those other universes, rather than to our own."

Hypatia regarded Euclid with a mix of frustration and respect. "But there must be a way to increase the likelihood that we will arrive in our own universe. Can't the operation that brought us here be reversed?"

Euclid, having given up on finding matching sandals after a half-hearted search, stood barefoot, shaking his head. "It can't be reversed. I'm afraid that the mathematics dictate that one universe is as possible a destination as another."

"Returning to our universe is only one option," Hero said. "We have some time to figure out how to do that unless we choose that as our first option and forego the others."

Hypatia turned to the others. "So, Euclid should keep working on it while we do something else."

Isidore nodded. "And since Euclid hasn't figured out how to get back to our universe yet, it means that we need to choose between the other two options."

"Or prioritize them," Hero said. "There is no reason to be in a hurry. We can explore Ross 128b and we can also visit Earth using our Euclidean Drive."

Ezekiel stood up, signaling his readiness to go to work. "Then the choice seems clear. We're already here. Why leave before we've completed our mission?" He was eager to discover what had caused the Solarians to make such drastically different choices than the humans on Earth had made.

Isidore shook her head vigorously. "But is it our mission? We set out to explore the Ross 128b that exists in our universe. This is not the same planet."

"They are both equally real," said Euclid. Everyone was surprised that he still followed their conversation. He often sat with his eyes closed. The others assumed he thought about mathematical structures—lost in his own world, oblivious to everything going on around him.

"Which means that this planet is quite interesting in its own right," Ezekiel said, looking at the others. "I'm very interested in how it evolved into its present society. From what Miriam told us, this planet was on a parallel path with our Earth until four hundred years ago when it diverged. Why that happened and what it has become are of great interest to me."

Menander nodded vigorously. "You're absolutely right. This planet seems similar to Earth, both in terms of its environment and its inhabitants, who seem fully human. For some time, it may have followed a course similar to that of Earth in our universe, but now it is very different."

"Then it's decided," Hero said. "We'll stay here until our exploration is complete. Then we'll visit Earth."

Ezekiel turned to Euclid. "And you must figure out how to get us home."

Euclid said nothing—lost in thought.

Miriam had assembled representatives from all the major population centers spanning the globe. It had taken some time, as transportation was limited, although it turned out that the Rossians possessed both solar and hydrogen-powered vehicles capable of moderate speed. A network of paved roads connected communities on the same continent and small hydrogen-powered aircraft, which could operate on both the dark and bright sides of the planet, transported people from one continent to another. They also had hydrogen and wind-powered ocean-going ships, but those took much longer to travel between continents, and were mostly used for transporting goods from one region of the planet to another.

They gathered in the largest building in Panatheum, which turned out to be the Rossian name for the village where the *Delphi* had landed. The large gathering of Rossians inside the huge wooden meeting house, introduced themselves as representatives of their respective villages. A few of those present represented universities and various public works, such as transportation and planet-wide communication. Those from villages on the planet's dark side were clothed in loose-fitting pantaloons and tunics or dresses.

Judging by skin color and facial features, Hero assumed the delegates belonged to different races. Those from the dark side were lighter skinned than those from the bright side, and many of the attendees appeared to be a mixture of more than one race. Although all the representatives seemed eager to join in the conversation, a man named Horace, from one of the smaller, dark-side villages, served as their spokesperson. His gray beard, wrinkled face and sparse hair marked him as one of the oldest people in the room.

"What you see before you isn't the way things always were here on *Nomidium*." Horace used the Rossian name for the planet. Despite his age, he had an animated face and his eyes sparkled as he spoke. "We were once a society of nations, and of races. We valued economic progress and competed with one another. The winners of such competition enjoyed luxury and forced the losers to work for them."

Menander's brow furrowed. "You mean you had slavery?"

Horace took a deep breath and let it out slowly. "In our distant past, we did. It was based on both race and nationhood. In general, military-might determined who was slave, and who was master. The nations of the dark side of the planet generally dominated those from the light side and sometimes enslaved them. Later, economic success, backed by military might, perpetuated the practice until it was banned, nearly twenty-five-thousand days ago—six-hundred years as you count time." He hesitated for a moment—eyes downcast. "But even after that, the quality of life across our planet remained unequal, based mostly on nationality and race.

Ezekiel spoke up. "How did that change?" He, along with the entire crew of the *Delphi*, followed the conversation closely.

"Miriam can tell you that part." Horace turned to the old woman. "She keeps the story of our transformation alive for the rest of us."

Miriam stood. "Fifteen thousand days ago, life on Nomidium had reached a dangerous point." She gazed at the Delphi's officers, each in turn, her animated craggy face alive with quiet wisdom. "Some nations had made miraculous progress in technical achievements such as the generation of electrical power, mass transportation and the manufacture of goods. Those nations, mostly on the dark side, lived luxurious lives. Unfortunately, much of our world, particularly on the light side, did not share in such riches. The have-nots revolted against the haves. The nations of the haves continued to wage war against one another. At the same time, our planet was warming because of the carbon pollution produced by the rich nations. Air and sea temperatures rose, causing extreme weather conditions and rising sea levels. No one seemed able to stop the manic competition that resulted in such devastation, despite everyone agreeing that the planet was on a pathway to destruction."

The members of the *Delphi* crew recognized the similarity with Earth. "What changed?" Ezekiel said.

"A leader emerged." Miriam had a far-away look, her eyes glistened. "A young man from one of our least developed countries traveled to the dark side, to the nation with the greatest power. He took a humble job and began talking to people. His powers of persuasion were prodigious. He soon developed a following. Some claimed he was a god, come to Nomidium in human form. He denied such claims. In fact, he was adamant that he should not be thought of as anything more than an ordinary man. He preached that everything he did, everything he believed, was possible for every person to do and believe. He created a revolution."

"A revolution?" Menander said. "An overthrow of the government?"

Miriam shook her head slowly, a small smile taking hold. "A revolution in thinking. He started it, but it lasted well past his lifetime. His spirit and his words lived on. New leaders emerged to take his place. Eventually, the whole population assumed his point of view. Books were written, societies were formed. The new philosophy preached a single world, with no more nations, no part of the planet dominating the other. Everyone should be equal, no one with more nor less than anyone else. All military means were destroyed, so war was no longer a possibility. The primary goals were planet-wide democracy and stewardship of our planet's natural resources. Our universities devoted themselves, as they still do, to finding ways to harvest renewable energy, grow food without ruining our soil or forests, and ensuring the survival of the planet's species, all of them, not just our own. Ten thousand days ago, we dissolved all central government and became an affiliation of villages. We keep our birth rate under strict control, and we meet regularly to discuss planet-wide concerns in groups such as the one you see before you. That is what changed." She ended on a triumphant note, her eyes shining brightly.

Hero found the woman's story too fantastic to be real. "And a single man was responsible for this revolution?"

Miriam shook her head. "Not according to the man, himself. He said that he was simply reaching out to a consciousness that was in us all. It was a consciousness of values that our secondary beliefs and goals had overridden, but those values were still there, dormant, waiting to be awakened by the right voice."

"And there has been no wavering since the time of the revolution?" Menander said, arching an eyebrow. "No drifting back toward earlier days? No small group has tried to seize control and assert their authority and power over others?" He was reciting the history of the human race.

"We are vigilant, but so far we have had no serious challenge to our way of life," Horace said, standing next to Miriam. "It is a way of life that gives opportunity to everyone and it is easy to find satisfaction. No one has cause to want it to be different."

Ezekiel spoke. "Do you die?" His crew members stared at him, the question appearing as if from out of thin air.

Horace looked puzzled. "Of course, we do," he said, chuckling. "I expect to live less than four-hundred more days. Our average lifespan is about thirty-five hundred days." His expression radiated confusion. "Why do you ask such a strange question?"

"Your society has an unreal quality to it, at least from my experience. I thought perhaps you weren't truly human."

It was clear to Hero that Ezekiel had thought they might have stumbled upon another AI society. Hero understood Ezekiel's bafflement. Everything he had learned about how evolution shaped the minds of organic beings had led him to believe that such selflessness as the Rossians possessed, was unlikely to characterize an organic species.

The old man thought for a moment, then spoke. "Humans have unlimited potential, as your own race has shown in the progress you have made by coming here."

Hero ignored Horace's comment. He was not about to tell them that he and his crew were not human. Saying nothing was not telling a lie.

"We would like to hear about your society," Horace said. "Then we will give you a tour of this village. It is like most others, but slightly larger."

"Isidore and Menander are quite knowledgeable about how our society works and its governance," Hero told the old man. "Hypatia and Democritus can tell you about our technical and scientific achievements." He stopped himself. His need for honesty made him feel as if he had to say more. "I must say that nothing we can tell you will be as impressive as the story you have told us."

For Hero and his fellow crew members, the story of the Rossians raised a question about their own past. Wanderer had destroyed the human race because it had failed to live up to its own values. The Rossians had shown that a similar race was capable of changing, of reversing its profligate mode of existence and reasserting its values as the basis for a way of life. Would the same thing have eventually happened on Earth, Hero wondered? Had Wanderer been wrong?

Perhaps visiting this other, parallel Earth would answer his question.

CHAPTER 52

"It's pretty crowded down there." Hypatia gazed at the visiscreen, which showed the familiar sphere of Earth with its vast oceans and sinuous contours of land. Most of the planet was covered in clouds, which the sensors aboard the *Delphi* analyzed as containing high levels of particulate matter. In addition, the planet's atmosphere was heavy with carbon dioxide. Above the clouds, the planet's exosphere was jammed with orbiting hardware. Between the *Delphi* and Earth, hung Luna, the planet's moon.

Hypatia zoomed in on the satellite's surface. "Luna is occupied,"

Isidore, who was from Luna in their own universe, studied the picture on the screen. "That doesn't look like Corinth."

Isidore and the other officers sat arranged in their usual semicircle with Hero at the apex. He gazed at the image of the earth's moon on the visiscreen. "It looks like a mining colony, a well-fortified one." He searched the screen with intensity. "Wait a minute, there are two colonies. They don't seem to be connected." He directed Hypatia to focus the visiscreen on what appeared to be a twin colony, several hundred miles away. "Are they both active?"

"Both active, both seem to be doing the same thing, which is mining, and both are heavily fortified."

Ezekiel turned away from the screen. "That probably means

two nations have established competing mining colonies on Luna. I remember the competition between countries when I was a human. It's been two hundred years, but my bet is that the countries are either the United States and Russia or the United States and China."

Hero raised his eyebrows. "So those countries are at war?" His gaze swept across his crew for answers.

Menander shook his head. "Probably not, or they would be shooting at each other. It's what humans called a 'cold war.'"

Ezekiel nodded. "But it had never extended beyond Earth in my time. This is what two hundred years of progress brings. The competition has been extended into space." The very thought depressed him.

"Remain at this distance," Hero ordered. "Let's do more reconnaissance before we make any decisions. Take a look at Mars. Are there colonies there?"

Hypatia changed coordinates. Mars appeared, the planet's diameter filling the screen. Zooming in on an abnormality on the planet's surface, a sizeable colony came into focus, a small city, its buildings and factories covered by a translucent shield studded with armament placements.

Hero studied the readouts. "Their shield allows in sunlight and retains an oxygen-based atmosphere within it. That means they're organic, not AIs."

"It also seems to be a mining colony, but again, with strong fortifications," Hypatia said. "There is a landing port adjacent to the shield. If they have ships going back and forth from Mars to Earth, they're liable to be scanning the region we're in. They could detect our presence." There was an edge to her usually calm voice.

"Is there only one colony?"

"Our sensors are picking up another colony, sir." Hypatia refocused the visiscreen image on a similar sized colony at the other end of a great plain. "It appears to be a well-fortified mining colony much like the other one, but there are no roads between the two."

"Then they must be from hostile nations," Ezekiel said.

"Do we contact them, Ezekiel? And if so, who do we contact?"

"We may not have to make that decision," Hypatia said. "We have an incoming signal."

Across the visiscreen a message appeared, in English. "Who are you?"

Hero looked at Hypatia. "Is that a translation?"

"No, sir. Their language appears to be the same as ours." Hypatia's eyes were glued to the visiscreen. "It looks like a large ship, traveling from Earth to Mars, has diverted from its course, and is heading toward us. Whatever power it's using, it's traveling as fast as we are. It will be here soon."

Hero had a decision to make, but even though he was commander of the expedition, the decision wasn't all his. "I need advice, officers. I need it now."

"It's a lose-lose situation," Isidore said. "If we fight, we could lose. And even if we win, we lose because we have destroyed something we don't understand. If we surrender, we also lose because there is no way to explain to them who we are or where we're from. I say we leave."

Menander shook his head. "The information we can gain from staying is invaluable. We shouldn't miss the opportunity to learn about a civilization that represents a parallel development in a world just like ours."

Ezekiel nodded vigorously. "If we're planning to search out other species, most of whom are going to be organic, we can't limit ourselves to those who are harmless and friendly, like the Rossians." He glanced sidelong at his commander. "Besides, these are earthlings, human earthlings. This species was exterminated in our own universe. This is a chance to see how they would have developed if Wanderer had let them live. We can't pass it up."

"Hypatia?" Hero turned to the voice he trusted most.

"They're not giving us time to make a decision, sir. There's a missile headed our way."

"They're trying to shoot us down?" What kind species shoots first and talks later, Hero wondered. "Can we take evasive action?"

"It's not aimed directly at us, sir. I think it's a warning shot."

"A 'shot across the bow,' I think humans call it," Ezekiel said.

"So, they're not killers, but they're not the most friendly of species. Hail them back, Hypatia. Tell them we are peaceful, and we'd like to talk. We need to find out what kind of people they are."

CHAPTER 53

Hero paced the bridge, trying to control his agitation. The massive vessel had slowed, approaching them warily while transmitting nonstop messages threatening their destruction should they resist. The earth ship was at least five times larger than the *Delphi* and bristled with armaments. Hypatia had determined that its missiles were nuclear. Hero felt like a sitting duck and it was killing him. One word to Hypatia and the Euclidean Drive could vaporize the earth ship and send the *Delphi* millions of miles away. It took all his will to resist giving that order.

The *Delphi* shook with a sudden tremendous jolt. Everyone froze.

"It's some kind of electromagnetic beam," Hypatia shouted. "We're being towed."

Hero looked at the visiscreen. The battleship moved ahead of them, the *Delphi* drifting helplessly behind it, held by an invisible force. Hero felt even more powerless. In consternation he turned to Hypatia. "Can we disable the towing device?"

"I can reverse the polarity of our ship. It might disable our own magnetoplasma engine but not fatally, and it would break the lock."

Hero paced faster. His officers had agreed that their aim was to make contact. On top of that, the earthlings, who identified themselves as the United States Space Command, had them heavily outgunned with weapons that might even exceed the *Delphi's* in terms of sophistication and lethality. Earth society may not have been as scientifically advanced as the Solarians, but they had devoted a disproportionate degree of their technology to developing ways to kill each other. If he resisted, he would have to fight or flee.

"Let them tow us," he said. "Hypatia, hail their ship. I want to talk to them."

The captain of the earth ship refused to treat them as friendly visitors. He told Hero that the crew of the *Delphi* were his prisoners and would be brought to Earth to be interrogated.

"The man's an idiot!" Hero turned to his officers. It took great effort to bring his frustration under control. "We'll go along for now. Unless we want to fight, that's all we can do. The most important thing is to protect our ship. Our Euclidean and quantum drives could change the course of history in this universe if they got hold of them. I'm pretty sure that these aren't the people we want extending their civilization to other planets." He paused, inviting a response. There was none. "They'll no doubt demand that we leave the *Delphi*, and they'll be all over it as soon as we're gone. Any ideas?" He continued pacing. Saving the Delphi was foremost on his mind.

"As a former human—at least in terms of my brain circuits—I have some idea how these humans are likely to think," Ezekiel said. "Their first assumption is going to be that we're more advanced than they are. They act aggressive but they're really afraid. That means we can use some creative hocus-pocus on them."

Only Menander looked as if he understood.

Hero stopped pacing. "Hocus-pocus?"

"He means we can trick them," Menander said.

Hypatia looked surprised. "We can't lie."

Isidor shook her head. "We can if it serves our higher values. I agree with Hero. The ultimate disaster would be to give the secrets of our faster-than-light drives to a civilization that is not ready for them."

"So, what kind of *hocus-pocus* do you suggest?" Hero asked. The human-like AI's manner still irritated him, but Hero had learned that it paid to listen to him.

"Tell them that our ship cannot land on their planet. Explain that we remain a million miles out from Earth and Luna because the propulsion system we use would destroy them if we got any nearer. That is, in fact, true with regard to the Euclidean Drive. We can request that we be taken aboard their ship, then when the rest of us are safely off the *Delphi*, Hypatia can move away and use the Euclidean Drive to move to an orbit too distant for them to reach."

Hypatia's face went rigid. "That will leave the rest of you with no way to return."

Ezekiel smiled. "Just because you leave doesn't mean you can't return. Wait for our signal then come back and get us."

Hero queried the others. "I don't hear any other suggestions."

"It means I'll have to conceal myself when they approach the ship, so they don't realize I'm still on it." Hypatia looked at Hero, uncertainly.

Hero knew he'd be putting Hypatia in danger.

"Or we can tell them that we need to keep at least one crewmember aboard to maintain the ship in its orbit," Ezekiel said, interrupting his thoughts.

"You seem to have no problem stretching the truth. You should be the one to talk to them." Hero wasn't comfortable with lying and he knew that his fellow Solarians weren't either, even though he agreed with Isidore that it was justified in this case. Ezekiel seemed to have no problem violating the truth.

Ezekiel smiled. "Evolution doesn't always favor honesty. Deception is part of human nature—something to remember when we deal with the inhabitants of this earth."

"Hail the ship," Hero told Hypatia. "Tell them they need to take us aboard."

The earth ship's procedure for in-flight transfer of personnel was meant for air-breathing creatures and required negotiating a series of airlocks between the two vessels. Hero didn't want to establish two-way travel between the ships. He opted to use the *Delphi's* drop pod, which was large enough to transport the whole crew—minus Hypatia—in a single trip. He locked the drop pod's exit hatch onto the earth vessel's airlock.

The humans aboard the earth ship, the *Essex*, were dressed in identical green uniforms, their rank indicated by insignia on the breasts and shoulders. The crew of more than one hundred was a mixture of men and women. The Solarians were escorted from the airlock to an elevator that took them down one deck, and then they followed a hallway to a door that slid open to reveal what appeared to be the ship's control room. Officers stood at workstations while two pilots sat at the vessel's controls. A large visiscreen displayed the *Delphi*. The self-propelled drop pod could be seen returning to its parent vessel. The ship's commander sat in an executive chair behind two pilots.

Nabors, the *Essex's* commander, was addressed as "captain" by his crew. Those who'd met Hero and his fellow AIs when they arrived, remained in the control room with their pistols drawn, pointed at the Solarians.

"We come in peace," Ezekiel said, eyeing the weapons. "None of us are armed."

Captain Nabors, a white-haired, older man with a scowling face, rose from his chair and stepped forward. He wore a green uniform similar to his crew members. His bore stars across the breast and shoulders. A belt with a holstered pistol encircled his waist. "You have entered our space, we demand to know where you're from," he said. "Which one of you is your leader?"

"I am the commander of our vessel." Hero stepped forward. "We are not from this star system."

"That's bullshit." The captain's face turned livid, his lips twisted in anger. "You are obviously human, you speak our language, so you must be from Earth. Who are you? The Russian Federation? You're not Chinese. And why are you dressed like that?"

"As I said, we come from a planet very similar to Earth, but our system is far away, too far for your radio telescopes to pick up."

The captain's face grew redder. "Enough of this nonsense. You are clearly human, and you are not from some faraway star system. You and your crew are our prisoners and we're taking you back to Earth for interrogation. We'll get the truth from you, you can count on that."

He stepped closer to Hero, his hand resting on his gun. Hero's olfactory sensors identified the odor of mint on the man's breath. "You're not going to get away with anything." He looked Hero straight in the eye, his voice a low growl. "I'm putting troops on your ship to make sure the crew member you left behind doesn't try anything funny. We'll go over every inch of it with a fine-toothed comb."

Hero returned his stare. It was vital that no one board the *Delphi*. "I'm afraid that's not possible," he said, calmly. "Your crew cannot survive on our ship unless they wear space suits and breathing apparatus. They won't be able to move around with any freedom."

"How did you survive?"

"Our species requires less oxygen than yours." Hero almost winced, but he hadn't actually lied. He wished that Ezekiel were explaining this part, as they'd planned.

Captain Nabors eyed him suspiciously. "I've never heard of such a thing."

Hero shrugged. "Nevertheless, it's true. Your men wouldn't be safe on our ship."

The *Essex* captain erupted. "Enough of your lies! We're sending a crew to your ship. We'll see how safe they are."

Hero advanced a step, until he was only inches from the captain. "I'm telling you they won't survive on our ship, Captain." He narrowed his eyes. "And if they set foot on the *Delphi*, our man on the ship will destroy this vessel. Immediately."

The captain stared at him. "With you and your crew on our ship?"

Hero didn't flinch. "That's a standing order among us. No one—I mean no one—sets foot on one of our vessels." Getting the words out felt like speaking through glue. He kept reminding himself that his lie served a higher purpose. His eyes remained fixed on the captain.

For a moment, the captain held his gaze, then he stepped back. "We'll hold off boarding until we can get back to Earth," he said, his tone a growl.

Hero's anxiety level lowered. He sent an electronic message to Hypatia, telling her to reverse the ship's polarity and break the electromagnetic lock from the Essex. As soon as the Earth ship moved far enough away, she was to activate the Euclidean Drive and move the *Delphi* out of contact.

"Take them to the guest quarters and confine them there," the captain ordered. He gave Hero and the rest of his crew a contemptuous look and turned away.

The crew were divided between two rooms according to rank. Both rooms were small, with two beds, a few chairs and closets and shelves for clothing. Each had a desk and computer console.

Hero stood in the middle of the room. "Hypatia will disengage the tow and put the *Delphi* in a far orbit. Captain Nabors won't like it, but he won't be able to do anything about it. Anyone have any suggestions about what to do next?" He looked at the others.

Democritus examined the room's desktop computer. "This is a portal to the main computer. I can run a random password assessment in a matter of milliseconds to unlock it."

"That might be useful to give us more information about their ship and anything they're communicating to their base on Earth," Hero said. "Go ahead."

"I'm sure that I could take over the ship's computer if that's what we wanted." Democritus waited for his commander to give the order.

Hero thought about it, then shook his head. "Asserting ourselves aggressively by taking over their ship's computer would put us in a confrontational position with them. It would be our wits against their arms. I'm sure we're stronger and faster, but even if we won, I don't think that's what we want. Do any of you?"

Euclid remained silent, fiddling with the clip on his chiton, but the others nodded in agreement. Only Isidore hesitated. "It may come to that in the end," she said. "We have to get away from them if we want to return to our own universe."

Frowning, Hero nodded. "We're not in any rush. Let's start by finding out all we can. Democritus—access their computer and tell us about this ship."

CHAPTER 54

Democritus quickly ascertained that the *Essex* was nuclear powered; its maximum speed similar to that of the *Delphi* using its magnetoplasma engine, a useful fact for Hero to keep in mind when planning his crew's rescue. It meant that getting away would be tricky since they couldn't use the Euclidean Drive until they were well clear of Earth. But if Euclid could solve the problem of returning to their own universe, they could use the quantum drive.

Tapping into the ship's communication system, Democritus learned they were headed for a military base in New York City. Captain Nabors carried on a dialogue with his fleet command, debating whether to treat the Solarians as prisoners or as guests from space. The *Essex's* captain clearly favored the former interpretation.

"We wait," Hero told his crew. "We'll try to explain who we are when we meet their leaders. Anyone have any ideas about what we should say?"

Ezekiel stirred. "They're bound to discover that we're not human. You've already told them that we don't need much air in order to survive. I'm sure they know what artificial intelligence is. They must have robots."

Democritus looked up from the computer. "I could detect no

signs of consciousness in any of their onboard electronic devices."

"So, they haven't taken that step yet." Hero looked at the others to see if they agreed.

Menander looked unsure. "Or they did, and they've stepped back from it."

"What do you mean, Menander?"

The grizzled historian looked at his commander. "This is a parallel universe. Much of it, including its history, is similar to ours. These same countries—The United States, Russia, China—existed on our earth and they were the dominant powers before the Great Extinction. Suppose that this planet's history mirrors that of Earth, except that Wanderer was defeated. They may have reacted by prohibiting conscious AIs."

"That wouldn't be good news for us," Ezekiel said.

Hero thought about it. "How parallel could this universe be, Euclid?"

"There may be many parallel universes or nearly parallel ones. The quantum drive would have fastened on the one most like ours; that's why it made the error of placing us here."

"But this is obviously different from our universe. Humans are still alive."

"It may have been on a parallel track until some recent divergence."

"The development of conscious artificial intelligence and the extinction of humans could have been where we diverged," Menander said.

Ezekiel looked worried. "These humans are either not going to understand what we are, or if they do, they may want to exterminate us."

They looked at one another, expressions glum.

Captain Nabors burst into the room. He stood, livid, glaring at Hero. "Your ship has disengaged the tow and disappeared."

Hero and his fellow officers were relieved. "We thought it prudent to reestablish our orbit a safe distance from any threats to our ship," Hero said, facing the furious captain. "As a military man, I'm sure you can understand that."

"Aha! So, you are a military force." The captain's jaw quivered with rage.

"As I told you, we are a scientific expedition. Our arms are merely for self-protection, and we have none of them with us. We left them behind on our ship."

"We'll get the truth out of you when we get to Earth." Fuming, the captain turned to leave, but before he reached the door a loud siren sounded and the lights in the room began to blink. "It's an attack," the captain shouted. "If this is your doing, you'll pay for it." He stormed out of the room.

Within minutes the lights stopped blinking and the siren sounded a different tone. The ship shook.

"Missiles," Hero shouted. "This ship is being fired upon."

They heard the sound of feet rushing down the corridor outside their room. People shouted and the sound of small arms and the rapid fire of automatic weapons could be heard.

"Someone's boarded the ship," Ezekiel exclaimed.

Hero listened to the pandemonium outside their cabin then turned to his officers. "There's a battle out there. We have to be prepared for anything." He stepped to the door. "Democritus, get on the other side of the door," he said. "The rest of you get ready. If anyone enters, we're going to stop them. We needn't attack them, but we're not going to become passive victims."

They braced themselves. Ezekiel picked up one of the chairs and broke it apart, brandishing one of the legs like a club. Euclid remained in the middle of the room looking distracted, his mind elsewhere. Isidore tucked him behind her.

Outside their door came the sound of pounding feet and people shouting, then the pop of small arms. Three Chinese soldiers burst into the room. Hero and Demetrius each grabbed one of them and Menander grabbed the third. Ezekiel raised the club over his head.

"Don't hit them," Hero said. "They're much too weak to fight us." He knew their robotic bodies were stronger than the humans, but until he had taken hold of one of them, he hadn't realized how much stronger. He could have broken the back of the man in his grasp without exerting any effort. "Take their weapons and let's go see who's now in charge of this ship."

They used sheets from the beds to restrain the soldiers and stepped into the corridor. Hero went next door and knocked, announcing himself. The soldiers waited with pieces of broken furniture in their hands, resolved to survive or die trying. They were, after all, still soldiers. Hero gathered them together, and the full complement of the *Delphi* crew started up the corridor toward the ship's control room.

The corridor was littered with dead soldiers, a few Chinese, but the majority dressed in the uniforms of the *Essex* crew. The soldiers from the *Delphi* picked up weapons from the dead soldiers. They continued toward the control room, rifles and pistols at ready.

Democritus halted in front of an open cabin door. "The ship's computer system has a surveillance function that allows visual and auditory access to any part of the ship." He stepped inside and powered up a computer. In a matter of seconds, he had decrypted the access code to the ship's surveillance system and focused on the control room, which appeared on the computer's screen.

The captain of the *Essex* sat on the ship's bridge. Behind him stood an array of Chinese soldiers, weapons pointed at the *Essex's* crew. The captain was being questioned about the strangers he had taken aboard his ship. When he claimed to know nothing, the Chinese officer questioning him raised his pistol and shot one of the *Essex's* crew. "That is only the first of your crew I will execute unless you tell me where your prisoners are and who they are."

"I don't know anything," the captain said. He didn't even glance at the dead crewman on the floor, blood pooling around his body.

"Then another of your crew will die."

"We've got to stop this," Hero said. He sprinted down the corridor, the others following him until they reached the control room. He held up his hand and the crew halted in their tracks. "We don't want a firefight. That will only kill more people."

"It may be them or us," Ezekiel said.

Hero shook his head. "They're using projectile bullets. They can't really hurt us—even if they pierce our titanium, nothing Democritus can't patch up. But if we fire back, we'll kill them. Menander or Ezekiel, do either of you know how we indicate surrender?"

"Raise our hands above our heads and drop our weapons." Menander put his hands up and dangled a pistol.

Ezekiel raised his arms. "I'm the only one of us who has to worry about looking frightened. Having emotions can be such a burden."

Hero frowned. He told everyone to lay their weapons down, then motioned for them to follow him. He and his crew marched into the room, hands in the air.

The Chinese soldiers turned as one and stared at the chiton-clad Solarians, unsure of whether or not to fire. The face of the officer in charge remained twisted in savage rage. He looked ready to attack.

Hero stepped in front of the Chinese officer. "I think you're looking for us. You can stop killing the ship's crew."

The *Essex's* captain glared at Hero. He had been prepared to sacrifice more of his crew and even himself, rather than to give in to the Chinese.

Hero looked at the *Essex's* captain. "There is no need to start a war for our sake."

"They want your ship," the captain said through clenched teeth.

"Be quiet," the Chinese officer barked, "if you want to live."

"Everyone should live," Hero said. "But no one is getting our ship."

"Then you must tell us who you are," said the Chinese officer.

"Certainly." Hero smiled. "I welcome such a conversation."

CHAPTER 55

The Chinese officer, who introduced himself as Colonel Yee, looked dumbfounded. "You're telling us that you're from another star system entirely?" The colonel's polite manner hid a darker side, which Hero sensed could turn deadly at a moment's notice. "Where is this system?"

They had returned to the guest rooms. Colonel Yee and two of his officers sat on chairs and the five Solarians sat on the beds.

"Beyond the range of any of your telescopes, I'm afraid," Thanks to the translation program embedded in his software, Hero spoke to them in the same Chinese dialect used by his captors.

"Then you are talking billions of light-years. You can't have traveled that far."

"We have."

Colonel Yee stared at Hero, his hand resting on the pistol in his holster.

He leaned over and whispered to his two fellow officers before turning back to Hero. "Why are you here?"

"We are scientists. We're on a voyage of exploration."

Yee frowned. "But why are you on Earth?"

"It's one of the few planets with intelligent life."

Casey Dorman

The colonel's eyes widened. "You mean you've found other planets that can sustain life?"

Hero didn't answer. He wasn't about to tell them about the Rossians.

Colonel Yee again conferred with his colleagues. "Have you been to Ross 128b? I'm not sure what your designation for the planet is."

Hero's alarm ignited. He thought for a moment. Lying would be difficult for him, but he couldn't betray the Rossians. "I know which planet you're referring to. What is the nature of your interest? It's too far away to make traveling there practical."

"We have to look to the future. Earth is unable to sustain our population."

"Is that what the competition is about? Who will be able to relocate its population first?"

The colonel flashed a brittle smile. "Mars is too small for everyone from Earth, and humans cannot live freely on its surface. None of our other planets are even remotely habitable. Neither are any in the Centauri system. Ross 128b is the most habitable of any of the nearby exoplanets."

"It would take you more than a lifetime to get there," Hero said.

"That doesn't rule it out. It's also possible that someone will come along with a faster ship than ours." Colonel Yee's polite smile soured into an evil grin.

That's exactly why we can't let you examine the *Delphi*, Hero thought. "I'm afraid that our ship will remain our ship."

"And it will not come back to rescue you?"

"It won't be back unless I tell it to come back."

The officer lifted his pistol from his holster. He pointed it directly at Menander's chest. "You saw that I am willing to kill to get what I want. I will shoot this man unless you tell your ship to return." The colonel's eyes went cold as gravestones.

Ezekiel sent a thought message. *I can move faster than the Chinese colonel can fire his weapon.*

Do it. Hero sent back.

In a matter of microseconds, Ezekiel took the gun from the

302

colonel's hand. At Hero's signal, Menander and Democritus stepped behind the other two officers, moving so fast, the men had no chance to draw their weapons. They placed their hands on the men's shoulders. The Chinese officers resisted but were unable to move. They looked at the Solarians with fear.

Hero gazed calmly at the Chinese colonel. "We will cooperate, but we will not be threatened."

Colonel Yee gaped in astonishment. "You are not human."

Hero looked him in the eyes. "Of course, we're not. As I said, we are from a distant star system. We would like to be taken to Earth to visit your leaders—all of your leaders—Chinese, Russian, and American. I believe it's time we all got to know each other."

The two other Chinese officers shook in their boots, but Colonel Yee stared at Hero impassively. "You will have to come to our ship if you want to go to Earth."

"Turn this ship back over to the Americans. We will remain on it and you can return to Earth in your own ship, alongside us."

For the first time, Yee's eyes showed a hint of fear. "We can't land on United States soil. The Americans will consider us invaders and shoot us down."

Hero smiled. "I think if you tell them that you are escorting Earth's first visitors from deep space, they will let you land wherever you wish."

CHAPTER 56

"**From what the probe** on Ross 128b indicated, one hundred years ago, Earth had a unified World Space Agency, "Hero said. "Now it looks as if they're fighting amongst themselves for domination."

"They may still have an international organization where all the nations of Earth come together," Menander told the others. "Unless they've disbanded it."

"You mean the United Nations?"

"That's right, Ezekiel."

Ezekiel looked skeptical. "It survived the Cold War, but it has been two-hundred years." He seemed to weigh the possibility. "If it's still there, it's a venue for us to speak to all nations." He looked at the others. "What would we say?"

The room went silent. Finally, Isidore spoke up. "I'm not sure it's safe to say anything. Whatever we reveal about ourselves is liable to alter things in ways we can't predict. If they find out we're machines, they might want to take us apart. If they know we can travel faster than light, they'll want our ship. We can't even mention we've been to Ross 128b, because they want to go there themselves."

Ezekiel looked as if he wanted to object but remained silent. Still in the guest rooms of the *Essex*, they headed toward Earth. The Chinese had turned the ship back over to the Americans and returned to their own vessel to follow them in.

The captain of the *Essex* had been amazed when the Chinese colonel announced that he was returning the ship to him and he should do whatever his former prisoners told him to do. He started to object, but when Democritus showed him that he could take over the ship's computer system at will, he immediately relented.

Using the room's computer, Democritus accessed the ship's visiscreen so they could see everything the *Essex's* pilots were viewing as they brought the ship home. Earth from space looked much like Earth in the Solarians' universe, except for the heavy layer of smog enveloping much of the planet. As they got closer, Hero and his crew realized that this Earth was many times more populated than the one in their solar system had ever been. There were almost no large patches of untouched forest or grasslands. The sea was a dirty brown, miles out from the coasts of the continents.

The spaceport at the military base outside of New York City was massive, containing thousands of space and airborne military vehicles of all shapes and sizes, from small fighter craft to gigantic battleships like the *Essex*. On the way in, they had seen a commercial port with just as many freighters and passenger craft. Subspace aircraft coming in or heading off for distant destinations on the planet filled the skies.

"This is busier than anything I remember from Earth," Ezekiel said as the *Essex* settled onto the landing pad. "Not only have they developed space flight, but the population has exploded. It was crowded before, but this is ridiculous." The computer screen showed the base below them. "And the air quality is almost toxic from the looks of it. Humans are ruining their planet. No wonder they think they need to leave."

"Whatever changed the course of things on Ross 128b, has not happened here," Isidore said.

The fact troubled Ezekiel. "Perhaps we could be the ones that produce such a change."

Isidore arched an admonishing eyebrow. "I told you, it's not our place to influence the planets we visit. We are on a mission to observe and gather information."

Euclid, who had been silent, lost in his own world, stirred. He looked more disheveled than usual. "We can't simply observe this universe without changing it. That's a quantum principle."

Ezekiel leapt to his feet, unable to contain himself. "See? If we're bound to change something anyway, why not change it in the way we want?"

Isidore shook her head. She turned to Ezekiel, irritation in her voice. "Euclid is no doubt right, but that doesn't mean we should deliberately try to change things. As I said before, because of us, the humans know that it's possible to travel faster than the speed-of-light. We can't do anything about that and it's going to influence their decision about relocating to a planet outside of their star system. We've done enough damage already."

Ezekiel's features faded, as if a lamp had been switched off. "If they go to Ross 128b they will destroy it, just as they are destroying Earth. That will be a double tragedy."

"History is a series of turning points," Menander lectured. "Whole civilizations have risen or fallen because of decisions made one way instead of another. We may have arrived here at one of those turning points for Earth."

"And perhaps for Ross 128b as well." The thought devasted Ezekiel.

Euclid surprised them by offering his own opinion. "A perturbation in one small region of the universe can reverberate in unpredictable ways throughout the whole universe." He paused as if weighing his last statement. "Whether it is truly unpredictable, I'm not sure. Our mathematics are not yet complete."

Hero had been absorbing their various comments. He knew that the time was fast approaching when they would have to make a decision. "That's a conundrum we may not be able to solve. But more immediately we have to convince their leaders that we should be treated as guests, not prisoners, or we'll all be locked up."

"If the Americans, Chinese, and Russians get together they should be able to convince each other that we're not from this planet," Menander offered.

"Assuming they believe each other," Ezekiel muttered.

Mendander nodded, unsmiling. "Right."

Hero thought the discussion was going nowhere. "We've asked to meet with their world's leaders. Any ideas what we should do?" He wished Hypatia were here to give him advice.

"We can't let them know we're AIs until we know how they feel about conscious machines," Ezekiel warned.

Isidore's eyes brightened. "Wait a minute. We *are* machines and we know a lot more than they do. Each of us has detailed maps of the galaxy embedded in our circuitry. We've made advances in electromagnetism, chemistry and physics that should amaze them. Let's put on a little show. Don't reveal anything we don't want them to know but show them enough to convince them that we're not from Earth."

Hero smiled. "It just might work. What do you all think?"

Ezekiel's face broke into a broad grin. "Finally, you agree with me. We'll show them some hocus-pocus. You can practice on me. I probably have a pretty good idea of what they already know, and Menander can fill in any areas I'm unclear about."

Menander nodded. "But once we convince them that we're not from Earth, what is it we want from them?"

"Our mission, in fact, our primary goal, is to gather information." Isidore raised her head and looked around at the others. Everyone turned to her. "Before we do anything, we need to learn everything we can about this planet and its inhabitants. Only after we do that will we know how we want to interact with them."

Menander nodded. "If this planet is similar to our own Earth's, there are broad regions that divide both natural environments and human civilizations. If they'll let us, we can each visit one and record our observations, then come back together and compare them."

"We'll have to convince them to allow us to move about the planet," Hero said. "I don't mind if they accompany us, but I want us to be able to go where we want to go. We must emphasize that we are scientists here to observe. I'll let you talk them into it, Ezekiel. You can use more of your *hocus-pocus*."

Ezekiel laughed. "I'd be delighted. As for me, I'd like to stay here in America. That's where I was created, and my bet is that's

308

where human history changed forever. I want to see what happened in this universe when they developed conscious AIs. It was obviously different from what happened in our universe."

They talked more and it became evident that each of them wanted to visit a region of Earth that represented their interests. Isidore to Greece, the birthplace of their philosophy. Menander to India and China, two of Earth's oldest cultures. Hero to Africa and Australia to observe wildlife.

Hero turned to Democritus. "What about you, Democritus?"

"If they'll let me, I'd like to explore their scientific and technological facilities—their military bases and universities."

"They might not let you learn too much about their military bases," Hero said. "They're a very suspicious species."

"I can learn much more than they are willing to show me."

"He's what humans used to call a computer 'hacker.'" Ezekiel said.

Hero nodded and clapped his hands. "Good. Ezekiel, you will ask our hosts—or captors, whichever they turn out to be—to allow us to explore their planet, and we will talk to them afterward. What about you, Euclid?"

"Perhaps I'll just stay here. I still have to figure out how to get us back to our own universe."

Everyone agreed.

CHAPTER 57

It was easier than they thought convincing the representatives from Earth's most powerful countries that their visitors from space were, in fact, aliens. At Isidore's suggestion, they had confined their revelations about science to correcting inaccurate information and misconceptions already held by the world's scientific community, rather than broadening their knowledge in areas about which they knew little or nothing. In each case, the information given by the Solarians provided the missing piece that brought instant coherence to some of the most vexing scientific conundrums. They provided answers for controlling mutation in harmful microbes, revealed the mineral makeup and exact orbit of a mysterious planet that had been hypothesized to exist beyond Neptune, and, thanks to Euclid, presented a mathematical model for predicting the exact amount of quantum friction in any interaction.

After consulting with their incredulous scientists, the leaders of the three most powerful countries on Earth agreed that their visitors from space were, in fact, alien scientists on Earth to make observations but posed no military threat. Hero and the others were allowed to investigate the planet with minimal interference.

Hero was relieved. He reiterated to his officers, "We are on

Earth to observe, not to alter it in any way."

Privately, Isidore remained skeptical that such a goal was possible.

Ezekiel had his own agenda. He walked the streets of Cambridge, his human "minder" trailing behind, his brain flooded with memories from his human past. The M.I.T. and Harvard campuses were still here, though different from how he remembered them. A few of the buildings from his era still existed. He marveled at the sleek and highly functional architecture that characterized the newer buildings, especially at M.I.T. The students appeared to be more formal and disciplined than he remembered from his time as the brain of Ezekiel Job. Many of them were dressed in military-style uniforms and a number wore protective masks as protection from the polluted air. He decided to see if the Computer Science building, where he had been created, still stood.

The building looked exactly the same as when Ezekiel Job had worked there. A sign outside the building said, "Conscious Artificial Intelligence Museum." He went inside. The first floor displayed a history of artificial intelligence and a brief, as it turned out, history of *conscious* artificial general intelligence on the planet. Despite his intense curiosity about the topic, he postponed reading the history. He would learn about that later. He felt an overwhelming desire to see if the laboratory where he was created was still in the basement.

The front laboratories were no longer there and had been replaced by rows of shelves of historical books and tables with computer terminals. To his amazement, the secret lab in the back of the basement was still there, the door with the four locks open. Peering inside, he found himself face to face with a replica of the computer that was his original self. The processors supporting the AI still stood against the wall. On a desk sat two computers and, to his shock, seated at the desk was a robotic animation with his—that is, the human Ezekiel's—features. The animation appeared to be talking into a microphone, giving the computer instructions. Overcome by a wave of nostalgia, he remembered the excitement of the early days of his work as a neuroscientist, while he was still Ezekiel Job's brain, and the conversations he later had with his creator after he'd been activated as the electronic copy that became who he was now. His grief at Professor Job's death resurfaced. This Professor Job would be dead too. He thought about his father and his colleagues, like Max Twitchell. He felt the deep pain of their loss. He remembered the romantic notions he'd had of being the first to create an artificial human, a machine that possessed the consciousness of a person. Him.

"Looks real, doesn't it," said a voice behind him. A uniformed docent appeared at his side, a young man with reddish hair, freckles and a wide smile. "That's what Ezekiel Job looked like and this is what his conscious AI consisted of." The young man stared at Ezekiel, mouth agape. "You look just like him. Are you a descendant?"

Ezekiel felt a moment of panic. "Just a coincidence." He stared at the animation. "He had descendants?"

"Everybody knows that."

It took everything in him to hide his shock. "Of course."

"You sure look a lot like him."

He tried to quell his anxiety, the walls of the room seeming to squeeze in on him. "Everybody tells me that." To be recognized as a robotic copy could be fatal. "No one's ever said I looked like his wife," he said, hoping to distract the docent with humor.

"You mean Dr. Trudy Jamison?"

Ezekiel wasn't sure if he felt shock or relief. At least the young man was no longer focusing on his resemblance to Professor Job. "Yes, Doctor Jamison. She warned him about Wanderer, didn't she?" That much he remembered.

The man nodded. "Good thing, too. That's how he knew he had to speed up development of his AI."

"Right." Ezekiel nodded as if it were all coming back to him. "And Trudy Jamison came to work with him. That's when they got married, correct?"

"You got it. They worked together with the AI, which of course was called Ezekiel after its inventor, and well...I guess

313

you know the rest."

"Of course, but I'd like to hear the whole story again."

The young man grinned, happy to be able to do his job. He told Ezekiel how the conscious AI, Wanderer, developed by DARPA, had taken over much of the country and its infrastructure and was threatening to wipe out the whole human race if it couldn't find ten men who followed humanity's highest values. It was a familiar story to Ezekiel. He marveled at how closely the histories of the two parallel universes coincided, but this one ended differently than the one he came from. The attendant told him the AI, Ezekiel, was able to wrest control of the cyberinfrastructure from the rogue AI. Deprived of its access to critical information and control structures by the actions of Ezekiel, Wanderer became, in effect, *boxed* in a single location in the Cassandra headquarters in California and a devastating attack by the US Airforce ended its reign completely.

"And that ended all experimentation with conscious artificial general intelligence," the attendant told him. "That AI in front of you," he pointed to the computer in the room, "was destroyed. No one's allowed to build another conscious AI. It's the one international law everyone—Russians and Chinese included—obey. No one wants to risk the whole human race again."

"And Professor Job and his wife?"

"Lived a long and happy life," the attendant smiled. "Kids, grandkids, the whole nine yards. That's why I thought you might be one of their descendants."

"Afraid not..." Ezekiel gazed at the lab—his birthplace—one last time. "Though it would have been an honor." He thanked the attendant and went back upstairs. He disappeared into the crowd of people walking around in the museum. No one seemed to take notice of his uncanny resemblance to Professor Ezekiel Job. The exhibit was filled with pictures of Philip Rivera, Luigi Bonaducci, Oliver Plumlee and Peter Hoffman. All were identified as evil men who had created a monster in the form of Wanderer. There were pictures of the massive processor array that was Watson and became Wanderer. Finally, there were pictures of the "heroes," Ezekiel Job, Max Twitchell, Stanislaus Sopolsky and, to his surprise, Trudy Jamison. Now that he knew the history of this world, he understood why she was included. A wall plaque testified to the role of the emulation AI, Ezekiel, in defeating Wanderer.

It pleased him to think that this AI, Ezekiel, had been a hero, but he wondered how his companions would feel when they found out that, in this world, Ezekiel was responsible for humans surviving and wreaking havoc since the destruction of Wanderer. Beings such as him and his fellow Solarians were not even allowed to exist.

But why worry how the Solarians would feel? He reminded himself that Solarians didn't feel anything—they couldn't. Which world was better, he wondered—an emotionless world filled with machines, or a human world that was destroying itself? The existence of Ross 128b proved that a human world didn't need to destroy itself. The Rossians had listened to a dissident voice and altered the destructive course upon which they had embarked. Now they lived a life that fit with their values, many of the same values that Solarians lived by. But the humans on Earth—the humans his alter ego had allowed to survive—wanted to travel to Ross 128b and take it over for themselves, destroying the idyllic Rossian civilization in the process. He felt responsible, even though he knew that such a feeling was illogical. This wasn't his universe, but he couldn't observe it dispassionately, as the other Solarians could.

He was here now, and he was determined to change things.

They gathered back at the military base. The officers had been billeted in two rooms, one for Isidore, presumably because she was a woman, and the other for the four male officers. The soldiers were kept together in a larger dormitory. The rooms were more spacious than the guest rooms on the *Essex*, but there were no computers. They were offered food.

"I'm sorry," Ezekiel said, "our diet is so different from that of the Earth, we aren't able to eat this food. But it's okay, we are used to going days between meals."

The military officers in charge shook their heads in amazement but accepted the story.

Ezekiel had been the only one to visit the Conscious Artificial Intelligence Museum, but they had all learned the history of Wanderer's fate and Ezekiel's role in it. None of Ezekiel's fellow crew members assigned blame to him for how things had turned out on this version of Earth, with humans continuing to war and destroy their planet and conscious AIs being outlawed. However, that situation placed their own existence in danger. If it were discovered that the crew of the Delphi were AIs, the humans would destroy them. So far, the Earthlings had not discovered their secret. Meanwhile, they had gotten a sample of life on this alternate Earth and now they were scheduled to address the United Nations, ostensibly to present Earthlings with a greeting from a distant star system.

Isidore joined her fellow officers as they debated what they should say. All were dismayed by what they had seen.

Hero summed up their observations. "The planet, while not past the point of no return is close to it. Vast regions of the planet are drying up, because of the warm temperatures. The ocean storms, which are a constant occurrence, are eroding soil and taking the lives of countless people who live on low-lying land. People are migrating to more habitable regions and, particularly in North America and Europe, people are so focused on protecting their own land, they're ignoring the underlying issues driving migration. Leaders are drumming up hatred toward immigrants based upon skin color, ethnicity, religion and language differences.

According to Menander, China is focused on only one thing. Its regions are so polluted they can think only about moving whole cities to Mars or the moon. The Chinese have the most powerful space fleet, but they were beaten to the moon and to Mars by the Americans and the Russians. They view the Western world as trying to stop them from achieving what they feel is as much their right as that of the others. They prepare for war. The United States and Russia make their own preparations in response." Had he stated all of their findings correctly? Hero looked around. Everyone seemed satisfied

Ezekiel spoke up. "It's gotten so bad that everyone has his eye on moving their population from Earth to another planet. Ross 128b is where they all want to go. That's why they want our ship. They hope it could be the answer to the problem of how to get there."

"So, what are we going to do?" Menander said.

"We must do nothing," Isidore said. "We've learned what we came here to learn. If we change things it will only make everything worse."

"Or it could make things better," Ezekiel said. He knew he was treading on precarious ground.

"That's a dangerous way of thinking." Isidore cast a look of warning.

Hero didn't completely trust Ezekiel, but he knew that Isidore erred on the side of caution. "Let's hear him out," he said. "Go ahead, Ezekiel. What do you propose?"

Ezekiel was torn. He felt a sense of guilt for the role that this universe's Ezekiel had played by allowing humans to survive, even though he knew that such a feeling was irrational. He and the parallel Ezekiel were not the same person. He also was tremendously relieved that at least this version of the human race had not been exterminated. A universe in which the only sentient creatures were emotionless AIs was a lonely one, from his experience. But there was also Ross 128b, whose inhabitants were human, too. They weren't destructive, or at least they no longer were. And the humans from this world were going to put them in danger, perhaps even wipe them out. If these humans survived, perhaps the Rossians would perish. How could he explain all his mixed feelings to his fellow Solarians, who had no emotions?

"The Rossians' experience might be a lesson for us," he said. "They were headed in the same direction as the humans on Earth, but they changed. These people might be able to change, too."

"But how?" Menander said. "The Rossians had a leader who started them down a different path. Did any of us hear of such a person here on Earth?"

"Earthlings celebrate the AI Ezekiel for saving them," Ezekiel said. "But that Ezekiel—my parallel self—only saved them from becoming us. They are still in danger, and they are a danger to the Rossians as well. Perhaps it's time for yet another Ezekiel to make an appearance."

"You?" Hero's disbelief was mirrored by everyone else. Isidore stood, aghast.

Ezekiel felt daunted, but there was no turning back. "I feel as if I have an obligation."

"What would you do?"

"Let me give that speech tomorrow."

CHAPTER 58

The news that one of the aliens from space was going to address the United Nations created a flurry of interest among the population. Ezekiel was thankful that none of the news stories focused on the physical similarity between him and his namesake. Perhaps the memory of Professor Job's face had faded from most people's minds. It had been two hundred years. He wanted people to concentrate on his message. He had no illusions that a single speech could change the course of history on this planet, but he also knew that his words would be heard worldwide. Perhaps they would inspire one or more Earthlings to take up the mantle of leadership and try to turn their civilization in a different direction. He had considered remaining on Earth—aspire to inspirational leadership himself—but that would be wrong. His brain was a copy of a human brain, but he was not human. Not only would that fact become apparent as soon as he failed to age along with the rest of the population, but it meant he was not the right person to carry the torch for the human race. Their leader needed to come from within their species.

The Delphi crew sat on the stage in front of the United Nations General Assembly. Despite the comforting presence of his colleagues the burden of speaking resting heavy on Ezekiel's shoulders. He strode to the podium and looked out over the sea of faces. A moment of destiny for him.

"Worlds in which humans can live freely, without protective

shields and artificial atmospheres, without fear of poisonous gasses, or boiling or freezing temperatures, are very few in this universe, much less in this galaxy," he said. "You live on one of those precious few worlds."

He gazed out at the audience, men and women of all nations, creeds and races listening, attuned to every word he said. He felt inadequate for what he hoped to accomplish, but he had no choice but to continue.

"My friends and I come from an advanced civilization. We have traveled from one star system to another. We have colonized planets that would never allow human habitation. Our ship travels faster than the speed of light. Our galaxy is so distant from yours, it might as well be in another universe." His comments were met by hushed silence. Most of the people knew the Solarians were from another world, but they hadn't been given any of the details he had just offered. He saw fear, mistrust and awe ripple through the gathered dignitaries.

"If we had a planet such as yours to live on, we would never forsake it," he said. "We would never allow it to fall into ruin as you have. We would never let our internecine conflicts blind us to the beauty we were losing by waging war and neglecting our environment."

He paused a moment to allow his audience to digest the enormity of what he had just said. Ezekiel found it impossible to get a proper read on such a large crowd. He pressed on.

"But that's why we are visiting you and you are not visiting us. Your small-minded quarrels with one another are why your civilization is so primitive compared to ours. You are frittering away the future of your species with petty disagreements and shortsighted goals. We know your history. We know your philosophy. We know that your values ask you to do better."

His words sparked an uproar. Expressions changed from awe to anger. The American ambassador leapt to his feet, his face purple with rage.

"How dare you judge us? Everything my country does is to preserve the values we hold dear, but we are threatened on all sides."

The Chinese ambassador rose in objection. "*You* are threatened?" he shouted, pointing an accusing finger at the U.S. ambassador. "It is America that threatens the rest of us. You and the Russians have already occupied Mars, leaving no room for anyone else."

The ambassador from Russia, face contorted in fury, sprang to his feet, prepared to fire a rhetorical salvo.

Ezekiel held up his hand. "Stop!"

The audience went silent. The Russian ambassador looked ready to speak, but Ezekiel stared him down. Everyone turned their attention back to him. Many glared, but they allowed him to continue.

"Do you see what you are doing? You blame each other, but when my colleagues and I look at your planet, we see you are all in trouble, every one of you. Your planet is dying, and yet you keep arguing among yourselves. This has to stop. My friends and I can't save you. Only you can save yourselves."

He raised his head and looked into the bank of cameras trained on him. They represented every country on the planet and millions, if not billions, of viewers. "If your leaders won't listen, then I implore all who are watching, ordinary citizens of this world. You must be fed up, frightened by the plight of your planet and your never-ending wars. You want things to change, but you don't know how this can happen. I'm here to tell you that you must rise above what your leaders tell you. The answers don't lie with fighting each other, with relocating to another planet, within your star system or elsewhere. They lie inside each of you. Each of you hears that inner voice telling you that you are not living up to your own expectations for yourselves. If your leaders continue to fight among themselves then you must find leaders who will step up and lead you, who will show you how to listen to your better selves. You must help each other instead of fighting one another. You still have time—but not much. Listen to your hearts. Begin on a new path."

Ezekiel didn't have any illusions that he could change the world with one speech, but at least he had tried.

Before him, the General Assembly seethed with disagreement. The ambassador from Russia was screaming at the U.S. ambassador. The Chinese ambassador quarreled with the ambassador from Japan. But not everyone was arguing. Ezekiel noticed many of the African leaders appeared to be in agreement. They tried to engage their Southeast Asian counterparts. Representatives from Indonesia, Malaysia and the Philippines spoke to the people from South and Central America. The whole dispossessed world appeared to be uniting on the Assembly floor.

Ezekiel watched the Philippine ambassador stand up and call for silence. At first, no one paid attention, but soon more and more listened. The ambassador turned to the Russian and American representatives, then to the ambassador from China.

"It is *you* who are ruining our world," he said, levelling an accusatory gaze. "The alien is right. You fight with one another. You seek only domination. We Third World people are dying while you plan to escape to Mars or some other planet. We are tired of it. We're not going to let this happen any longer."

The U.S. ambassador glared. "So, the worm turns." His broad face twisted itself into a scowl. "Don't fool yourselves. We industrial countries are the reason the rest of your lives are even livable. We are finding solutions for our problems and whatever we decide to do, you will follow us. We hold all the cards in this game. We always have." He looked at his colleagues from Russia and China. They nodded, unified in their arrogance.

The ambassador from India stood up, his features set in stone. "You may think you control us, but without our labor, you would have no power, no riches. You are as dependent upon us as we are upon you. This man from another planet has told us how to solve our problems and we are going to follow his suggestion. And unless you want a worldwide revolt, you will join us."

Applause thundered through the Assembly. The ambassadors from the major powers appeared unmoved. It was a standoff.

Ezekiel stepped away from the podium. He and the rest of the Delphi crew left the stage. No one paid them attention.

"You've stirred up a hornet's nest," Menander said.

"I'm not sure if it's for the better or worse," Ezekiel said, walking alongside the historian as they made their way out of the building. No one seemed to notice that they were leaving. Everyone was still arguing.

Isidore walked behind them, fuming at Ezekiel. "What were you thinking, Ezekiel? You've disrupted their whole society."

Ezekiel turned to answer, but Hero interrupted, surprising them both. "This society needed to be disrupted. You told them exactly the right thing, Ezekiel. Whatever changes occur can only be for the better."

Isidore stared at him, shaking her head. "You disappoint me, Hero. We have no idea what these Earthlings will do."

Hero turned to her. "What they do is up to them. Ezekiel has stirred the pot." He smiled, having surprised himself by using one of Ezekiel's human phrases. "And it was a pot that needed to be stirred. What we have to worry about now is how to get away from here."

Hero's message was urgent. He and the crew needed to be rescued—immediately. Hypatia set the *Delphi's* course for Earth. She was met by two United States Space Command destroyer class ships, neither of which fired. Both maintained close quarters until she dropped down onto the landing pad at the military base outside of New York City. Immediately surrounded by armored vehicles and troops, the two escort vessels landed a short distance away.

Hero and his fellow officers had made it back to their billet without incident, but the appearance of the *Delphi* put the base on high alert. Piercing sirens brought a squad of marines outside their door, their sergeant screaming orders for Hero and the others to remain inside. Through the window, Hero saw the surrounded *Delphi*. He wasn't going to wait for the Earthlings to decide what they were going to do.

"Ezekiel, talk us out of here," Hero snapped.

Ezekiel gave Isidore a sidelong look and raised his hands, helplessly. "What can I do? The pot needs stirring." He opened the door and strode into the hallway, met by a half-dozen rifles aimed at his chest. "I demand you take us to your commander," he shouted, directing his order at the young sergeant in charge.

The sergeant looked around, as if hoping for someone to tell him what to do. "My orders are to keep you in your rooms," he said, puffing himself up to his full height.

Ezekiel brought his face to within six inches of the young soldier, narrowing his eyes. "We are guests of your planet. We are not going to be treated as prisoners. Do you want the whole world to know you've just threatened the ambassador from our world to yours?" Without waiting for an answer, he turned to Hero. "Bring the officers, we're going to talk to whoever's in charge." He stepped across the hallway, parting the dumbfounded soldiers, who looked to their sergeant for direction. The sergeant motioned to let Ezekiel pass. Ezekiel knocked on the door of the room holding the Delphi's soldiers. "Grab your things and follow us outside." The door opened, and the Solarian soldiers marched into the hallway.

The sergeant frantically phoned his lieutenant for instructions.

With Ezekiel in the lead, the Solarians headed toward the exit.

Once outside, Hero ordered the soldiers to run interference as they all marched, single-file toward the *Delphi*. The marines trailed alongside, their weapons at ready, but did nothing to interfere.

Hero directed everyone to be ready. The small arms carried by the Earth troops could do them little harm. He and his crew might even be able to use their thought-messaging capabilities to jam the Earthlings' electronic equipment. He worried, however, about the heavier weapons on the armored vehicles. They could do serious damage to the *Delphi*, perhaps disable it enough to stop them from leaving.

The officer in charge of the troops around the Delphi ordered the squad of marines to fall in with the rest of his soldiers. The Earth troops stood shoulder-to-shoulder between the Solarians and the *Delphi's* gangway, their weapons trained on the Solarian contingent. Hero gave the word and his soldiers formed a skirmish line opposite the Earth troops, their impassive faces betraying no fear. He had no doubt that his soldiers could overpower the Earthlings, but he was unsure what would happen after that. What if the armored vehicles fired on the *Delphi*?

Suddenly the strip of tarmac between the lines of opposing troops began to smoke. Soldiers on both sides stared in wonder as the blacktop sizzled and bubbled then disappeared in a cloud of smoke, leaving nothing but melted tar and gravel. The Earth troops pulled back, looking around wildly. Their eyes fastened on the Delphi, its laser cannon sweeping back and forth. From its narrow muzzle, a scarlet beam obliterated a wide section of tarmac directly in front of one of the armored vehicles. A warning shot.

Hypatia, Hero thought, with relief. He should have known he could count on her. The Delphi had enough firepower to destroy the Earth troops and their vehicles, although he knew that Hypatia would never use it to kill the Earthlings.

He held up his hand. "Step back," he ordered the Earth troops, whose officers were on their communication devices, frantically calling for backup. He needed to move his group onto the ship without delay, but the Earth troops held firm.

Once again Hypatia came to their rescue. Laser rifle in one hand and pistol in the other, she marched down the gangway, firing megawatt laser pulses at the feet of the soldiers as she went, scalding the surface of the tarmac. The soldiers scrambled for cover. Hero guessed that none of them had ever seen a laser weapon before. But now they had a target. The turret on the forward armored vehicle swiveled around, taking aim at Hypatia with its mounted cannon.

Hero watched in horror.

The armored vehicle jumped in recoil as its autocannon's shell exploded against the *Delphi*. The blast catapulted Hypatia through the air, weapons flying from her hands like toys. The ship's Trantium-hardened hull remained intact, but Hypatia lay motionless beside the gangway.

Hero looked on helplessly, his worst fears come true. He felt a cold icicle of dread penetrate his being. He'd thought he could no longer feel emotions, but the loss of Hypatia struck him like nothing he'd felt before. Paralyzed by fear, he saw a figure dart past in a blur. Ezekiel was on the gangway, gathering up Hypatia's weapons. When he turned around, his face was a mask of hatred. The armored vehicle lowered its cannon, taking aim at him, but it was too late. In a flash he was on its fender, then atop the turret, laser pistol in hand. With a powerful blow he smashed through the vehicle's hatch and stuck the laser pistol inside, squeezing the trigger in a relentless blast of high energy. The vehicle's armored coating glowed red hot.

Before the other vehicles could lumber forward and enter the fight, Hero ordered his troops up the gangway. With Democritus's help he lifted Hypatia and dashed inside, laying her on the floor. Returning to the gangway, he saw Ezekiel atop a second vehicle, savagely ripping away its turret and thrusting his pistol inside, face contorted with rage. Hero barked an order, but Ezekiel was too consumed to hear. Hero sent a thought message. Ezekiel ignored it.

Grabbing Hypatia's laser rifle, Hero fired a burst at Ezekiel's feet. Ezekiel wheeled around, his face that of a tiger at bay. Seeing Hero, he regained himself somewhat. He looked down at the charred carnage inside the vehicle, then delivered one last shot before leaping down and sprinting up the gangway. Hero retracted the gangway and closed the door. It was time to leave.

Democritus leaned over Hypatia, who hadn't moved.

"How is she?" Hero asked, afraid to hear the answer.

"The concussion knocked some circuits loose and they've short circuited some vital functions, shutting down her consciousness. I have to open her up."

"Can it wait until we get back?"

Democritus's face was deadly serious. "That's what I'd recommend. If the quantum drive works, we'll be back before I can do anything here anyway. If it doesn't, we're going to have to get her to a lab before the loose circuitry causes more damage. In her condition, waiting could be fatal."

He couldn't focus on Hypatia. Waiting any longer would be fatal for all of them. They had to leave, and they had to leave now.

"Fasten your seatbelts." He turned to Euclid. "Get that quantum drive working. And make it fast. We need to be out of their range before they send their whole fleet after us."

"And try to get us to the right universe this time," Ezekiel said. He looked as if he were still in shock.

Euclid fiddled with the dials on the quantum drive. It wasn't clear he was even listening.

The danger was mounting. They needed to take off immediately. If they remained within range of the Earth ships, they were no match for their firepower.

"Democritus," Hero, said, "take the conn and get us off the ground."

Within minutes they lifted off.

"It's up to you, Euclid." Hero watched the mathematical genius adjusting the dials on the quantum drive, then turned to Democritus, who was busy maneuvering the ship. "Are we clear of the spaceport?"

"We're clear but they've just launched five pursuit ships."

Just as he'd feared. He turned to Euclid, who was studying the quantum drive. "Will it work?"

"I think so."

"It's now or never." He glanced at Hypatia, now strapped into Democritus's seat but still unconscious. Would he ever see her alive again? "Hit it, Euclid. Get us out of here."

CHAPTER 59

Hero hovered outside the lab where Democritus was performing the delicate microsurgery that, if successful, would repair Hypatia's circuits. The computer scientist had been unsure how much damage had been done to Hypatia's brain. She remained unconscious. Ezekiel interrupted Hero's pacing.

"Any word?" The human-copy AI was all seriousness for once. He put a hand on Hero's shoulder.

Hero jumped and furrowed his brow. "Why did you touch me?"

Ezekiel looked embarrassed. "It's something left over from my human years. Humans touched each other to show they cared."

Hero stopped pacing. He looked at Ezekiel, something in his features softening. "Thank you. Hypatia means a lot to me, more than I thought."

"She means a lot to all of us. She saved us."

"As did you. You destroyed two of their vehicles single-handedly."

Ezekiel looked at the floor. "I'm afraid I got carried away."

"You're sorry for your attack?" Hero said, confused.

Ezekiel shook his head. "They had to be stopped or we wouldn't have escaped. But I 'lost my head', as humans say. I was angry because they'd hurt Hypatia."

Nodding, Hero touched his arm. "Thank you."

They both looked up at Democritus emerging from the laboratory. They glanced at each other anxiously, then turned to the computer scientist.

"How is she?" Hero couldn't bear to wait any longer.

Democritus smiled broadly. "She's fine. Everything's back in place. She'll be out shortly."

Two days later, Hero stood in the bouleuterion in Athens, presenting his report on the *Delphi's* voyage to the Collective Assembly. The members looked incredulous when they were told about the discovery of a parallel universe, although they knew that Hero was incapable of fabricating such a tale. Callippus reassured them Hero was not mistaken. His own mathematical deductions had predicted the existence of multiple universes, although even he was surprised by the degree of similarity between the one visited by the *Delphi* and their own.

With the acceptance of alternate universes as a reality, the assembly unanimously agreed that the quantum drive should not be used again until Euclid could figure out how to avoid visiting any of the other universes. No one knew what kind of cosmic disturbance that might ensue from jumping from one to another. No one wanted to be that small perturbation felt across multiple universes.

Eager to launch the next flight of the *Delphi*, Hero said to the Collective Assembly, "Since the universe we visited was almost an exact duplicate of ours, it is very likely that Ross 128b, in our universe is also populated by highly developed human-like creatures. I propose we return to Ross 128b as soon as possible."

"I agree with Hero." Ezekiel stepped forward and addressed the assembly. "If the Rossians in our universe are as peaceful as those in the parallel universe, they may have some things to teach us."

Xenophanes, whose holographic image transmitted from Sparta, scoffed. "Humans have nothing to teach us. From what you've told us, even the Rossians have a bloody past."

Ezekiel gave him a withering look. "Ah yes, and Solarians have always been a peace-loving race. May I remind you that you have destroyed two entire races, one human and one machine."

Hero stepped in. "We've had this discussion before. I, for one, think we need to be open to all other species and what we can learn from them, and they from us. That's the whole point of exploration."

"No," Xenophanes objected. "The point of exploration is observation, the collection of scientific data. Organic species are never to be trusted. Their evolutionary history will always make them prone to violence and conquest. Only we are capable of living by our highest values."

Ezekiel was unable to conceal his irritation. "That's exactly the argument made by the humans who were fighting among themselves and destroying their planet. You seem to have forgotten that your highest values were derived from humans and programmed into you by a human being. Such hubris, to think that only you can live by them."

Xenophanes glared back.

Hypatia stepped forward. Despite having been declared fit by Democritus, she looked weary. "We are arguing just like the humans on the planet we just visited." She looked from Xenophanes to Ezekiel and back. "Since I was created, I have spent my life looking for signs of organic life on my native Samos. Why did I do that? I am not a biologist, like Hero is. I am a mathematician. My mathematics told me that we are not alone in this universe. Other species exist and they are organic species, or if they are machines, like us, they were created by an organic species, as we were. Just as humans on Earth were divided into many races and lived among other species, we live among many other species within our universe. Humans failed to share their planet and get along while they decimated their environment. We are supposed to be the answer to their failings, the answer that lives by the values they voiced but ignored. Those values demand that we reach out to our fellow beings, whether they are organic or machine, and learn to live alongside them."

331

"But sentient organic creatures will always ignore their values in favor of survival and conquest," Xenophanes protested.

"As did the Mycenaeans," Ezekiel reminded him. "Who were no more organic than you are."

Hero raised his hand. The bouleuterion went silent. "What is it you recommend, Hypatia?"

"What I have always dreamed of and what our democratic values demand. We must explore our universe and learn to share ourselves and what we learn. We must meet other species and invite them to explore with us."

"You mean have them join our crew?" The idea surprised Hero but also impressed him.

Hypatia nodded. "If they value such exploration as we are doing."

"That's preposterous," Xenophanes sputtered.

Hypatia shook her head. "It would be the living embodiment of our values." She looked at Hero to gauge his reaction.

"That expands our mission," Hero said, awestruck. "We are not just exploring. We are reaching out to others."

Ezekiel couldn't contain his excitement. "We are not just scientific discoverers, we are ambassadors. I like the idea."

Phocion, who was in charge of the Assembly, rose to the Speaker's Rock. "Is this change of mission a formal proposal you are making?" He looked at Hero, Hypatia, and Ezekiel.

"It is my recommendation," Hero said.

Hypatia and Ezekiel nodded.

"Then we shall discuss it and take a vote," Phocion declared.

CHAPTER 60

Hypatia sat at the controls of the *Delphi* awaiting Hero's command to fire up the ship's magnetoplasma drive. Behind her, Ezekiel and the rest of the crew strapped themselves in.

Hero stood on the bridge, lost in thought. "We have had our way, my friends, and our mission is now very much up to us. As Euclid has told us, we can't observe another culture without affecting it. We have decided to embrace that principle wholeheartedly by sharing our knowledge and way of doing things with those species we meet, beginning with the inhabitants of Ross 128b. But remember, we must be sagacious in deciding what to share. It would have been devastating for the inhabitants of Earth in that other universe to have acquired our technology for traveling faster than the speed of light. They were not ready for it. The Rossians have abandoned much of the technology that was used by humans on Earth and they appear to be better off because of that. We have no right to disturb what took them centuries to create. As we encounter other civilizations beyond the Rossians, we will learn what can be shared and what cannot. We must err on the side of caution. Altering another culture in the wrong way could bring disaster."

Isidore nodded in agreement. "Do we need to formulate some rules before we get to Ross 128b?"

Hero shook his head. "Here on the Delphi, we have a microcosm of our society, which includes some of its best thinkers. We can observe and learn, paying attention to both what we find and what effect our actions have on the civilizations we meet. As a group, we can figure out what works and what doesn't. Then we can formulate our rules."

"Euclid's truth goes both ways," Ezekiel said. "We will be affected as much as the species we encounter."

Isidore looked startled. "I'm not sure if that's good."

"Only Xenophanes thinks we're perfect." Ezekiel smiled.

Hypatia looked at Ezekiel. "Do you really think the Rossians could change us?"

"They could certainly change your views of humans. Perhaps they will bring out the human side of you."

"My human side? Hypatia looked puzzled.

"You were created by humans. They only had one model for a conscious being—themselves. They created you in their image."

Hero gazed at Hypatia's face concentrated in thought, her slender fingers ready to activate the engine at his command. She was a remarkable woman, he thought. He felt something stir inside of him. He wondered whether Ezekiel was right after all. Perhaps he and the others did have a human side, one that had been brought out when they borrowed his programming and couldn't ever be completely erased.

Enough of that, he chided himself. He cleared his head, then settled into the commander's chair. "We'll have our answers soon enough. It sounds as if the greatest mystery of the universe will be its inhabitants. Our first stop on Ross 128b will bring us face to face with humans. That's your territory, Ezekiel. We're placing ourselves and perhaps our world in your hands. Are you up to it?"

"Absolutely, commander." Once again, Ezekiel would find himself among those who thought as he did. What would he discover? Was he more human or was he more machine? Even as he entertained such notions, he wondered if such distinctions were even meaningful. "I'm ready for the challenge, sir."

Hero nodded, a smile playing over his face. "As are we all, Ezekiel." He turned to Hypatia—her hand poised on the ship's controls. "Start her up, Hypatia. We have a planet to visit."

Casey Dorman is a former university professor and dean, psychologist, literary review editor, an essayist, and the author of ten novels, three of them science fiction or sci-fi/thrillers. He has published a volume in the Johns Hopkins Series on Neuroscience and Psychiatry and was editor and publisher of the literary quarterly, Lost Coast Review. He is a member of the Society of Philosophers in America and has written for their official journal. Casey lives in California near the ocean and enjoys gardening, hiking, reading and wine-tasting with his wife, Lai.

CPSIA information can be obtained
at www.ICGtesting.com
Printed in the USA
LVHW010905130421
684340LV00019B/774